ALSO BY DAVIS MACDONALD

The Hill *(set in Palos Verdes), Book 1 in the Judge Series*

The Island *(set in Avalon, Catalina Island), Book 2 in the Judge Series*

Silicon Beach *(set in Santa Monica and L.A.'s West Side), Book 3 in the Judge Series*

The Bay *(set in Newport Beach), Book 4 in the Judge Series*

Cabo *(set in Cabo San Lucas), Book 5 in the Judge Series*

The Strand *(set in the South Bay beach communities of Southern California), Book 6 in the Judge Series*

The Lake *(set in the Lake Arrowhead community of Southern California), Book 7 in the Judge Series*

The Cruise *(set on the open sea), Book 8 in the Judge Series – Due out in the Fall, 2020*

Recipes and Philosophy from A Los Angeles Semi-Serious Epicurean and Bon Vivant. *(Recipes from Certain Memorable Dinners Prepared by Amazing California Chefs and Cooks)*

I hope you enjoy The Lake, and if you do, please drop a brief positive review on Amazon for me. Your review will be greatly appreciated.

Watch for announcements for future books on my Website: **http://davismacdonald-author.com/**

Enjoy the Read

THE LAKE

A Mystery Novel

BY

DAVIS MacDONALD

In 1797, J. W. von Goethe wrote a poem about what can happen when men tinker with a technology they don't understand and can't control. The technology in that day was called black magic:

"And now come, thou well-worn broom,
And thy wretched form bestir;
Thou hast ever served as groom,
So fulfil my pleasure, sir!
On two legs now stand,
With a head on top;
Water pail in hand,
Haste, and do not stop!

See! he's running to the shore,
And has now attained the pool,
And with lightning speed once more
Comes here with his bucket full!
Back he then repairs;
See how swells the tide!
How each pail he bears
Straightway is supplied!

Oh, thou villain child of hell!
Shall the house through thee be drowned?
Floods I see that wildly swell,
O'er the threshold gaining ground.
Wilt thou not obey,
Oh, thou broom accursed?
Be thou still, I pray,

And thy nimble wood so tough,

With my sharp axe split at last.
See, once more he hastens back!
Now, oh, Cobold, thou shalt catch it!
I will rush upon his track;
Crashing on him falls my hatchet.
Bravely done, indeed!
See, he's cleft in twain!
Now from care I'm freed,
And can breathe again.

Woe, oh, woe!
Both the parts,
Quick as darts,
Stand on end,
Servants of my dreaded foe!
Oh, ye gods, protection send!

And they run! and wetter still
Grow the steps and grows the hall."

From *The Sorcerer's Apprentice*, by J. W. von Goethe (1797)

****

She had a need to feel the thunder,
Chasing lightning from the sky.
Watch the storm with all its wonder…
Raging in her lover's eyes!"

Lyrics from *That Summer*
by
Garth Brooks, Pat Alger and Sandy Mahl

A Note from the Author

This story, and its characters, organizations, businesses, events, locations and scenes, are completely fictional.

Chapter 1
Saturday Morning 1:30 a.m.

The Judge couldn't sleep. He quietly shifted the covers off and stuck one bare foot and then the other off the antique four-poster bed and onto the cold wood floor. From there he raised his considerable bulk to sitting, slid off the bed, tiptoed across the floor, and tottered out into the hall and down the stairs to the cabin's main floor. At the foot of the stairs he passed the tall antique clock that had belonged to his great, great grandmother. It read 1:33 a.m. He let his breath out in the living room, apparently successful in not waking his young bride, twenty years his junior.

The cabin was old. Even older than the Judge. Built in 1908, it stood testimony to the pioneer spirit that settled Lake Arrowhead in the early 1900s. It was originally a two-story cottage, built at the bottom of its lot, hanging over the Lake and its private dock. It was a place of plywood interiors aged in golden brown and a huge fireplace in the great room crafted from local stone.

The Judge's family had modernized it here and there over the generations: forced air heating, new kitchen, basement built out into a game room and a bedroom-attic, now turned into his office. The footprint hadn't changed, but the space had grown to some 2,500 square feet.

The Judge had inherited the cabin when his mother died. *Whispering Point* was its name. And although his busy schedule precluded him from visiting Lake Arrowhead often, it was still a sanctuary of sorts. Clean air, the crystal-clear lake reflecting sparkling blue skies, and nights filled with a thousand stars. The cabin was set on a semi-peninsula jutting out into the Lake. In the evenings the lapping water of the lakeshore whispered up through the pines to the cabin's interior, hence its name.

In the great room were the old almost floor-to-ceiling windows opening over the lake, wide open now to let in the soft night air. The Judge stood before them, looking out. There was a large yellow moon shooting a broken yellow ribbon across the Lake surface, the ribbon rippled by a gusty wind. Winter would be here soon. He could hear, almost taste, the quiet lapping of the Lake's edges against the shore, sending a calliope of sound floating up around the cabin. It was very peaceful. Like an empty church.

A boat started up across the Lake, over toward Lake Arrowhead Village. A speedboat with big engines and noisy pipes, droning like a distant bee in the background, making the surrounding silence even more precious. Someone was up late. Perhaps heading home on the water after a pub-crawl in the Village.

The Judge took deep breaths, sucking in scents of the Lake, the trees, and the intermittent brush, feeling his soul replenished in some measure by the air and the silent romance of the place and the night.

But there was a gradual disquiet from somewhere. What was it? The damn boat across the Lake with its buzz-saw engine. It had initially settled down directly across from him on the opposite shore. But now it was tearing across the Lake's surface again, drawing closer, invading his pristine silence like a noisy thief. He wished the guy would get to his dock and shut his damn engine off.

The buzz grew closer, and noisier, and closer and noisier. It felt like the damn boat was under his feet. His cabin seemed to pulsate in step with the boat's racket.

Then, suddenly, there were ripping, tearing, screeching sounds. Fiberglass and aluminum ripping through a wooden dock below. His dock. The night was lit by bright orange flames leaping skyward beneath him, up, up, higher than the cabin in a mini fireball. The thunder of the explosion engulfed the Judge, the blast of hot air knocking him back on his heels. His hands went up instinctively to protect his eyes.

Shit. Someone just crashed into his dock!

Chapter 2
Saturday Morning 1:40 a.m.

The Judge stabbed his bare feet into his nearby shoes and pounded down the stairs, out through the game room to the deck, and down the ancient stone stairs toward his dock, his progress illuminated by dwindling flames on oily water.

There was a boat there, or what once had been a boat, more like two thirds of a boat now, upside down in the water, its smooth under-belly immodestly exposed for the world to see. Bits and pieces of what had been the whole were nearby in puddles of burning fuel. Small flickering flames licked experimentally at the fiberglass and wood remains.

The Judge dashed down the wooden steps that led onto his dock, or what was left of it. The outer half of the float was no longer there, its loss defined by a jagged boundary of broken wood and shredded float.

That's when he saw what he feared. A lone man floating face up beside the overturned hull, half submerged, one arm thrown over a piece of floating wood from the wreck.

Not moving.

The Judge jumped into the water beside the dock, gasping with the cold. Fortunately, the Lake was shallow around his dock. He quickly waded forward, almost to his neck, splashing aside the puddles of burning fuel. With a long reach he collared the back of the floater's Tommy Bahama shirt and stumbled his way back over the slippery seaweed bottom to shore, dragging the man up onto the small sandy beach. The Judge sank himself onto the sand and pulled the man's head over to his lap.

There was a deep searing wound down one side of the man's skull at the back. But his chest was worse, one broken rib sticking through a gash in his side pumping blood all over the Judge and into the surrounding sand.

The Judge recognized the man. He was a friend, a fellow attorney, a neighbor from across the Lake in Shelter Cove. It was Jerry Stone.

Jerry's eyes fluttered open and he seemed to recognize the Judge. He reached up to pull the Judge's head down, closer, and in a hoarse voice whispered, *"Find Cindy… Thousands will be killed… Stop it…"*

Then Jerry sank back, exhausted. A rattling gasp came out of his mouth. His eyes rolled back into his head. Jerry was gone. The Judge could feel it. Jerry's body suddenly felt lighter, the sense of his aura fading to nothing, muscles limp, skin suddenly flat and cool, all energy evaporated. Gone!

The Judge heard faintly, and then louder, the sound of sirens on the highway further around the Lake. A patrol boat was also setting out from somewhere across the Lake, a spotlight sweeping an arc from its bow across the water's surface. Lights were going on in cabins on either side of him, concerned residents nosing out to see what had happened.

Katy, his bride, emerged on the edge of the terrace above him, Annie the Dog at her side. Katy peered over the edge, her blond hair tousled, a robe thrown around her.

"Are you okay, Judge. What happened? You didn't fall in the Lake again, did you?"

The Judge sighed. One small slip off the dock two years ago and he'd been forever marked by his wife and dog as prone to falling in the Lake. Someone who needed to be watched carefully. And scolded periodically lest he forget his brush with a watery grave.

The Judge looked down at the face of his friend in his lap. Jerry hadn't missed his appointment.

He gently laid Jerry's head back down on the sand, stood up, brushed sand from his soaked PJs, and began a slow ascent of the many steps which ran up the side of the lot to the street. He waved his hand in the air to attract the attention of firefighters scrambling off their truck above, arms filled with equipment and spotlights, trying to assess how to get down to the wreck. The glow of their truck's strobe light alternately washed the surrounding pines in red, lending an unreal macabre atmosphere to the scene.

The fire team came tearing down the steps, meeting the Judge halfway, then tearing past at his direction. Later a team member came down with a collapsible stretcher. Soon all three came back up, two hauling the stretcher, unfolded and flat, occupied, a clean sheet tucked over poor Jerry. The night seemed lonely now, dark and empty.

The sheriff's department showed up in the form of an older officer sporting a large paunch that made it difficult to clamber down the narrow stairs to the dock. Too many years, too much stress, too many donuts.

"Hi Judge," muttered the cop. He almost looked relieved to have something exciting to do on the night shift.

"Jack Prentis." Answered the Judge. "I'll be damn. They haven't retired your number yet?"

Sergeant Jack Prentis smiled and extended a meaty paw which the Judge took to shake.

The Judge stated what he knew. Then Jack asked him to repeat it again. As though the Judge were some ancient who had forgotten something. Friends were friends, but police procedure was police procedure, supposed the Judge.

"Did Mr. Stone say anything to you before he died, Judge?" asked Jack Prentis.

The Judge paused, perhaps a tad too long, then responded, "No. No, nothing."

Twenty minutes into their conversation a second sheriff showed up, pounding down the steps to flank Prentis and listen in. He was younger, late twenties, a redhead with a pink face and freckles surrounding his somber blue eyes. Jack introduced him as Pete Campbell. Campbell nodded briskly at the Judge.

"You took a while to get here, Pete," said Jack.

"Yes, sir. I was over on the other side of the Lake. North Shore."

Jack turned back to the Judge.

"Okay, Judge, just for the record and for Pete's sake, go through it one more time." His eyes twinkled at the little pun he'd made.

The Judge started over but stopped as the threesome turned in unison to watch the patrol boat pull up beside the splintered dock, more red and white lights flashing back on the Lake. The crew set up booms to corral the floating fuel. This was a resort community, making its living off the surrounding opulent second homes of the rich and the powerful. And the hordes of weekenders and day-trippers enticed up the mountain from the Great Los Angeles Plain. The Lake had to stay pristine at all costs.

After he finished his statement for the third time the Judge thought he was done. But the Lake patrol boat pulled back to the half of his dock still floating and a young woman leaped off onto its deck. She bounded up the stairs to the top of the bluff below the Judge's cabin, waving for him to come down. Dressed in tan uniform and peaked cap, with *Arrowhead Lake Association* emblazoned on one shoulder, she cut a pretty figure, tall, slim and buff. As she got closer, he saw black curls tucked under her hat, pale white skin, heavy eyebrows, and dark brown eyes that held a twinkle, even at this ungodly hour in the morning. Her eyes suggested Middle Eastern, or perhaps Turkish roots.

"You're the Judge," she called as she got closer, an engaging smile lighting her face. "Least that's what everyone calls you."

"I am," said the Judge, smiling back despite the weariness enfolding him like a blanket.

"Is that 'cause you're a Judge?"

"Used to be. Been retired by the voters for some years now, but the nickname still sticks."

"Well, Judge, you need to take better care of your dock."

"Yes. Half of it seems to be missing, doesn't it?"

"Seriously, though, without the front floats the balance of the dock is likely to sink into the Lake if the wind comes up any further. Best call your dock contractor this morning. We don't want it going into the Lake, do we?" He got the big smile again, softening her words.

She was face to face with him now. She smelt faintly of florals, fresh fruit, and mildew, perhaps a combination of *Daisy Eau* and dock lines. Her eyes looked openly into his, filled with interest and concern. He had a feeling they might have met in a former life, been something more than friends.

She perhaps felt it too. She blushed and looked down for a second.

"Okay, Judge. I'm Ally Monroe. Commander of the Lake Patrol." She stuck out a small hand to shake, slender fingers and clear nail polish, the hands of a concert pianist. He took it into his gnarled paw, noting the feel of the calluses here and there from working rough lines and driving boats. There was a slight electric shock to her touch, a mini-current, not unpleasant; in fact, arousing. And then it was gone. She pulled her hand away quickly and looked over his shoulder to the right.

The younger sheriff, Pete Campbell was there, practically on top of the Judge, glowering over his shoulder at Monroe.

"Hi Pete. Long time no see," said Monroe, producing an infectious smile, trying to look encouraging.

The Judge could feel tension between them.

Pete just nodded slightly, turned on his heel and, stiff-necked, followed Sheriff Prentis back up the stairs. Ally Monroe watched Pete's back with troubled eyes, then, pulling herself together, bounded back down the steps to the water and danced her way across the remainder of the Judge's dock to her waiting boat.

The Judge made his way back up to the cabin's lower level, chilled to the bone now. As the Judge moved off the stairs and onto the main floor, still dripping a little, he saw Katy sitting on the antique sofa, her aqua robe clashing with its dark wood and tufted red velvet upholstery.

Katy was tall and slender, all arms and legs, despite carrying and birthing their son, Ralphie, now almost seven. She had long brown hair, askew right now from sleeping, and small delicate features, emblazoned with smile lines that lent character to her alabaster face. Her nose was a bit long and narrow, but in that it matched her head, also more oblong than round, but all very delicate. Katy had the most extraordinary eyes, vivid blue like the Caribbean, large and intelligent, with long lashes.

But Katy's eyes were wet right now. She was holding a limp handkerchief to her mouth, stifling soft sobs. Of course. Jerry's wife, Marie Stone, was Katy's best friend in Lake Arrowhead.

He sat down beside her and she turned to him, nestling her head into the hollow of his shoulder, her whole body quivering. Finally, she muttered into his shirt, "Oh, Judge. Poor, poor Marie. Who's going to tell her? What's she going to do? And poor Jerry. Oh God, poor Jerry. I saw him before they covered him up on the stretcher. His battered side, his empty eyes staring up at me. Gone! Just like that. Gone."

"I'm so sorry, Katy. We've lost a good friend. And no, I don't know what Marie's going to do."

"They were so in love, Judge."

"Sometimes life just happens that way, Katy. You just never know."

The Judge tucked Katy back in bed after watching her down a brandy. He'd jettisoned his wet PJs for a dry pair but was still chilled. He finally climbed back into bed about four a.m. He moved his icicle feet over against Katy's warm thigh, seeking solace, only to be met with a yelp, and a firm hand pushing them back to his cold side of the bed. The frontier values of sharing discomfort and grief with your spouse were apparently lost on Katy.

Annie the Dog jumped up on the bed to the rescue. Practically any excuse would do for her to leap onto their bed and take her rightful position by their feet, despite the Judge's efforts to discourage her. But her fur and heat on top of the blankets over his feet lent much-needed warmth. He drifted off, his dreams tinted with visions of a goddess dressed in a tan uniform arising from the flames of a watery hell.

Chapter 3
Saturday Morning 10:00 a.m.

The Judge awoke to find himself alone in the high old-fashioned bed, the original four-poster that was a part of his family's legacy. Katy and Annie the Dog were long gone. Liquid gold sunlight streamed into his face through the open window. He heard his six-year old son, Ralphie, outside the window and below three stories, trying to corner a squirrel. Katy wouldn't like that. But she wasn't around at the moment and Ralphie was having serious fun.

He heard the ancient door chimes one floor below, and then the creak of the front door and voices. Katy's, and someone else, a woman's voice. Their conversation trailed across the living room beneath his feet and into the breakfast room. He heard the rattle of tea service. Then the creaking of the stairs as Katy came up the stairs to roust him. His rest for the day was done.

The bedroom door opened part way and Katy stuck her head in. Seeing him awake she whispered, "Marie is here, Judge. Can you come help?" Marie Stone was Jerry Stone's wife, now his widow. And Katy's friend.

The Judge nodded his understanding, stretched, and crawled out of bed, making his way to the suite's bathroom for a quick shower and shave.

Fifteen minutes later, still tasting of mint toothpaste, he made his way downstairs in his light brown corduroy pants and Pendleton bronze and blue plaid shirt. He fancied the Pendleton brought out the blue in his eyes, eyes red and swollen from too little sleep

The breakfast room was two sides glass, looking out over the Lake and out over the pine trees to the side. The two women were sitting at the circular glass table, quiet, teacups in hand, staring out at the Lake, crystal blue now, matching a blue sky dotted with puffy clouds. If they looked down, mused the Judge, they'd see the remains of his splintered dock, and the upside-down hull of Jerry's cherry-red boat. He tucked the unpleasant thought away.

Marie was mid-thirties, five foot seven, willowy, hazel hair, with large brown eyes which conveyed warmth and emotion. She was the great great great granddaughter of one of the landed Spanish Dons of Old California. The money ran out generations ago. But the style never does.

She wore a black sweater over black jeans and black boots, a grey silk scarf tucked into her collar. No makeup; she didn't need it with her porcelain white skin, strong eyebrows and chiseled cheekbones. But her face was pale, her eyes ringed with fatigue and sadness.

"Oh Judge. What am I going to do?" Marie's voice was thin, reedy, not its usual robust self. She was in shock.

"I'm so sorry, Marie. Words aren't worth much right now, but you can count on us for help and support. Just tell us what we can do."

She rocked back and forth slightly, staring into her teacup, as though reading its swirling debris of jetsam, bits of leaves and a floating stem atop the last bit of liquid at its bottom. The Judge's grandmother used to read tea leaves for him so very long ago at this very table. The floating stick on top suggested a new visitor would arrive. Life had been so simple back then.

"How could it have happened, Judge? Jerry was way too young to die... Jesus, I feel so alone so abandoned."

A small tear eased down one cheek, circling part of Marie's jaw and resting there, not large enough to drip. Katy jumped up from her seat and wrapped her arms around Marie, giving the Judge the 'get out of here' look.

The Judge stood, patted inconsequentially at Marie's shoulder, and left the breakfast room, moving slowly, distressed, thinking about the good friend he'd lost. He wandered down to what was left of his dock and surveyed the scene. The ski boat must have been going full bore. The front half of his dock was mostly kindling, much of it washed up on the beach, some still floating in the water, parts of the debris charred from the after fire.

What had happened last night? A mechanical accident, the throttles jammed full on, Jerry losing control of the boat.

Or maybe substance abuse? Jerry out on the lake drunk, unable to react in time to avoid collision with the shore? Jerry was something of an alcoholic, although a cheerful one. He was an amazingly funny guy, even funnier with a few drinks. Full of jokes, funny stories, and good cheer, warm and personable.

Or was it maybe something darker? Suicide, perhaps. Going out in a blaze of crash and fire, intentional self-destruction. The Judge had noticed none of the signs of depression sometimes a precursor to suicide: excessive moodiness, long-lasting sadness, mood swings, unexpected rage, hopelessness, sleep deprivation. But then, come to think of it, he hadn't actually talked to Jerry in some weeks. Their paths just hadn't crossed. And Jerry might have cleverly covered up his depression, as people do. It was difficult to see what was going on in the heads of complicated homo sapiens.

Jerry's fiery crash could have been something even darker... a homicide. But for why? Humans kill for a limited number of reasons. Someone once simplified it down to the four 'L's: Lust; Love; Loathing; and Loot. There were other reasons of course, the fear of being caught, for self-protection, killing for sport, killing as collateral damage in connection with another crime.

Was this something more than an accident? The thought circled through the Judge's mind, and came back to the front, to his attention. It was just all so neat for an accident.

Chapter 4
Saturday Evening 5:00 p.m.

That evening the Judge and Katy settled into bent hickory chairs in front of the almost floor-to-ceiling windows opening out over the Lake. They watched the shadow of the cabin creep out across the water as the sun set behind the structure. Katy had whipped up some gin and tonics, Bombay Sapphire. The Judge could feel the tension leave his body as he sat with her sipping his drink, contented as the sky turned from a vivid blue to a light violet and the early stars made their appearance.

"Katy."

"Yes, Judge?"

"As I was holding Jerry down there and he was dying, he whispered a very private message to me. His last words. It was a message he wanted me to give to Cindy. Do you know who Cindy is? Was there a Cindy in Jerry's life?"

"I don't know any Cindy, Judge. But we can ask Marie."

"I don't want to upset her even more. Perhaps Jerry had a mistress or something. That's why I didn't bring it up this morning."

"I don't know, Judge. Don't know any Cindy here at the Lake. Or even down on the flats for that matter. Maybe it was his secretary or his paralegal, or something. Or maybe Jerry had a sister. What was the message?"

"I don't think I can tell you, Katy. It was the dying man's last words, given in confidence. There's even an attorney-client relationship. I did Jerry's estate plan."

"Oh, pooh, Judge. You're no fun at all. Isn't there a pillow talk exception or something?

"No. And we're not even on pillows, Katy."

"We could be." Katy giggled

"I like that idea, but it wouldn't help." The Judge smiled, drawing her in closer for a hug.

"Let's go see if there's still any life left in the springs of that old four-poster, Judge."

"I'm really tired tonight, Katy. Can I give you a rain check?"

Katy bit her lip, but almost covered it, then said brightly… perhaps too brightly, "Sure, Judge. I'm always on call and available." She got up from her chair and marched herself across the great room and up the stairs alone. The Judge watched her go, wishing he had more energy for his twenty-years younger bride.

He got up from his chair and lit the old stone fireplace, vintage 1909, supplemented now by a gas pipe at its back, and a blow-it-off-the-wall forced-air heating unit downstairs. There must have been a lot of chopped wood and a lot of blankets piled here in November of 1909. He settled into his favorite overstuffed leather chair by the fireplace. It had been his dad's chair too, recently re-sprung, re-stuffed, and reupholstered. He liked that things changed here some but still stayed much the same.

His thoughts turned to Jerry Stone. Jerry's older brother, Jake, had been the Judge's fraternity brother at USC. Jerry, fifteen years younger, had been just a toddler when they'd first met. A stork's surprise for parents older in years and not expecting another child. Jerry'd been a happy little guy. The Judge had seen him now and then through his puberty, turning into a likable teenager and then a galloping college man. USC both undergrad and then law. He'd been a serious law student but never lost his playful nature, quick witted with a devilish sense of humor. It had carried over into his career as a young lawyer.

Jerry had a knack for telling the rankest of dirty stories to make them funnier than hell, leaving the cadre of guys he always had around him howling with laughter. Even better, at a social function with females present, Jerry would boldly launch into the very same sordid story the guys had heard earlier in the day, the males all cringing at the presence of the women and what they would think. But Jerry would cleverly twist the ending, so the story was both clean and twice as funny. The men would be totally flummoxed.

He'd joined the small boutique law firm of McCarthy, Jenner & Smith, based in downtown L.A. but run mostly by pedigreed, monied lawyers from San Marino, the place where Jerry had grown up. Jerry had thrived, becoming a litigation partner at an early age, charming his way around the firm's clients, its lawyers, his fellow lawyers at the bar, and the judges and juries who perpetually gave Jerry the benefit of the doubt on the close questions, swayed by his likable charm.

If there'd been a downside for Jerry, perhaps it was a too-large tab at one or another of the local watering holes around the courthouse, starting at around four in the afternoon each day. An effort to decamp the built-up stress of the litigation law practice Jerry carried. But that was a common problem for much of the litigation bar. It was so bad that the California State Bar added mandatory Substance Abuse Training to the continuing education requirements for all lawyers. But then, Jerry had been even funnier when he was high. The trouble was, Jerry was high a lot.

Jerry's monied grandparents settled behind the iron gates of the exclusive Shelter Cove neighborhood of Lake Arrowhead for their second home in the late forties, just after the war. Jerry had grown up on the Lake, spending most summers and holidays here. With the death of Jerry's parents a few years back, the Shelter Cove estate had been handed down to Jerry and Jake. But Jake had become ill and died, leaving no heirs. So, it was Jerry's estate now, or had been. He and his wife Marie were at the property most weekends and holidays. Oh, and Jackson, the housekeeper, and a large Siberian Husky that had belonged to Jerry and Jake's dad.

The Judge had first brought Katy up to the Lake seven years ago as his new bride. Up to Whispering Point, his family cabin. Katy had fallen in love with the Lake as he'd hoped. He'd arranged the dinner that first weekend with Jerry and Marie Stone, people closer to Katy's age. They'd clicked immediately. Katy and Marie became fast friends both on the Lake and on the flats below.

And now Jerry was gone. A reminder of how fleeting life was. The Judge stood and unsteadily trod his way upstairs to their bedroom, feeling older now. And far wearier than his fifty-six years excused.

Chapter 5
Sunday Morning 10:00 a.m.

The next morning Katy left early to meet Marie for breakfast, and later returned to pick up little Ralphie. Ralphie was going down the hill to visit his grandparents for a few days. Giving Katy and the Judge some well-earned alone time.

There was suddenly a rapping at the front door of the cabin. The Judge creaked open its ancient door to expose the smiling face of Jack Prentis, the older sheriff who'd been a casual friend around the Lake for years. The Judge showed him into the great room and then disappeared into the kitchen, returning with a cup of freshly brewed coffee, Starbucks vanilla, with two cubes of brown sugar as requested.

"So, Judge, I just thought I'd drop by and bring you up to date. On last night and all."

"Yes. Do, Jack."

"Well, first off, our friend Jerry Stone was pretty loaded when he died. His blood alcohol concentration, or BAC, was 0.11."

"That contributed to the accident, Jack?"

"That's the thing, Judge. It wasn't an accident. We think it was murder!"

"What?"

"We think it was a homicide. The coroner says there was a blow to the back of Stone's head, not consistent with the trauma he expected to see from a boat accident. Left Stone either unconscious or semi-conscious. Anyway, disabled."

"That's what killed him?"

"He says no, the blow wasn't fatal. He speculates Stone was hit from behind with a boat paddle. Someone then mounted a semi-conscious Jerry Stone in his boat, propped him up in the helm chair, threw the boat throttles into full ahead, and set the boat off across the Lake. The explosion sent pieces of sharp fiberglass into his chest, causing his death."

"But why?"

"To make it look like an accident."

"Oh, I understand that, Jack. But why Jerry? Why kill Jerry?"

"That's what we're trying to discover, Judge. We wondered if you could help."

"Any way I can."

"I've heard a rumor that Mr. Stone said something to you as he died in your arms. Is that true?"

"Yes. Boy, news travels fast around here."

"I guess you told your wife, and she told Marie, Jerry's widow, and Marie crawled up my ass, demanding to know what her husband said."

"I see."

"So?"

"So?"

"What did Stone say, Judge?"

"I wish I could tell you, Jack, I really do. In fact, the words made no sense. But Jerry was one of my estate planning clients. Anything he told me in confidence I can't disclose. It's privileged under the attorney-client privilege rules."

"But Stone's dead now."

"The U.S. Supreme Court decided more than a decade ago in Swidler and Berlin v. United States, that the attorney-client privilege survives the death of the client. I have to follow the law, Jack, just like you. Besides, Jerry's words were muddled.."

"Do you know anyone who might have wanted him dead, Judge? You two were pretty close."

"We were good friends, although I hadn't seen much of him of late. Practicing lawyers are busy lawyers. There's not much time for socializing. But I think everybody who met Jerry liked him. He had an amazing sense of humor, if a bit risqué. He was a warm, friendly, outgoing guy."

"He had a drinking problem I understand."

"He sometimes hit it a little early in the afternoons, Sheriff. But hell, he was a litigator. You'll find a lot of them in bars around L.A. late in the afternoon. The job is extraordinarily stressful."

"Blowing a 0.11 in your blood is usually indicative of more than a 'little problem.' "

"I suppose it is, Jack."

"Do you know of any big cases Stone was working on, Judge? Cases someone might want to kill over?"

"I did hear he had a major case he was litigating. Some non-profit animal rights outfit, or something. There was money in it; they were paying him well. It wasn't pro-bono. But it doesn't sound like the sort of case someone would kill over."

"What about his social life, Judge?"

"What about it?"

"There's rumors of a free-wheeling club here on the Lake. Back in my day we called them swingers clubs. There's some talk maybe Stone and his wife were members. You ever hear anything about that?"

"I haven't. I'd be surprised if that were the case. But I suppose in the end we never really know anyone, do we Jack?"

"I heard a neighbor was up in arms last summer on the North Shore, Judge. Seems Stone stuck his quill in the neighbor's ink well. Ended up with a lot of drama and a divorce."

"There's always idle gossip in a small community like this, Jack. Often not much to it. I wouldn't put much currency in a rumor like that."

"So, you didn't hear anything about that?"

"No. didn't."

"Stone was seen in the village earlier on Friday, Judge. He left the Papagayos Bar about midnight. That's where he got loaded, apparently."

"Okay."

"So, where was he between midnight Friday night, and one-thirty early Saturday morning, when his boat left his North Shore dock and bombed over here into your dock?

"That's a good question, Jack. I was home here. I haven't a clue what was going on in the village."

"Home with your wife?"

"Yes."

"And you don't know why your dock was chosen to crash into?"

"I don't. But I'm right across the Lake from Jerry. The boat had to end up somewhere. I think it was just random it was my dock. Random and bad luck for me."

"We immediately searched the shore over there, Judge. Looks like there was a party for two on Jerry's dock. But we didn't find anything else. Fingerprints were wiped. No telltale footprints in the sand, nothing discarded into the bushes, no one lurking around. No one was heard to drive away. No taxis or Ubers called. Makes us suspect either a family member or neighbor was involved. Someone could have hiked their way out, but it'd be a long walk."

"It would, Jack. But you'd not necessarily hear a car departing if you were inside one of those big homes."

"True…. So, that leaves us with very few clues, Judge. We're wondering if Stone told you something about who did this to him. You sure you can't give me some idea of what he said before he died?"

"Sorry, I can't."

"That's not real cooperative, Judge."

"It's what has to be."

"Okay, I'll get out of your hair. Have a good afternoon, Judge."

"You too, Jack."

As the Judge watched the Sheriff trudge up the long steps from the cabin to the road above, his cell phone rang, going off with a wolf whistle. The damn cell rattled around in his pocket all day. And got even by changing his ring tone at random… or was at malice? He wasn't sure.

"Hello, Judge, this is Tim McCarthy, the managing partner at Jerry Stone's law firm. We met a couple of times at Jerry's big parties, and at Bar functions."

"Of course, Tim. I'm so sorry about Jerry. He was a good friend."

"Yes. Our firm is distraught. I understand you were with him when he died."

"Yes."

"How did it happen? A boating accident I heard."

"The police have determined it was homicide, Tim. Jerry was murdered. Someone set him off in his boat after they bludgeoned him with a boat paddle."

"My God! Oh, my God. Did he say anything to you before he died, Judge?"

"Like what?"

"I don't know. I heard a rumor he gave you a mysterious message or something."

"If he did, since I was his personal lawyer, it would be privileged."

"Of course, of course. It's just Jerry was working on a big case, a whale of a client for our small law firm. I thought he might have said something about it."

"I think Jerry knew he was dying, Tim. It wasn't the time to be thinking about his big case."

"No. No. Of course not, Judge. Of course not. Thanks for your time and sorry to bother you. Good-day."

The phone went dead. The Judge scratched the back of his head, a habit he'd picked up since he'd discovered he was developing a thinning spot on top. Sort of a nervous reassurance he supposed that he still had some hair back there. The way he was going he'd soon look like Friar Tuck.

Anyway, it was damn curious how quickly word had spread that Jerry had spoken to him before died. He had his ‘loose lips sink ships’ wife to thank for that. Damn!

Chapter 6
Sunday Afternoon 3:00 p.m.

When Katy returned, the Judge was in his rocker by the windows looking out over the Lake, reviewing a contract for a client on his laptop.

"How'd it go, Katy? Was Ralphie happy to be dropped off? And how are your parents?"

"It was all okay, Judge. The traffic was a mess. But Ralphie was happy to go and be spoilt. And my parents were quite looking forward to doing the spoiling. So now it's just us up here. And of course, the dog."

"Your dog, Katy, grabbed the packaged loaf of bread off the counter after you left, dooming my craving for toast this morning. My ex-pet!"

Katy smiled briefly. "So, Judge, you know what date it is, right?"

"Aha, your birthday? Ouch!" the Judge gasped. Katy's sharp skinny elbow dug into his ribs with a vengeance.

"You know my birthday is next month."

"Oh, that's right. Sorry, Honey. Is it our anniversary?"

"You don't remember?"

"Well, kind of, I mean yeah, sure, it's our anniversary." The Judge put on his best smile, trying to look pleased with himself. Trying to bluff his way through. Always amazed how quickly things could go

South with Katy. And even more, how quickly these damn anniversaries kept reappearing.

Katy harrumphed. "You got flowers? A gift? At least a card?" Katy stood up, standing over him, arms crossed. She didn't look happy.

"Shortly, Katy. All that. I was planning to go out a little later this afternoon and prepare."

"Sure, you were, Judge, sure you were. Seven years. Seven long years. Sometimes I feel like my youth is just gone, just slipped away, used up on you." Katy pointed an index finger at him. He felt like he was looking down the muzzle of a gun.

"Oh, now Katy. Wait a minute. We've had a wonderful time. And now we have Ralphie. Think about all the good memories."

"It was fun to start with, Judge. We were so romantic."

"We were hot, Katy, hot for each other. I couldn't keep away from you."

"You couldn't keep your hands off me, Judge."

"Well, there…"

"But that's all worn off, Judge. We have sex now and you just roll over and go to sleep. It's all just physical release. We used to talk for hours afterward, about our plans, our dreams. Don't you ever miss that?"

"We still talk about that, Katy, a lot."

"We do. But now it's in the car, dashing somewhere. Or over coffee in the morning, desperate to get out and on with our day. It's not the same, Judge."

"That romantic, infatuation period can't last forever, Katy."

"I suppose not, Judge. Such a shame. It's like the past of somebody else I vaguely remember, someone not me. I remember it was exhilarating. And I know it'll never come back. It leaves me sad."

"I'm sorry you're not happy."

"I'm not unhappy, Judge. Not exactly. I'm certainly not unhappy with you. I'm just wistful for something else in my life. Something we had. Something that faded. Something that'll never come again."

"I'm happy, Katy. Happy with you. Happy with our relationship." The Judge gave her his best smile again, trying to sound encouraging. Concerned now.

"I know that, Judge. But it's like we both put less effort into us than we used to. Not because we don't care. But because we've become comfortable. We each know the other better than anyone else. And we've just settled in. It feels to me more like I'm hanging out with my best friend, rather than my romantic partner."

"Oh no, Katy. That's not true. I love you dearly. And you're really hot. I don't think the passion's gone."

"I have questions in my head, Judge. I can't help it. Are we truly close anymore? Am I really happy? Am I as attractive as when we first dated? Am I bored with our routine? Is there something missing in my life? "

"For me, Katy, it's our shared interests that make me feel close. Our Ralphie, or traveling together, your insights in the cases I take and the crimes I try to solve, our enjoyment of old friends and our making of new, our conversations about the issues of the day."

"But you left out sex, Judge. You just left sex out...."

"Err, well, of course sex. Sex with you is wonderful."

"It's been seven years, Judge. Some marriage counselors say seven years is the average amount of time a relationship continues before the honeymoon phase completely ends. It's then the real emotional wounds of each partner emerge."

"The Seven Year itch, huh?"

"You laugh, Judge, but statistically there is such a thing. The numbers don't lie. On average, couples are likely to experience a romantic burnout around seven years in. They often assess the relationship as failed because they've 'lost that spark.' And they split."

"What emotional wounds are you talking about, Katy? You said, 'emotional wounds.'"

"Well, for instance, look at you, Judge. A first wife who left you for another man. You don't think that left scars? I believe your fear of abandonment carried over into our relationship. Perhaps a distrust that any relationship can be permanent? That it can last."

"I suppose, Katy. I suppose you're right. But then you have scars too."

"Me?"

"Sure. A financially successful dad exploring for oil all over the world, but rarely home. No live-in father-figure. No opportunity to learn about men firsthand from a dad active in your life on a daily basis."

"Did that create a scar do you think, Judge?"

"It certainly made you strong, Katy. But perhaps a little distrusting as well. Perhaps you also distrust that a relationship can be permanent."

"No, Judge. I believe we can be permanent. The issue is whether this permanent relationship is enough. What am I sacrificing for it? What am I losing, missing? What's happened to my youth?"

"We all get older, Katy. Youth is just a fleeting chapter in what, hopefully, is a long life."

"Yeah. We all shrivel up and die, don't we?"

"Wow, you are in an unhappy mood. Is it the time of the month, or…?"

"Oh, fuck off, Judge. Just fuck off." Katy got up and marched from the room, followed by Annie the dog, her tail curled in the air, leaving a silence that spread like a cloud, filling the Judge's heart, making him want to weep.

The Judge did what he usually did when they'd had a fight like this. He fled. Up all the damn steps outside the cabin, up to the road, up to his car . He headed over to Cedar Glen to nurse his wounds with a drink at RB's Steakhouse. There would be people to watch there. He wanted to feel like he was in a crowd, but not be part of it.

Chapter 7
Sunday Evening 9:00 p.m.

The downstairs bar at RB's Steakhouse was crowded. Too many people wedged into too small a space in a three-story structure that had once been the whorehouse of preference for Cedar Glen's loggers at the beginning of the last century. An elderly patron finished initialing her credit card bill and slid off her seat at the bar, opening a single slot. The Judge dived in to take it, just ahead of a burly guy with a red face who gave the Judge a look of pure menace for beating him to the prize.

As the Judge settled on to the still-warm seat, he felt a brush of something soft as the scent of cinnamon wafted around him. He turned to find a pretty blonde snuggling her rounded tush on the stool next to him which likewise had suddenly vacated. She looked vaguely familiar. His instinct was confirmed when she whispered under her breath, "Hi, Judgee. Didn't know you were a fan of the Lake."

She was a petite young thing, short but well proportioned, except across the chest, where she excelled. Her face was framed by long blond hair, and she had large brown eyes, which regarded him now with a twinkle. She wore a green skirt, shorter than the law allowed by an inch or so, a white blouse unbuttoned one too many buttons, exposing a lot of pink chest and large, barely covered breasts. This seemed the new style with young women these days, a style the Judge admired but couldn't really approve of. He knew he was a bit old fashioned. Over her blouse she wore a green corduroy sport coat. Her cell phone was tucked into the breast pocket of her sportscoat, rather than in her back pants pocket as most females and kids seemed to do these days. Likely so as not to spoil her posterior lines, speculated the Judge. If the Judge wore his cell phone in his back pocket, it'd be crushed every time he sat down. He really needed to give up ice cream for a while.

"You don't remember me, Judge. You don't remember me. Guess I didn't make as much of an impression as I thought." One small hand with perfect pink nail polish was laid atop the Judge's arm, sending sparks through his system. "You clearly need another dose."

The Judge stuck his hand out tentatively, admitting by his smile he didn't remember. It was his best boyish smile. He suspected the smile looked more that of an aging crocodile to this young thing, all teeth, but it was the best he could manage tonight.

"I'm Claire. You know, Jeffrey Simpson's old girlfriend."

By God he did know. It was his last major case. Jeffrey Simpson had been found in the maintenance room of The Strand Pre-School, hanging by his neck. The Judge and Barney Malone, dynamic duo lawyers that they were, had gone into play for the defense. They'd had a hell of a time getting their clients off.

"Claire Henderson." It was the Judge's guess at her last name.

"Got it on the second try, sweetie," Claire said, placing her small hand with perfect pink nail polish softly into his paw and lingering it there a tad too long for a handshake. "Going to buy me a drink for old times' sake?"

"Sure." The word popped out without a thought. He remembered she'd had this effect on him before.

They sat there for a while watching the ebb and flow of people into the bar, sipping their drinks.

"So, you remember my program for men, right Judge?" asked Claire.

The Judge, in the middle of a large slurp, almost spilt his beer on his lap.

Recovering, he said, "Three guys, each blind to the others' existence, covering a third of your support. Did I get it right, Claire?"

"Very good, Judge. I like men, and men like me. So, I always have two or three guys, sometimes four, to have fun with and to pay the rent and life's other little expenses. I have a significant relationship with each of my men. You know, deep conversations, ego-stroking, and lots of love and sex. These are natural things. It's how we're built. It's very normal to want sex with a lover, to spend time with him, to make him happy with your smile. To display your intense interest in him, in his workday, and of course, in his body. To be tight together. It's how the human race evolved. If you're going to do it with one, it's as easy to do it with three."

The Judge felt himself getting hotter, his face flushing. Someone should open a window. Perhaps just hot flashes.... Maybe guys went through the change too. At any rate, he felt at a loss for words, tongue-tied. It didn't seem to matter. Claire filled in the spaces quite cheerfully.

"Remember, Judge, we discussed how you might be one of my 'men.'" Claire batted her eyelashes at him, then winked.

"I... I don't recall that Claire."

"Sure you do. We discussed it at length. My male friends take me out. Show me a good time. I receive an expense allowance to cover my clothes and makeup and stuff, so I'm sure to look good for you, Judge."

"You look great to me, Claire." The Judge clamped his jaws shut, mentally slapping himself on the side of the head for uttering what he was thinking.

"That's what you said last time. We talked about going out together, you and me. We were going to have a great time. Fancy dinners, travel. I was going to hear all your lawyer stories. You were going to get all my attention. I was going to rub your shoulders, make you relaxed, release all your tension. You know, the way a woman can. And you were going to give me an allowance each month, to help cover some of my expenses.... But Judge, you never called!"

"Oh no. No. *You* talked about all that. But I never agreed to any such involvement."

"Oh, Judge. I could see you wanted to. I could see it in your face. Just like now."

"I'm married, Claire. I think I told you, I'm married, happily married. We have a son." The Judge sounded a little desperate now, even to himself, like a drowning man.

"Of course. You told me, Judge. I like honest men. And that's why it was going to be so perfect. Because I don't mind. And I'm so very, very discreet. Besides, I've recently lost one of my three benefactors, and I have room for you now, Judge."

The Judge looked around nervously. Did anyone know him here? He couldn't believe he was having this conversation. This was just the sort of situation where Katy would turn up unexpectedly. Some feminine instinct guiding her to the kill.

"Now, Claire. You're trying to have me on here, and we both know it. You told me what you do and how you work, but we never discussed my participating in such an arrangement."

"Oh, Judge. I would like to have you on, and we both know it honey. But perhaps our conversation was more implied than explicit. Or is the word *complicit*? And you never called. So, nothing was consummated. Course, as my mother used to say, 'Sometimes we're lucky; we get a second chance.'" Claire gave the Judge another eyelash bat. "I've had an opening suddenly in my triangle I need to fill. It could be you, Judge."

"You had one lover you thought was dangerous, Claire." Their conversation was coming back to the Judge.

Claire blinked, the smile dropping from her face, replaced by something else… what? Terror…? Then it passed, the smile pasted back with determination, lighting up her face again as she casually looked around the room over her shoulder. Looking carefully. Was she counting exits? By God he thought she was.

"Sorry, Judge. Not usually this jumpy." Claire leaned forward to whisper, "Just that I'm up here with one guy friend, and my other guy friend happens to be up here too. Fuckin' bad luck! They both want a piece of me. I'm starting to feel like a Goddamn ping pong ball. The Lake is 'small town USA.' I'm desperately trying to assure they don't meet. And don't see me with the other. Each one thinks he's the only one, as he should. Makes it very tricky. Like being a controller at LAX, shuffling planes around the sky."

"Last time we talked you were concerned with your friend who'd migrated from Chicago. A mob guy. Still seeing him?"

"Tony. Yes. I shouldn't have said that about him. He'd get mad. He's very secretive about his family. But we're still an item, Judge. He's very, very generous with his financial help."

"You said he was jealous."

"Yes, very. Makes it hard for me to get around."

"You mean sneak around?"

"Judge! What kind of woman do you think I am!" But Claire was smiling now, her soft brown eyes dancing. "Anyway, it's perhaps best we don't start something, you and I, Judge. My other lover, not Tony, is really into me. He's very powerful, and he's coming into oodles of money. He wants to retire my number, marry me and whisk me away to a new life. Perhaps to some island in the South Seas." Claire gave the Judge her big smile, showing all her teeth.

"What happened to your third lover, Claire?"

It was then the Judge felt the small hairs on the back of his neck twitch, as though eyes were boring into the back of his head. He spun around on his bar stool to face the crowd, his knees almost plowing into a man standing right behind him at the bar. staring at him with small, hard eyes.

Claire started, a nervous smile appearing on her face. "Hi dear. Are you ready to go to dinner?"

"Who the fuck are you?"

The man had a low, menacing voice. Shorter than the Judge by about four inches, but powerfully built, muscular arms and shoulders over the squat compact body of a wrestler. He wore designer jeans and an expensive caramel cashmere sweater over a Brooks Brothers pin-striped shirt, open at the collar to expose a hint of curly black hair. He was mid- thirties and looked rough and ready under his fancy clothes. There was a hint of Neanderthal in his face, heavy brow and slightly triangular shaped head, wider across the forehead and narrower at the jaw. The Judge sensed ruthlessness and barely contained violence in the man.

"Oh, this is the Judge, Tony. An old family friend of my mother's. Judge, this is my special friend, and the love of my life… this is Tony Roselli."

The Judge extended a hand as Tony relaxed a little, easing off his toes and back onto the balls of his feet, extending a meaty looking paw to shake, exposing a sparkling Rolex, a GMT Master II Ice. It made the Judge's Yacht-Master look puny.

"Let's go, Claire. This yuppie crowd is too noisy for me." He gave the Judge one more measured look, part warning, part disdain, threw a hundred-dollar bill down on the bar in front of Claire, and spun around into the crowd, heading for the door. Expecting Claire to follow. And she did, scrambling off her bar stool, giving a final wink at the Judge with her small chin up, trying to look brave rather than fearful.

Jesus, thought the Judge. *We seem to just naturally create our own complexities, our own messes. Then we spend all our time and energy trying to extricate ourselves from what we've created. Homo Sapiens, the animal walking on two feet with opposable thumbs, and a mind that spins webs better than a spider.*

The Judge stayed on at the bar another hour, watching the flora and fauna, sipping Laphroaig on the rocks, wondering through the gathering haze what he should do about Katy. He loved her dearly. But she wasn't happy… unhappy with him...? Unhappy with life?

The Judge finally left the bar at 11:45 p.m. He'd thought about leaving his car in the Village Parking structure and taking an Uber to his cabin. The Scotch had hit him harder than it should have, perhaps because he'd lost his appetite during his dispute with Katy and had skipped dinner. But he decided he was sufficiently sobered up to drive. He'd nursed a single drink for the last hour and a half, and filled up on salted peanuts, French fries and popcorn at the bar. Food Katy wouldn't allow him to eat for reasons beyond his ken. It was almost midnight. He figured Katy would be sound asleep, which was good. He wasn't up for more intense discussion about their relationship.

God did women like to use their words. To talk about feelings and emotions, conveying these things in the minutest of detail, sliced thin, like salami. Sometimes Katy's cascade of words seemed like a cascade of hammer blows. He supposed that was the female's main line of defense. And also, their main technique for aggression. What else did they have, generally being smaller and lighter than men?

The Judge parked his car at the side of the road, and stumbled his way down the thousand steps, holding securely to the rail all the way as he tripped unsteadily here and there. All he wanted was to collapse in bed and sleep.

He quietly used his key to open the kitchen door, and then crept upstairs and down the hall toward the master bedroom door, leaving the light off and hoping Katy wouldn't wake up. Christ it was dark. The moon had gone behind a cloud.

His final step before reaching the closed door came down two inches short of the floor on something corded, like a snake. It was yanked away with a yelp of pain. It threw him off balance and slammed him into the bedroom door. The door was just pulled to and naturally gave way, sending him spinning into the bedroom where he fell in a heap at the foot of the four-poster bed, banging his head against the frame.

"Shit… Shit… Shit!" he muttered. He'd just stepped on Annie the Dog's tail.

Katy's head flew up from her pillow. "What the hell's going on?"

Damn, now Katy was awake.

"Did you step on the dog again, Judge? Are you smashed?"

"I don't wish to dismiss it… I mean discuss it," muttered the Judge, picking himself up from the floor with what little dignity he could muster and heading for the refuge of the bathroom to brush his teeth.

Chapter 8
Monday Morning 9:00 a.m.

The Judge did the thousand steps from his cabin up to the street the next morning, panting like an old bull at the top. He called them the thousand steps, although there weren't near that many. Because of the high altitude, and because of the paunch he carried around and didn't seem able to diet off, the steps always left him winded and gasping for breath. They may as well have been a thousand.

He climbed into his car and headed off around the Lake toward Arrowhead Village. It was a sparkling day, blue lake, verdant green pines and azure sky, with just a hint of a puffy cloud here and there. It relaxed him to sluice around the turns on the narrow two-lane road. He pulled into the Arrowhead Village parking garage and maneuvered his car up to the empty upper level, picking a spot on the top end, protecting his car from dings. He turned off the engine and stretched as a prelude to clambering out and up the stairs to the upper level of shops. His private P.O. Box was there, a consequence of no residential mail delivery in the mountains.

It was dark in the garage; the silky sun didn't reach here. An SUV pulled past him, drab-green and dusty. It took a spot three up from him on the empty level. The driver didn't get out. He just sat there in the deeper shadows of his tinted-car, motionless.

The Judge shrugged and crawled out of his car, a Mercedes E Class, silver with a dark blue canvas top which he'd run up. A car he was proud of. It was several years old, but still looked powerful and sleek, maintained to perfection as befitting the German marvel it was. He turned back to fumble with his key in the dark, finding the button to lock its doors. As he did so, he felt a stirring in the air, part draft, part movement, part premonition, and then the painful thrust of a gun barrel into the middle of his back. The cold steel pressed hard into his spine.

The other driver must have been nimble, sliding out of his car and covering the handful of steps up behind the Judge while he'd dawdled.

"Don't turn around," hissed a male voice, deep and malevolent. "Just put your hands on your car's fancy blue top and stay still."

The Judge sucked in his breath; felt his pulse racing, his heart doing flip-flops, as adrenaline surged in his body. *Shit.* What was he going to do now?

"My wallet's in my back pocket," the Judge said, his voice sounding hoarse, far away, small.

"This isn't about your wallet," Mr. Deep Voice hissed, cuffing the Judge on the side of the head with his other hand, pushing metal deeper into the Judge's spine, making him gasp.

"You're very close to being dead, Judge. Very close. I'm going to ask this once, and I'd better get a complete answer. Otherwise you're going to join your ancestors."

"What? What do you want?"

"Jerry Stone's last words. All of them. What did he say? Spit them out… Now!"

It took the Judge half a second to decide, privileged client information be damned. "Jerry was dying. He knew it. He said, 'Stop Cindy.'"

"What else?"

"Nothing. That's it."

"Cindy, huh. So, it was about Cindy."

"Yes. That's all Jerry said."

"Shut up. Listen, Judgee. Now you've spilled your guts… just leave this boat accident alone. Let the cops handle it. Else you might join your friend. Clear?"

The Judge nodded his head.

"Now start walking down the parking lot. Don't turn back, don't look back or it'll be your last look. Just keep walking to the far end of the parking structure and out the door into the village. Go."

The Judge did as he was told, trying to memorize the voice.

When he reached the exit door at the other end of the garage, he made a dive through it, then braced himself against the interior wall of the hall leading to the lower village stores, gasping for breath, trying to control his heart rate.

After a minute, the Judge edged back around and peeked up the garage floor. No one was there. His Mercedes sat as before at the top. The balance of the floor was empty. The SUV was gone. Mr. Deep Voice must have driven up the level and out the other exit to the upper level Village shops. *Damn.*

The Judge forced his knees, suddenly weak, to move. He retraced his steps up the parking level to his car, his PO Box mission forgotten. He moved around to the driver's side of his convertible and saw to his horror someone had used a key or something to scratch a message in the paint across the driver's side door. An ugly message.

"Chicken Shit."

Chapter 9
Monday Morning 10:30 a.m.

The Judge felt rage building as he maneuvered his victimized car out of the parking garage. He could taste his anger like bitter tea. He hadn't wanted to get involved in this Jerry Stone mess. He hadn't asked for Jerry's boat to randomly demolish his dock, nor for the attention he was getting because he'd heard Jerry last words. He was sorry he'd mentioned to his wife that Jerry had said something before he died.

But he'd been humiliated back in the parking garage. And the damage to his car was the final straw. Nobody could treat him like that, abuse his favorite car with impunity, treat him like a schmuck! He was damn well going get to the bottom of what happened to Jerry, and why. He was going to bring down this shadowy shape that shoved a gun into his spine. He winced, feeling the pain of bruised vertebrae throbbing against the leather seat.

He swung the car in a wide arc and headed back out to the Village at the garage's lower level, across its parking lot, then turned on to Lake Edge Road, the direction for the community of Blue Jay at the Lake's western end. Driving slowly now, feeling old, vulnerable and angry. The sun didn't seem so bright as he edged around the Lake, the trees weren't so green, and the Lake wasn't so sparkly. He'd been thrust into a different world. A world of meanness, violence, and death. A world that co-existed with the lighter world around him. But it was a shock to be so violently jerked away from touristy Lake Arrowhead and into the world of dark garages and gun-barrels.

At North Bay Road he turned right. This road wound around the shore of the Lake to its North Shore, to Tavern Bay, and to Shelter Cove, the 'old money' section of Lake Arrowhead where Jerry and Marie had their posh estate.

Jerry and Marie had gotten married seven years before. They'd hosted a huge shindig of a reception at the Santa Anita racetrack in Arcadia. The Judge still remembered the mother of all mothers of a hangover the next morning, though the party itself was hazy in his memory.

As the Judge rounded the Lake on North Bay Road, catching intermittent views of blue through the trees along Totem Pole Point, Meadow Bay and Hamiltair. He wondered what Marie Stone would do now. Fortunately, they had no kids, just the dog, Muffles, a Siberian Husky with cold blue eyes which always stared at the Judge suspiciously.

Marie had gone off to Notre Dame after growing up in 'Lower Sub-Marino', the San Marino area of more modest homes south of Huntington Drive. Occupied by old California families with connections but less money. Not that anything was cheap anymore there, or anywhere in L.A.

Raised Catholic, Marie'd left the Church one night in the back of a Lincoln Convertible in her second semester at Notre Dame, or so she'd say with a wink and a nod. Taking a degree in marketing, she'd come back to L.A. and joined a large advertising firm, moving up the ranks to Account Manager with surprising speed. There had been rumors her success had been partly earned in unorthodox ways outside the office, but her friends chose to ignore them. Marie still dabbled at the Agency, but Jerry had more than enough money to support them in a grand style after his parents died.

Money wouldn't be a problem for Marie now the Judge supposed. Jerry and Marie got married after a whirlwind campaign by Jerry to win her. They'd originally met online through a dating service, but that was a well-kept secret only a handful of people knew. Marie preferred to refer vaguely to an introduction through an old uncle, twice removed. It had taken Jerry a year to convince Marie to marry, and had played havoc with his law practice, leaving his law partners relieved when she finally said yes. There'd been hope that after his marriage Jerry would spend more late afternoons in the office or at home, and less in the watering holes preferred by attorneys ringing the courthouse. And that had been the case… for a while.

The Judge cut down Voltaire Drive, and left onto West Shore Road, taking him past the UCLA Conference Center to Tavern Bay, and then left again at the Tavern Bay Beach Club to the little bridge and the access gate to Shelter Cove and its monied residences. He knew the gate code and extending an arm out his car window, punched it into the small box at the entrance. He watched the gates dutifully swing open like the ancient Doors of Solomon's Temple, allowing his car access.

He drove for another quarter of a mile on narrow, partly one-way roads, past vintage mansions of size and quality, perched at the top of wooded, gently sloping tracts that meandered down to the Lake's edge. This was old Lake Arrowhead. Occupants referred to their weekend get-aways here as lodges, or chateaus, or by fanciful names like Trees & Clouds, Versailles Gardens, and Trail's End. But never as 'cabins'. And he supposed rightly so.

The Judge turned onto a long sweeping driveway, ending in a circle in front of a large two-story Victorian-style mansion, roughhewn grey stone with a black slate roof. Its manicured grounds and lawn shouted net worth and privilege. It had been in Jerry Stone's family for three generations. The Judge doubted he could afford the gardening staff required to keep up the grounds, much less the taxes and utilities. There was no mortgage, the Judge knew from preparing Jerry's estate plan.

He got out of his car and marched up the steps to the twin oversized doors, each with large brass knockers in the shape of the Lake. He raised a knocker and struck its pad several times, venting some of the hostility swirling inside him. He even smiled, remembering the scene in the movie Young Frankenstein when Gene Wilder marched up to a similar set of doors, and said, "What knockers!" causing the bountiful Teri Garr who then opened the door to blush and say "Thank you."

A voice inside shouted, "Coming."

Chapter 10
Monday Morning 11:00 a.m.

Thirty seconds later the big door swung open to reveal Marie, Jerry's widow. Great knockers she wasn't. But standing perhaps five-four now in her flat slippers rather than heels, she still conveyed an image of elegance and wealth. Her slender frame was kitted out in a white blouse over a soft apricot skirt cut discreetly below the knees. No black mourning colors for her.

But her eyes didn't have their usual sparkle. They had a shell-shocked look to them, as though she couldn't quite grasp the situation around her.

"Oh, Judge. Just the person I need to talk to. Come in. Come right through in here to the sitting room. I'll get you a Scotch. Single malt as I recall, and neat, no rocks. Is twelve-year-old good enough for you?"

"Yes, oh yes." said the Judge, perking up at the thought of Scotch. The Stone's living room was of immense proportions, high ceilings, dark wood paneled walls and ceiling beams. A moose head was mounted on one end, an elk antler chandelier hung over an antique card table at the other. The upholstered furniture was all plaids. It felt like a Scottish hunting lodge of some prince or king.

Marie returned to the hall, dragging a check out of her pocket and shoving it at the tall black lady who had appeared there looking distressed. It was Jackson, the Stone's housekeeper. "I wish you good luck, Jackson," Marie said in a low voice the Judge could barely make out. I hate to let you go, but I think it's for the best."

Jackson shrugged, tucked the check into a small satchel she had over her shoulder, picked up a suitcase at her feet in the other, and marched out the door.

The Judge settled in on one of the sofas, feeling himself sinking down, down, into the upholstery. Jesus, it felt like a six-inch plunge. He wondered if he'd be able to get up without the help of a crane.

Marie handed the Judge a crystal tumbler of Glenfiddich twelve-year-old, no ice. The Judge preferred Laphroaig, but this Scotch would do just fine. Marie slumped into the sofa across from the Judge, tucking one leg under the other. He wondered if she'd sink so far that she'd disappear into the fabric too, like those quicksand movies of old. But she bobbed on top of the fabric like a small nesting bird. Perhaps his enormous weight was sinking him down. It was a discouraging thought. *Okay,* he silently said to himself, *No more ice cream for a week.*

"I still can't believe he's gone, Judge. Some part of me still expects him to come through the back door from the Lake, that infectious smile on his face. I can't get my head around not seeing him again, ever. Oh, God, Judge, it makes me sad."

Marie reached up and dabbed at her eyes with small alabaster hands. She got up and drifted over to her window, leaning her forehead against the cool glass, eyes drifting across the Lake. "I was very fond of him in my own way, you know. We often didn't agree. But I'm going to miss him."

She hung there for a while against the window. Quiet, like an injured bird trying to regain its strength. Then she gave a shuddering sigh and turned back to the Judge, some part of her pain boxed up and put away to a corner of her brain.

"The police were here, Judge. I guess you heard the awful news. Someone killed Jerry. Slugged him in the back of the head with a bat or something."

"I heard, Marie."

"It makes me so angry. Who would do such an awful thing?? Everybody loved Jerry."

"You said you needed some advice, Marie?"

"Yes. I don't know how to put this. It's kind of delicate."

"Just jumping in works best, Marie."

"Yes. Well. They asked me where I was the Friday night, the night Jerry died."

"Who?"

"The police of course."

"And where were you, Marie?"

"Well, that's the problem, Judge. See, I was with a social group."

"And you told this to the police?"

"Yes, I did, Judge."

"So, where's the problem?"

"The police wanted to know where our social group met, what it's about and the names of the other people there."

"So, you told them."

"No, Judge, I didn't."

"Didn't? Didn't what?"

"I didn't tell them the physical address where my event took place. I declined to give names of the other members or explain what it was about. I couldn't, Judge. I just couldn't."

"But Marie, you have to give them some names. Standard procedure. That provides your alibi. The job of the police initially is to eliminate suspects."

"I can't, Judge."

"Why on earth not, Marie?"

"It's complicated."

"I'm listening."

"I don't want to tell you either."

"But Marie, you're making this sound suspicious." The Judge raised his hands, palms out to Marie. "I know, I know, you'd never hurt Jerry. But the fact is that almost half of all homicides are committed by someone who knew the victim, often someone in the immediate family. So, it's the first place the police look. And suddenly you're being very cagey about where you were the night Jerry died. And who you were with. And why."

"I should have told them I was just here, Judge, at the house. By myself. Can I tell them that now?"

"You can. But the cat's out of the bag, Marie. You've told them you were at this social function. It will be equally suspicious if you change your story. You were either lying before, or you're lying now. Either way, there's a lie. So, they're going to wonder why you would lie."

Marie slumped further back into the sofa, her eyes misting. "Oh, Christ, Judge, what a mess."

"Tell me what's going on, Marie. Even though I technically don't represent you, at least right now. I'm an attorney and anything you tell me in confidence is protected by privilege."

"Aw shit, Judge. How to start?" Marie sat up straighter, resigned now, letting her gaze drift over the Judge's shoulder, out the window again to the Lake.

"See Judge, Jerry and I've been married for seven and a half years. And… I don't know. I guess the newness just kinda wore off. Last year, after a couple of bouts of marriage counseling which didn't go anywhere, the therapist suggested trying an open marriage arrangement. To spice things up a little, she said."

"No way. What kind of marriage counselor gives that sort of advice? Who picked her?"

"Well, actually, I did, Judge." Marie gave a wan little smile.

"And you knew of the counselor's proclivities?"

"Well …yes. I did, Judge. Anyway, Jerry and I talked about it. And we decided to give it a try."

"An open marriage?"

"Yes. You know. We are together as a couple and committed to each other and all, but we each can have flings on the side."

"Sexual flings?"

"Judge. Of course."

"Wow. I am surprised."

"You're more than surprised, Judge. You're shocked. I can tell. And so everyone will be if this gets out."

"And did you, Marie?"

"Yes. Jerry got involved with someone right off. And then he switched horses and got involved with another woman. And I ended up joining this social club."

"Was either of Jerry's side-bets named Cindy?"

"Not the first one. I don't know about the second one, Judge. He never told me her name. I heard him talking on his cell to her about a month ago when I walked into the room unexpectedly. He called her 'C'."

"So, her name could have been Cindy?"

"I suppose."

"So, what's the social club about, Marie?"

"You know, Judge, just a social club."

"I don't know, Marie. Tell me. You need to level with me if I'm going to help."

"Well, it's social club, sort of. I suppose in your day, Judge, it was called a swinger's club."

"Oh." The Judge sat back in his chair, taking time to digest this information. To rearrange his impression of Marie, and of the Jerry-Marie relationship.

"But don't you have to bring a partner if you're in a group like that, Marie?"

"Huh," snorted Marie. "If you're a guy, sure, you've got to bring your partner, or at least a woman friend willing to participate. But if you're a single female, you're always welcome, Judge. I guess that's just nature's way." Marie gave the Judge another soft smile.

"And that's where you were last night?"

"Yes. At Sharon Langley's house."

"The widow."

"Yes. You know her? She has that beautiful mansion looking over the Lake out on Rainbow Point. Three stories and six bedrooms. She throws quite a party."

"I'll bet." The Judge smiled. Sharon Langley was mid-forties. She'd married and then lost a very wealthy husband twenty years her senior. She was well known around the Lake for throwing lavish parties, often, and for any reason or cause that could be drummed up. She was a big knocker girl if ever there was, with something of a loose reputation.

"How many people were there?"

"There were twenty of us, the usual group, plus two guests from below."

'Below' was the name for the flat lands at the base of the mountain, spreading off from San Berdoo across the great Los Angeles plain through downtown L.A. and out through Hollywood and the Valley beyond.

"And they all can testify you were there?"

"Yes. Of course. But I don't want them telling everybody I was running around a party butt-naked for Christ sakes. Particularly while my husband was getting himself murdered somewhere else on the Lake."

"Well. So, you were there over what time period?"

"We got started at nine. I left at twelve-thirty, sharp. I was worn out."

"You participated in the play?" The Judge knew he was being snoopy now, actually more of a voyeur he supposed, but he couldn't resist.

"Oh yes."

"You came and went by yourself?"

"Yes. I came… and I came… and I came... And then I went." Marie's eyes twinkled for a moment.

"Yes, well…"

"So, you see, Judge, I can't tell the Sheriff about this. This is a small gossipy village. My reputation would be trashed. My woman friends wouldn't allow me to talk to their husbands. You wouldn't be allowed to sit here having this conversation with me if Katy knew. At least not alone."

"It's a bigger problem than that Marie. Even if you let your secret slip, you still wouldn't have an alibi for the period when someone piled Jerry into his boat half unconscious and sent him careening across the Lake."

"How so, Judge?"

"It was one-thirty when I heard Jerry's boat on the Lake. You'd left the party about twelve-thirty, you said."

"Oh."

"You came straight home?"

"Yes."

"You left the party by yourself?"

"Yes."

"Did you see Jerry? Was he here?"

"No."

"Was Jackson here?"

"No."

"Did you and Jerry sleep together in the same bedroom?"

Marie sighed. "No. Not anymore. Not for two months now."

"What happened?"

"I don't know. I mean I know, but it wasn't fair. We had this open marriage deal, see. So, it was okay for him to have his mistress, and I was supposed to have open privileges too. I guess he thought I'd get a pool boy or something."

"He didn't know about your 'social' club?"

"No. Not till the sister of his law partner's paralegal happened to come to our social club as a guest two months ago. I guess she went back and spilled her guts. Anyway, Jerry stormed up here that weekend loaded to the gills. Said he'd just heard I was screwing half the men in the village. Said I had the right to an affair, but he'd never agreed to my dicking a whole damn village. Course it wasn't like that, but his imagination ran wild. Anyway, we had this big fight. He decided he wasn't sharing a bedroom with me anymore. Just like that."

"Was he threatening a divorce?"

Marie hung her head. "Yes," she whispered. "He filed two weeks ago."

"I have to ask, Marie. What would have happened if Jerry were still alive and you two had completed a divorce?"

Another sigh from Marie. "Not much. I signed a separate property agreement when I married Jerry. My asshole father-in-law insisted on it. We have no kids. I'd get some alimony for a few years, then be cut off."

"Do you have any money of your own?"

"No. Jerry has... had all the money."

"But Jerry's dead, now. So, there is no divorce. What happens under Jerry's will?"

"I think it all goes to me under some trust form or something, unless he changed it."

"Yes, I did Jerry's estate plan. That's how I recall it too. Did Jerry change his will or trust recently? Perhaps because of this divorce?"

"No. I don't… I… I guess I don't know."

"I'm sorry, Marie, but that does give you motive. The police will see it that way." Marie looked even more stricken. "Is there someone special you're intimate with when you do your social club, Marie?"

"That's private, Judge. Give me a break."

"When this all comes out, and I'm afraid it likely will, Marie, that's the question the police are going to ask."

"Why? Why does it matter?"

"Because the threatened divorce gives you motive, you have no alibi over the time period Jerry was attacked, and you were in the vicinity. But, you're hardly strong enough to hoist an unconscious Jerry into his boat. If you'd done it, you'd have had an accomplice."

"Oh."

"Is there someone special at your social club?"

"There's a Spanish guy, from Granada. Younger than me, very sweet. We've been spending a lot of time together at the group, talking, sharing dreams."

"And being intimate?"

"Of course. You're supposed to spend some experimental time with at least two people at each event. It's an informal rule. It's what the club's about. But lately I've been spending most of my time with him."

"What's his name?"

"God, Judge. You don't think he'll be dragged into this? It's not fair. It's like I'm on trial. And I haven't done anything."

"Would he be jealous of Jerry? Perhaps like to see Jerry off stage so he could have you all to himself?"

"No, Judge. It's nothing like that. We're just friends."

"And lovers."

"And sometimes lovers, but nothing exclusive. We just enjoy each other's company and each other's bodies, that's all."

"What's his name?"

"Judge..."

"If you want my help you have to give me the full picture, Marie."

"Juan. His name is Juan. He's an architect with Hambro and James, the architects in Blue Jay."

"How old is he?"

The Judge could see the color rising now in Marie's face.

"Twenty-four... But he's very mature for his age."

"It sounds like it," said the Judge, covering his smirk with a cough. "What was Jerry working on at his law firm? Any big cases?"

"This animal rights thing... God, it's all Jerry'd talk about."

"His case?"

"Yes, his case. His big case. He ate, slept and breathed the damn case."

"Was he litigating for the protection of animals, or defending against someone's claim, Marie?"

"You know, Judge, sometimes it was hard to tell. I mean, Jerry started off defending The Foundation."

"The Foundation?"

"Yeah, The Foundation for the Advancement of Animal Rights and Education. It goes by FAAR, I think. Anyway, Jerry said a disgruntled ex-employee claimed the bulk of the money contributed to The Foundation was used to pay big salaries and to fund illicit research on animals. The employee tried to blow the whistle and now claims he was fired because of it. He's the one who has sued."

"And this Foundation has the money to hire a big-time law firm like McCarthy, Jenner & Smith?"

"Oh yes. The Foundation raises lots of money for its work; it's very well endowed."

Marie said, "It could afford to pay Jerry and his team to come in and run paper circles around the small law firm representing the ex-employee. It was a suit The Foundation couldn't afford to settle, Jerry said. What would their donors think if The Foundation lost, or settled?"

"And Jerry was still working the case just before he died?"

"Well, yes and no. He was working it on Thursday. He visited their corporate offices, which they maintain on some ranch up here in the mountains above the Lake."

"So why do you say, 'yes and no'?"

"Cause, Jerry came back that night all steamed up. I guess they'd had a big fight or something."

"Jerry and The Foundation?"

"With its director, I think. Jerry was really angry. Told me he was withdrawing from the case. Said there was no way he'd represent those bastards. Said they were diverting funds to do dangerous things."

"What things?"

"He didn't explain. Said it was better that I didn't know. Oh, God, Judge. It's all so sad. I wasn't much of a wife to him in the end. I think I need to be alone now. I… I just can't cope." Marie stood up, emphasizing his interview was over, and slowly padded to the front door, the Judge in tow.

"If I can help in anyway, Marie, just call," said the Judge. Marie nodded, not saying anything, watching him with glazed eyes as he stepped out into the fresh air and sunshine. Then she softly closed the door.

Chapter 11
Monday Noon

The Judge started for his car, hesitated, then set out across the brown grass to the left, around the house, toward the Lake. It was the way to Jerry's dock. He ducked through the trees on a well-worn trail behind the house which meandered down toward the Lake, smelling the faint odor of pine, admiring the daylilies riotously growing along the trail. The trees gave way to a small sandy hill, sloping down to the water's edge. Down to the dock.

It was a single dock like the Judge's, but twice as wide, with an ancient set of rock-hewn steps leading down to it, framed by white fencing with a slight oriental flare as it swooped to the water. At the shore end was a green clapboard cabana, providing storage at its back and a wide bar with sink facing the water. Panels at the bar's front, facing the Lake, lifted to display the most amazing volume and assortment of alcohol in colorful bottles and decanters. The Judge remembered at least five single malts he sampled here at a summer party. At the other end of the dock a double lounge was positioned under a large red umbrella, one of those new-fangled side-supported affairs with a pole sweeping out from behind it.

There was a mass of yellow police tape strung across the dock's entrance, clashing with the reds and greens of the dock and the blues of the water. But no one was around.

The Judge gingerly stepped over the tape and took the steps down to the dock, feeling it give slightly as he stepped aboard. At the front of the cabana the Judge could see someone had lifted the set of bar panels and latched them to the roof. The bottles on display glowed in the late Fall sun as it crept ever closer to the rim of hills surrounding Arrowhead Valley. A bottle of Jack Daniels sat on the bar, open, its cork beside it, along with two empty tumblers. Jack Daniels was Jerry's drink. But he'd never ruin good whisky by leaving the top off. The Judge wondered why the little display hadn't already been swept up and off to the lab for fingerprinting.

The dock slip was empty. A heavy canvas sling stretched across the inside nose of the slip, there to stop forward motion before a boat could crunch its bow into the shore side of the dock. It rocked idly as the dock balanced from small ripples on the Lake. An empty dock line was wound around a cleat there, its bitter end disappearing into the Lake where it'd fallen. The cleat was wobbly; its outside screws set into the dock lifted two-thirds out of their mountings.

The Judge dropped down on one knee and considered. The boat belonged bow-first in the dock. That's how the lines were set up, how the bumpers were located. And the boat did less jumping around from the waves of the Lake when the waves rolled in and under the stern first. But Jerry's boat must have been backed in, since it had come out nose first and straight across the lake. Backing a boat into a slip took a little more dexterity and skill than driving a boat in bow first. It was… what? Curious.

The Judge wondered if the police had searched the Lake and the bushes for a boat paddle or a bat. Wondered if they'd found traces of Jerry's blood on the dock. It was a vicious crime. But had it been planned? Or was it a crime of opportunity? Or even of passion; someone so upset they couldn't stop themselves from going after Jerry with a paddle?

Did they lie in wait for Jerry here, perhaps on the sand at the side of the steps? Or did they come back with Jerry in his boat, watch while he artfully backed it into his slip? Perhaps attacking as he bent over to tie the dock lines?

Chapter 12
Monday Evening 5:30 p.m.

They sat in the living room, feet up on the sills of tall windows that dropped almost to the floor, wide open despite the chill. They watched the shadows fall across the Lake as the sun eased below the mountains behind the cabin. Katy had mixed some Campari and sodas. The Judge had picked up smoked salmon and crackers. The Lake and the air, and Katy, were like a soft balm, soothing the Judge's soul. The Campari helped too, though he would have preferred scotch.

"So, Judge, have you figured out who did this to Jerry?"

The Judge smiled. "Often the facts, once uncovered, are quite simple to explain. But digging out what is true can be complex. Much of the confusion in this case turns on where the crime was initiated. Jerry's boat left his dock and came tearing across the Lake to smash into our dock and explode. Jerry unconscious at the helm. But where did the crime start, Katy? That's the first question. Where was Jerry when he was bashed across the back of his head with a boat paddle? The police assumed this initial attack occurred at Jerry's dock. But is that right?"

"I don't know, Judge. What do you think?"

"Well, Katy, consider. There's a half torn out cleat near the back of Jerry's dock. Someone tied the boat up with the bow pointed out, revved the engines hard, then let go the restraining rear dock lines so the boat tore out of the slip. What does that mean?"

Katy looked at him. "That's not normally how you dock a boat, Judge."

"You're right. It means someone had to negotiate the boat around out in the Lake, in front of the dock, and then back it into Jerry's slip. It's always a little tricky to back a boat into a slip. There's no tide on the Lake, but there was a twenty-mile an hour wind blowing crossways to the dock that night. Jerry wasn't the best of boatmen in sober times, and much less so when he was three sheets to the wind. The police lab results showed Jerry was highly intoxicated when he was hit from behind. So, what do we conclude from that?"

"Someone else maneuvered the boat backwards into it slip."

"Right. Who was that someone? And where were Jerry and his boat before it was backed into the slip?"

"What do you think, Judge?"

"I heard Jerry's boat out on the Lake that night, Katy. Thinking back, when I consider it, I think it sounded like the boat started up over at Arrowhead Village. The boat continued across the Lake to Jerry's dock, did some maneuvering there, lingered in idle for perhaps three minutes, then started up again, becoming louder and louder as it raced across the Lake toward us. From the sounds I heard, I believed this all started at the Village dock."

"It happened in the Village," gasped Katy, sitting straighter in her chair now, playing the game.

"Let's suppose the attack was initiated at the Village, Katy. And the killer drove the boat across the lake to Jerry's Shelter Cove dock and set things up there How did the killer get away after he or she released the boat from its dock lines? It's a long walk to anywhere from Shelter Cove. And no taxi or Uber was ordered that evening for Shelter Cove. The police checked."

"An accomplice," said Katy.

"Yes, Katy. It suggests there was someone else involved. Someone who took a car from the Village, around the Lake to Shelter Cove and picked up our killer after he or she released the boat. Two people. Two people were involved in Jerry's death. One or both of them disabled Jerry on the community dock in the Village, knocking him unconscious, loading him onto his boat. One of them drove Jerry's boat across the Lake to his dock, staging what appeared to be a boating accident. As though Jerry took off from his dock and then lost control in his inebriated condition."

"So, the other person drove their car around the Lake to Shelter Cove and picked the killer up," said Katy.

"Right. Removing the killer from an area that would be heavily inspected by the police a half-hour later. Transporting the killer away. I think we have a crime initiated at the community dock in the Village with two people present. The question then becomes, who?"

Chapter 13
Monday Evening 11:00 p.m.

Later in the evening after Katy had toddled off to bed, the Judge lit the fire, mostly for cheer since the forced air heating had vanished the chill. He poured himself a generous couple of inches of Laphroaig, an eighteen-year-old single malt Scotch from the Isle of Islay and settled in at the old carved dining table that had belonged to his great-grandmother. He powered up his laptop, determined to learn more about Jerry Stone's client, or former client. A client Jerry had apparently abandoned mid-stream, something a good lawyer hardly ever does. And Jerry was a superb lawyer.

Clients of course fire their lawyers all the time, and for a variety of reasons. But lawyers, once committed to a case, were under an ethical obligation to follow through to its conclusion, subject to only certain exceptions. For example, clients refusing to listen to the lawyer's advice, clients failing to pay for their legal services, unanticipated conflicts of interest arising in a case, and, sometimes, clients continuing or contemplating illegal actively. The Judge was curious why Jerry had felt compelled to abandon this client.

The internet was helpful, disclosing myriad details about The Foundation for the Advancement of Animal Rights and Education, or FAAR, or just The

Foundation. And even more about its Director, the honorable Dr. David Francis Branden. But it hadn't been easy to dig out.

At first the Judge had run into a lot of expensively prepared eyewash about how wonderful the good Doctor was, how dedicated to animals; and how modern science, research and food processing were treating animals in inhumane ways. The Foundation apparently had plenty of money to hire the biggest and best press agents and internet manipulators, and to initiate sustained broad web campaigns touting The Foundation's work and the importance of its Director. All very glowing and self-laudatory. And no doubt helpful for raising charitable contributions for The Foundation's cause.

There were several photos of Dr. Branden, or 'The Doctor', as he was called. He had premature silver hair, long and flowing; he could have been a conductor for the Philharmonic. His sideburns framed a deeply tanned face with a gregarious smile, set off by perfect teeth. Bright blue eyes twinkled from under bushy eyebrows that arched in a devil-may-care way. He looked a little like Ralph Lauren, except that he was a big man, perhaps six-foot two, with broad shoulders and an expanding paunch. He obviously liked la dolce vita and could afford to live it.

But going farther back, to the earlier postings on the internet, and then further back, into the archives of the Los Angeles Times, and then the New York Times, a different picture emerged.

David Francis Branden, contrary to popular legend, was not a self-made man from humble upstate New York beginnings. He was rather a Long Island native, the scion of a famous New York surgeon who'd been an early researcher into the repair of patients' hearts. Dad had gotten his young man into Yale, but David didn't have the grades to pursue medical school, opting instead for a Masters in hospital administration at NYU. This was followed by a stint of tours as assistant administrator, and then finally administrator, at various SurgiCenters up and down the Eastern Seaboard. He'd left a trail of bad feelings at several of his jobs if press reports and internet chatter were to be believed.

Somewhere along the way, 'Dr.' started appearing in front of Branden's name, although there was no indication he'd ever earned a doctorate, anywhere.

At the turn of this century, Branden had taken a job as administrator of a Los Angeles SurgiCenter in Boyle Heights, a poor and tough neighborhood of almost 100,000 residents east of Downtown L.A. That's where his fortune had turned.

He'd become involved with the San Gabriel Protection for Animals Society, a charitable group down on its luck with mounting bills and dwindling support. The Society was on the verge of dissolution. He'd stepped in as its director on a volunteer basis and discovered he had a flair for charitable fundraising. He built back the nonprofit's finances and then left his SurgiCenter job to become the Society's full-time 'paid' Director. He then took the non-profit on an amalgamation spree that snapped up similarly purposed small animal rights non-profits around Southern California and then up and down the state.

As finances improved, he renamed his organization The Foundation for the Advancement of

Animal Rights and Education, or just 'The Foundation'. He replaced the Board of Trustees with people of his own choosing and brought in an Advisory Board that read like a who's who of Hollywood activists who were always clamoring for something new and liberal to lavish their time and money upon.

The stated purpose of The Foundation was to create public awareness, and support legislation and litigation to protect animals, and combat their use as test subjects, their use and abuse in the feedlots and in the meatpacking industry, and the not so gradual extinction of many species on the planet through over hunting, over harvesting, neglect and climate change.

Branden initiated a series of galas at major cities up and down the state to support The Foundation, hired the best ad agencies, and rolled out well-oiled campaigns that brought in the social elite of Los Angeles, San Francisco, Sacramento, San Diego, Monterey, Napa, and even the Chowchilla Valley. People with money who all wanted to hear his story and drink his Kool-Aid. The Foundation's liquid reserves swelled above one hundred million of dollars, surprising for a non-profit that was essentially an animal rights group. The Judge wondered if there were other sources that contributed to so much cash.

Branden's rise hadn't been without controversy. There were rumors of illicit affairs with wealthy married patrons, gambling debts that early on had almost put him into a personal bankruptcy, and accusations that much of the money raised was used to support the extravagant lifestyle of its Director. There were also hints of tax audits, at one point a threatened removal of The Foundation's non-profit status, and rumors of a Foundation Ranch somewhere in the San Bernardino Mountains where secret research was carried out. What the research was about wasn't clear.

Branden had taken over an older corporation, now a sort of sister organization to The Foundation if the online gossip was believed. This other corporation, Replace/Repair Corp, was a for-profit corporation that seemed to have lucrative contracts to provide consulting services to The Foundation. Replace/Repair Corp was originally privately owned by David Branden. But then Branden had taken Replace/Repair public. Its shares were now publicly traded on the Pink Sheets Over the Counter Market. Its Dunn & Bradstreet Report suggested Replace/Repair's revenues were in the high nine figures.

The Judge turned to a search of the court records for current cases pending in Los Angeles Superior Court, searching under Jerry Stone's name as principal attorney. The pleadings in Lawrence Wildman v. The Foundation for the Advancement of Animal Rights and Education made for interesting reading. Wildman, a former bookkeeper for The Foundation, alleged that The Foundation was a sham and a fraud, raising money from non-profit contributions supposedly to help protect animals; but then turning the money over to capitalize Replace/Repair's for-profit business. The last count in the complaint alleged The Foundation was funding illicit research conducted by Replace/Repair Corp. There were no specifics in the pleadings as to the nature of the research.

The Judge sat back in his chair and considered the complaint, and then The Foundation's response. The Foundation's answer was a form of general denials, without specifics. Interestingly, there was no mention of the lawsuit and its nasty allegations, in the local press. No doubt the result of a full court press to stymie any release of information. Jerry Stone, as lead defense counsel, had quickly sought and successfully obtained a gag order, precluding either side from releasing information to the press or giving press conferences about the lawsuit.

Chapter 14
Tuesday Morning 9:00 a.m.

The morning showed crisp and bright with a temperature in the low sixties. The leaves still left on the deciduous trees had turned to burnt reds, golds and yellows, providing a riotous flash of color among the deep green pines.

The Judge climbed into his jeopardy and headed into the village for coffee, looking at his watch. He wondered if McCarthy, Jerry's managing law partner, would be in his Los Angeles office yet. He found the law firm number on Google and called from his cell.

"McCarthy, Jenner and Smith," rattled off the receptionist.

"Is Tim McCarthy in?"

"Let me see sir." There was some static, then some obnoxious jazz, played way too loud, filling his car with discordance. Finally, three more clicks, and then McCarthy's golden tones, smooth, like honey.

"Tim McCarthy here, how can I help you?"

"Hi, Tim. It's the Judge. Jerry's friend. We talked on Sunday."

"Of course, how are you? What a tragedy. And I was aghast to hear the police think it might have been a homicide."

"Yes. They do. And I've decided to investigate it myself. I was hoping we could meet and talk about Jerry and his law practice at your firm."

"You know I can't talk about specific cases. Client confidentiality precludes that."

"I understand. But perhaps you could give me a feel for Jerry's state of mind. Who his friends were? What was going on in his life. How he was bearing up. Your firm has big, important litigation cases, Tim. The stress of handling those cases must be enormous."

"Well, it's certainly no bed of roses, as you can appreciate, Judge. And we take our legal work quite seriously here. We never cut corners. But I don't see how I can be of any help."

"Marie tells me Jerry's major ligation client might have been planning something illegal. Of course, Jerry would have to withdraw if that were the case." The Judge was bluffing, but it was worth a shot.

"Oh no. That's ridiculous. We don't represent clients like that. I'm sure Marie's mistaken, Judge. She shouldn't go around spreading false rumors. I'll have to talk to her."

"Well…then if you consider Jerry's last words, Tim…it just gives me pause."

"Look, Judge, I don't mind grabbing coffee and talking off the record for a few minutes, just to clear the air. Are you up at Arrowhead, perchance?"

"I am."

"I'm about to leave my office here in L.A. and head in your direction. To Arrowhead. I'm going to visit Marie. She's asked me to help in handling Jerry's funeral arrangements if the damn police would release his body. Would you like to meet for lunch today, in the mountains?"

"Great. That's perfect. Let's meet at twelve at the Belgian Waffle Works. They serve a great lunch."

"Done. See you then, Judge." There was a quick click. The great man had signed off.

At 12:15 the Judge strode into the Belgian Waffle Works in Arrowhead Village, wading through the inevitable crowd lingering outside waiting for a table. They were supposed to meet at 12:00, but the Judge was hoping McCarthy had arrived on time and put their names in. He detested lines and waiting around for a table.

Tim McCarthy waved him over to a corner table with one side to a wall and one side against the string of windows looking out on the Lake. It was a perfect table. A nice view, yet discreet. McCarthy chose to sit with his back to the side wall.

"How you doing Judge? It's been a year or so since I saw you last. I think it was at our Marina Yacht Club."

The Judge nodded, pulling out a chair with his back to the view wall, adjacent to McCarthy's chair. Funny how lawyers liked to sit with their backs to a wall. You couldn't be too careful.

McCarthy was out of uniform, no traditional grey or blue shark-skin suit and fraternity tie. Today it was a bright green polo shirt under a white cashmere sweater, and matching green golfing pants, masking a paunch even larger than the Judge's. McCarthy's belly gave the Judge petty satisfaction. McCarthy's ensemble was anchored by green socks and brown loafers.

The Judge thought loud colored pants were best worn by small boys, but he'd learned to keep his opinions to himself, only venting occasionally when Katy went too far in her efforts to snazz him up. The tried and true-blue blazer over a blue pinstripe business shirt and tan slacks were the Judge's uniform for all occasions. Except for funerals, where he wore a black sport coat over the tan slacks. He supposed he'd have to get his black jacket out for Jerry's funeral. Depressing.

Paunch aside, McCarthy looked fit for his fifty odd years, his tan face relaxed in a smile. He had thinning hair in a uniform color of store-bought light brown. His eyes were dark and intense, set under bushy brows of the same uniform brown. At least his eyebrows matched, mused the Judge.

"Thanks for meeting with me, Tim. I was sorry to hear about you and Marge," said the Judge. Tim and his wife Marge had completed their divorce the summer before. Rumor was it had been quite ugly. And expensive for McCarthy. After twenty-five years of marriage how could it be anything but?

"Life happens, Judge." McCarthy smiled, showing a set of perfect white teeth, so perfect the Judge wanted to take them home and put them on his piano. "As to meeting with you, I'm up here anyway to see Marie and also meet with a client. So, it has all worked out well."

"The client Jerry was handling litigation for?"

"Err… yes. How'd you know?"

"Marie said they had corporate offices up here, somewhere on a ranch."

"Yes. Well, that's confidential. No one's supposed to know about their facilities here."

"Oh. Why so secretive?"

"There's a lot of money at stake for them. Like everybody, they have a public face, and a private face. Their ranch property is very much part of their private face."

The Judge wondered what that was all about. He could tell his asking was making McCarthy nervous. McCarthy sat straighter in his chair now, alert, eyeing the Judge much the way a snake-charmer watches his snake.

"Are you staying over, Tim?"

"No. Just up for the day. Wish I could stay over. I love Lake Arrowhead. But duty calls back in L.A. I'll drive back this evening after the traffic."

"What can you tell me about the case Jerry was defending, Tim?"

"You know the answer to that, Judge. Only what's in the public record. Everything else is covered by attorney-client privilege."

"And there's a gag order precluding public comment or release of information by either side," said the Judge.

"You know about that? You do your research, Judge. But there is a way I could tell you more."

"I'm listening."

"You could come aboard as our replacement litigator, Judge. Be of counsel. Take over where Jerry left off on The Foundation Case. Defend their case from here forward on behalf of our firm."

The Judge's mouth dropped open, but no words came. He was taken aback. He slid back in his chair and reached for his cup of coffee, his eyes narrowing in thought. He could see McCarthy watching him with keen interest.

"You must have younger people far more qualified than I to step in, Tim."

"With that Strand case you made quite a name for yourself as a defense lawyer, Judge. Our client would be very receptive if you wanted to take over his case."

McCarthy was referring to the recent Strand Pre-School case where the Judge and his co-counsel, Barney Malone, had gotten their two criminally charged defendants off on a hung jury after a very contentious trial, and despite a smear campaign that had tried to convict their clients in the press.

"I'd have to know more about the case and the client, Tim." The Judge was being evasive now. And Tim knew it.

"I can enlighten you, but it has to be covered by attorney-client privilege, Judge. You can't repeat anything. All information I supply must remain strictly confidential, whether you agree to take the case or not."

"Agreed."

"Okay, then, Judge. Here's the deal. Lawrence Wildman was an employee at The Foundation. He worked at The Foundation ranch here in the mountains. He was basically an assistant accountant. But he decided he was a boy wonder bean-counter and started asking questions about payments made by The Foundation to a third party. He spoke out to management about certain of the adjusting entries used to book the payments. The Board of Directors formed a committee. The committee determined there was no tax issue, no tax risk, no conflict of interest, in connection with the transactions Mr.

Wildman questioned. Mr. Wildman didn't agree with the Board Committee's findings. He went to the IRS.

Then Mr. Wildman was let go for tardiness in showing up for work. Mr. Wildman now alleges he was fired in retaliation for whistleblowing. He is demanding damages for his alleged illegal firing."

"That's the entire suit?"

"Well, no. Mr. Wildman also shot his mouth off to fellow employees, to neighbors surrounding The Foundation Ranch, and to the press, telling folks The Foundation wasn't really a non-profit entity. Claimed people might get a tax audit if they tried to deduct their contributions they'd made to The Foundation. He said the story about how The Foundation was protecting animals was hogwash. His communications were a clear breach of his employment contract which specified that his work was to be kept completely confidential and he would not disparage the Company or its personnel in any manner."

"So, The Foundation cross-complained for breach of contract."

"You've got it, Judge. Breach of contract, tortious damage to reputation, everything we could think of. David Branden, The Foundation's Director, was absolutely livid. We're seeking twenty million dollars in damages from Mr. Wildman as a result of the harm done to The Foundation's reputation."

"What about the claim of illegal research?"

"Oh, that." McCarthy looked startled. "How'd you know about that?"

"A little bird."

"Sure, Judge. Well it was just a throwaway claim. Wildman's attorney threw everything but the kitchen sink into his complaint. Pure fishing expedition, no substance to it."

"So, there's no illegal research going on at The Foundation's facilities?"

"No."

"I saw Jerry was able to get a gag order, precluding either side from going to the press or making statements outside of court."

"Yes. Jerry was our best litigator. We're going to sorely miss him."

"But in the end, Jerry wanted to withdraw as legal counsel, Tim?"

"So one or two people have said, Judge. But Jerry never told me he was going to withdraw. I don't think he intended any such thing."

"Was there friction with the client? With David Branden, its director?"

"Perhaps some. But it was a tempest in a teapot. Jerry got some burr under his saddle about something, not quite sure what. We had a conference scheduled in the office yesterday, Monday, to discuss his concerns, but of course he never made it."

"Perhaps that's why he didn't make it."

"What do you mean?"

"Jerry was murdered. Someone wanted him dead. Maybe The Foundation people."

"That's ridiculous. I've known David Branden for twenty years. He's been my client for fifteen of those years. He'd never be involved in homicide. You've got the wrong idea there, Judge."

"Tell me about Replace/Repair Corp, Tim."

Tim looked startled again. The Judge could see their conversation was moving, step by step, into more sensitive territory.

"Look. David merely took over an earlier business started by his dad. It was really his inheritance. He was perfectly legal in doing so. His employment contract with The Foundation is only for three-quarters time."

"That's true if the business is legal. And if there is no illicit sharing of capital or facilities which converts non-profit contributions to profit oriented expenditures for personal gain."

"There's nothing like that, I assure you, Judge."

"What exactly does this other business of David's, this Replace/Repair Corp. do?"

Tim sighed. "David's father was a famous surgeon and conducted research into the replacement of organs for people in need."

"You mean he was researching the replacement of human kidneys and human lungs?"

"No. Nothing so esoteric. His dad was a leader in the use of pig valves to replace human heart valves."

"Pig valves?"

"Yes. Not very exciting, is it? Replace/Repair Corp is in the business of harvesting pig valves for delivery to surgeons around the world who need to replace heart valves in patients with diseased hearts."

"Why would someone use a pig valve?"

"Good question, Judge. I was pretty surprised when I first heard about it myself. By some amazing twist of evolution, human heart valves and pig valves are very similar in structure and function. As a result, pig valves, also called porcine valves or bioprosthetic heart valves, have been used in transplantation beginning all the way back in 1965, over fifty years ago! Their use was revolutionized in 1972 when the Hancock Porcine Valve was introduced. The Hancock pig valve is sewn into a plastic ring, reinforced with a metal ring and covered with a Dacron polymer. A newer generation of this valve, the Hancock II Pig Valve, is now manufactured."

"But I thought you would just get a mechanical heart, if you needed one, Tim."

"And you have that option of course. But if you use a mechanical heart replacement, you must use blood thinners for the rest of your life. Some patients don't tolerate the blood thinners well. And the use of blood thinners is found to increase the odds of other health problems, like infections and further heart disease. Further, mechanical hearts often are noisy, producing audible clicking sounds as they operate in your chest."

"Like the crocodile in Peter Pan."

"Yes, well, anyway, with a pig heart valve you don't have to use blood thinners. And there is no noise. Newer pig heart valves used as replacements typically last seventeen to twenty years before they wear out and require replacement. As a result, for older patients, they make a lot of sense."

"Where do you get pig valves?"

"Pig valve replacements have traditionally come from pigs that have been raised to eat. Johnsonville Sausage and Smithfield Foods are two companies that harvest pig heart valves for sale. Replace/Repair Corp has taken a different tack. It actually raises its pigs solely for the purpose of harvesting their heart valves."

The Judge looked down at his half-eaten ham and Swiss sandwich. He thought he might be sick.

Pulling himself together, he asked, "Does Replace/Repair Corp share facilities at the Ranch with The Foundation?"

"It leases its separate space there at a fair market rate." Tim sounded defensive now.

"Does Replace/Repair Corp employ research scientists?"

"I don't know."

"Does Replace/Repair Corp conduct research into modifying the pigs for better results?"

"I don't know."

"You don't seem to know a lot about your client's business, Tim. Did Wildman have anything to say about Replace/Repair Corp?"

"According to his deposition, he knows nothing about the organizational structure. He got his paycheck from The Foundation."

"Isn't it a little incongruous, that David is the Director of The Foundation for the Advancement of Animal Rights, and at the same time is operating a business raising animals for the purpose of selling their parts around the world?"

"It's perfectly legal."

"But the big donors to The Foundation don't know about it."

"Well... no."

"And the same big donors, for instance the Hollywood crowd, might be upset, might reduce or even eliminate their charitable contributions to The Foundation, if they knew."

"That's idle speculation and you know it, Judge."

"It also might be a motive for murder."

"I can see you're not interested in taking this case, Judge. I shouldn't have broached the subject." Tim slid his chair out from their table and got up to leave, snatching the check to pay before the Judge could reach for it, clearly agitated.

"Thanks for lunch, Tim. I hope we have the opportunity to talk some more about this."

Tim glowered at the Judge, spun on his heel, and stomped off to the cash register, leaving the Judge to watch after him with thoughtful eyes.

Chapter 15
Tuesday Afternoon 1:00 p.m.

The Judge sat in the restaurant for a while, pondering what he knew, what he suspected, and what he didn't know. Gradually his eyes focused across the room, and on the middle-aged black lady finishing her waffles at a small back table. Jackson, the ex-Stone housekeeper. He got up and moseyed over, settling into the chair across from her.

Jackson glanced up at him cautiously, recognition spreading on her face. "You're the Judge.

"Yes. Sorry you got let go over at the Stones."

"Twelve years. Twelve years of my life. First the parents, then just Mr. Jerry Stone, then Mr. Stone and that… Cat Lady."

"Cat Lady?"

"Yeah, the kind of cat you can trust to screw you in the back, every chance they get."

"You didn't get along with Marie Stone?"

"Oh, publicly we were great friends. She's a liberal Democrat you know. Always protecting the downtrodden women of color. But underneath, she hated my guts. Hated I'd been there before her and was so entrenched. Hated Mr. Stone was so fond of me; he never would have let me go. Hated I knew secrets about her and her fantasy boyfriend, Juan something. That's never going to last. He's just playing with her. Hated I knew secrets about Mr. Stone."

"Like what?'

Jackson looked cagey.

"I'm trying to find out who did this to Jerry Stone, Jackson, and why. If you know something secret about Jerry, tell me. It may help catch a murderer."

"I don't go blabbing stuff about the dead. It ain't my style."

"Fact is, the dead don't care. They're just dead, Jackson."

Jackson brushed a tear from her eye, then leaned over close to the Judge and whispered, "Mr. Stone had a mistress."

"How do you know?"

"Bout two months ago, Mr. Stone had her over on a weekend. When Mrs. Stone was out of town."

The Judge sat up straighter on his stool. "You know her name? Was it Cindy?"

"He just introduced her as 'my special friend' is all. She was a cutie though. Not very tall, but girlie, blond and brown eyed. Mr. Stone says, 'She'd be staying the weekend, Jackson, but you never saw her. Right? You never saw her.' That's what he said. Course I said, 'Yes sir.' Mr. Stone, he marches her into the master bedroom, and that's where they mostly stayed, Saturday evening, Sunday morning. There was a lot of loud goings on in that bedroom. Had a lot of fun, sounded like."

"So, you never heard her name?"

"Nope. Just Honey this and Honey that. And Sweetie here, and Sweetie there. Like a couple of love birds."

"Did Marie… Mrs. Stone, find out?"

"Oh Lordy, yes. Using the master bedroom was a big mistake. Mrs. Stone came back Sunday afternoon. Came storming out of her bedroom yelling god almighty. Calls Mr. Stone a bastard. Says her bed smells of cheap perfume and sex. She's really angry."

"What'd Jerry say?"

Jackson snorted. "He just left, slammed the big door behind him. Made the knocker rattle. It was very cold between them after that."

"Between Mr. Stone and Mrs. Stone?"

"Yep. She hated him after. You could see it in her eyes when she looked at his back. Glowered like a cat. Whatever it was going on with them before, it was different after that. Guess Mr. Stone crossed a line."

"Did Mrs. Stone find out you knew about it?"

"It was pretty obvious, Judge. I was there. Why you think I got fired?"

"You said you know things about Mrs. Stone and her boyfriend."

"Sure, I heard a lot in that house. Mrs. Stone cooing like a sick dove to this Juan guy on her cell. I saw him when he picked her up several times. Young enough to be her son. And when the Stones got into it over their separation of property, boy did the fur fly. They were yelling at each other or not speaking; it was either one or the other.

I even heard Mrs. Stone raging on her cell to her Juan friend about what a bastard Mr. Stone was. How he was trying to cheat Mrs. Stone out of what she was entitled to for staying in their marriage so long, what with him drinking, and womanizing, and all. How it'd be simpler if the asshole just died and I could be done with him. "

"Marie actually said that?"

"Yep. Swear to God."

Jackson rubbed her eyes again. "Mr. Stone was a lovely man. Don't care what they say about him. Had a sweetheart. He maybe drank a little too much, but living with the Cat Lady, who wouldn't?"

Jackson folded her arms across her chest. "I ain't saying no more. Saying bad 'bout people just bring bad back on you, Judge. Don't do no good."

Jackson picked up her check, slid off her seat, and headed for the cash register and then the door, not looking back.

Chapter 16
Tuesday Afternoon 1:15 p.m.

The Judge settled back in his new seat at Jackson's table and waved the waitress for a coffee refill, digesting what Jackson had said. And perhaps more important, what she hadn't said. His view of the room was suddenly darkened by the bulk of Sergeant Jack Prentis. The burly old sheriff was walking like his feet hurt. Jack plopped into the vacant chair facing the Judge and flagged the gal for another coffee.

"How you doing, Judge?"

"Doing, Jack, just doing. How about you?"

"Lots of leg work, Judge. My feet hurt." Jack smiled.

"Still working on the Jerry Stone homicide, Jack?"

"I am. Heard you might be looking into it a bit too."

"News travels fast."

"Small town, Judge. Hard to keep secrets."

"I'd have thought so, but now I wonder."

Prentis studied the Judge with tired eyes. Too many nights, too many beats, too many years, too many senseless crimes. "Want to trade some information, my investigation for yours?"

"Sure. But don't you have a detective assigned to work this?"

"Yeah. A young kid, fresh out of school. He's kind of nosing around but he's pretty haphazard."

"We all were like that once, Jack."

"Damn right we were, Judge. Maybe it was more fun, more romantic back then. Before we'd seen it all."

"What have you found out?"

"Jerry's wife, Marie, doesn't have an alibi for the period when Jerry Stone was killed."

"So I heard, Jack."

"And she consulted old Smitty Harper in Blue Jay a couple of months ago. You know, the divorce lawyer. Interested in how a divorce would work out for her. Left pretty steamed at how little she'd get, I'm told."

"I hadn't heard that," admitted the Judge. "Smitty tell you?"

"His receptionist." Jack winked.

"Oh. Shame on her."

"I know. Like I said, small town. Also Mr. Stone was in the Village that evening till pretty late, mostly at Papagayos. Pretty sloshed too."

"What time did he leave?"

"He stumbled out about midnight. We figure he went down to the community dock, took his boat there, and motored back to his dock in Shelter Cove. Probably shouldn't have been driving on the water. But that's not the most interesting part."

"Tell me."

"Mr. Stone had an altercation with another man at the bar before he left. Someone from downhill. No one knows who he was. Paid cash for his drinks. But lots of anger and heat, yelling, threats, nothing physical.

There was a petite blonde there too who might have been the subject of the dispute. I'm getting conflicting stories"

"What sorts of threats were made?"

"Just threats to tromp Jerry's ass. No death threat or nothing."

The Judge nodded, picturing it. But it wasn't like Jerry to provoke a fight.

"You get a description?"

"Short guy, rugged face, well built, mid-thirties, had a slight accent, maybe Midwest."

"Who told you?"

"Martha, the barmaid there. And the server witnessed it too. Happened about 11:45 Friday evening. So, it's your turn, Judge. What do you got?"

"Not much. Someone accosted me in the Village parking structure, wanted to know what Jerry's last words were to me. Shoved a gun barrel into the middle of my spine."

"You tell them?"

"Damn right I did. In a heartbeat. Funny how clear your thinking can be when you have the cold muzzle of a revolver stuck up your ass. Told him whatever I needed to get unstuck."

"Get a good look at him?"

"No. No look at all, Jack. Came up behind me in a dark corner of the garage. Convinced me to keep walking down the lot and not look back until he was clear. Did as I was told."

"You didn't report it."

"I just did."

"Okay. What'd you tell him? You said before there were no last words."

"No. I said any last words were protected by attorney client privilege. But I wasn't going to try to dodge a bullet with my superpowers, Jack. "

"So, what did Jerry Stone say?"

"He clutched at my face, pulled my head down to his mouth, whispered, '*Stop Cindy… Thousands will be killed… Stop it…*'"

"Anything else?"

"No."

"What the hell does that mean, Judge?"

"Don't know."

Prentis sighed. "What else?"

"Jerry was defending a big case, Jack. His client was the big animal rights foundation. That's David Branden and his group. The day before he was killed, Jerry decided to withdraw from the representation."

"I know David Branden. Nice guy. Contributes to the Police Memorial Foundation big time, every year. You know why old Jerry quit the case?"

"Not yet. I'm working on it."

"You think it was such a big disagreement, it might have been a motive for murder?"

"I don't know."

"Okay, Judge. Maybe you and I can compare notes here and there as we go along, see if together we can puzzle this thing out."

"Deal," said the Judge.

The Sheriff shifted his bulk out of the chair, gingerly putting weight on his feet, and ambled off, leaving the Judge with his coffee tab.

Chapter 17
Tuesday Afternoon 2:15 p.m.

The Judge toted his laptop up the two flights of stairs in the cabin to the attic, which had been converted to his office. He could stand upright down the middle of the room, but the sloping roofs restricted access to its sides. At the end of the room, next to a large window inches off the floor that opened out for side views of the Lake, was his table desk, a large piece of thick glass on finished oak sawhorses. He went online to the SEC website and looked up Replace/Repair Corporation, flipping through its Securities Reports, 10Ks, 8ks and form 3s and 4s, with the experience of the securities lawyer he was, quickly digesting the information.

The legal counsel representing Replace/Repair Corporation was the law firm of McCarthy, Jenner & Smith. Surprise, surprise. He read with interest the business description, which talked about the company's Dog Community business, operated to provide veterinarian blood supplies for pets. And its production and harvesting of pig valves for use as human replacement valves in open heart surgery.

He stopped when he got to the 'Capital Table' in the latest Company filing. He noted that David Branden controlled the Board of Directors, and thereby the company, through a cleverly designed Class B Voting

Preferred. Scanning the information on ownership of large blocks of Common, he focused with interest on an offshore entity, Melilla Investments, which owned 30 percent of the outstanding Common stock. The balance of the shares was scattered in the hands of some two thousand small shareholders, none of whom owned 5 percent or more of the Company's stock. The Company's shares were traded over the counter on the Pink Sheets Trading market.

Flipping to the Form 5s, the Judge found one for Melilla Investments which listed its address for mail as:

Attention Managing Director
Explanada de San Lorenzo, s/n,
52004 Melilla, Spain

The Judge pulled up Melilla on Google. It turned out to be a Spanish autonomous city located on the north coast of Africa, sharing a border with Morocco. Melilla, one of two permanently inhabited Spanish cities in mainland Africa, sat directly across the Mediterranean from Granada. Marie's new lover, Juan, was from Granada. Interesting.

The Form 5 had been filed on behalf of Melilla Investments by its U.S. legal counsel, the Law Firm of McCarthy, Jenner & Smith. So, Jerry Stone's law firm represented everybody it seemed, The Foundation, Replace/Repair Corp, David Branden, and Melilla Investments, this mysterious offshore investor.

On a whim, he shifted to the California Secretary of State's office, and looked up the corporate information for McCarthy, Jenner & Smith. To his surprise the Law Firm just recently filed for dissolution. The Law Firm was breaking up. The Judge wondered why. Successful firms didn't break up. A breakup was usually about money. If the money wasn't there to support hefty draws for rain-making partners, they would leave. Their absence could have a cascading effect on the finances of the law firm, turning its cash flow upside down in a heartbeat.

He Googled Walter Jenner, the second named partner and found he'd recently left to join a New York law firm with a satellite office in Downtown L.A. Rupert Smith was also leaving according to the internet gossip, moving to Orange County to open an office with three departing McCarthy, Jenner & Smith partners and two associates. Tim McCarthy's law firm was falling apart.

The Judge looked out at the Lake, its blues deepening now as the sun, past its zenith, began its slow transit back down to earth, considering. The law firm needed to keep The Foundation, a proven money-paying client, in its fold. The Judge could understand Tim McCarthy's desperation to sooth the client with a strong replacement litigator now Jerry was gone.

Chapter 18
Tuesday Afternoon 4:00 p.m.

The Judge clambered down the steep stairs from the loft, wondering where Katy had gone. It was strange. Once you had a significant other, each partner was expected to report to the other before leaving, and to report back on their return. It wasn't written anywhere. There was no contract executed by the couple. But it was an unwritten rule most couples seemed to take for granted.

Unless you were having a fight. Then it was considered 'fair' to ignore this convention. It was an indication you weren't speaking, or barely speaking, or still antagonized. Katy wasn't here. Nor was the dog. But Katy hadn't said she was leaving. It didn't bode well. She must still be pissed, even after their civil discussion over Campari and soda.

The Judge decided to duck out and visit Papagayo's Cantina, where Martha Lowell worked. He wanted to hear firsthand what she'd observed the night Jerry died. He climbed the thousand steps with difficulty, wheezing halfway up, stopping to gasp for air, then continuing. He needed to lose weight. God, he might even have to add exercise to his daily routine. No. Surely that wouldn't be necessary. He'd just eat less.

Again, he vowed to give up ice cream, starting next month.

Papagayos was a long-time bar and restaurant in Arrowhead Village, favored by locals and tourists alike, marked by a human-sized cutout of a parrot outside its door. It was acclaimed for serving the best Margaritas around the Lake.

It was 4:30. The bar and restaurant would get busier and noisier later. There wasn't much to do on the mountain in the evenings for locals except bar hop and drink. There was one movie theater, a handful of bars and restaurants, and an ice rink. And, the Judge supposed, Marie's social club. Maybe that was part of the reason for the club.

Papagayos would get its share of the bar crowd soon. They'd come straggling in, starting in another hour, the afterwork crowd. Lonely people with nothing else to do, preferring a little alcohol, and some conversation with other members of the herd to sitting home alone watching some artificial Netflix drama on a flat screen. But for now Papagayos was almost empty, silent.

Martha was behind the bar, washing glasses, preparing for the night's onslaught. She was mid-fifties, tall, big boned, and angular. She had the look of a weathered farm girl, deep tan skin, leathery lines around her eyes and jaw, and bright brown eyes circled by crinkly edges. Her honest smile was reminiscent of simpler times out on the Prairie where she'd grown up. She wore loose-fitting jeans and a Pendleton shirt under her bright green apron with a parrot logo splashed across its front in white.

"Haven't seen you in a while, Judge. How's your pretty wife?"

"Doing great, Martha. Perhaps we'll both come for a drink later."

Martha and the Judge went back a long way. As kids they'd played swing together on the rope ladder over the creek feeding the Lake. That had been when her family had first come to the Lake from Montana, and seven had seemed enormously old and adult to them both. They'd never been that close again, but they'd remained friends.

"I was talking to Jack Prentis. Said you had some excitement here the night Jerry Stone died."

"Sure did, Judge. You looking into it too?"

The Judge gave her a rueful smile.

"Thought so. Heard Jerry gave you a charge to do something out there on the beach, before he died."

The Judge just nodded. "What happened, Martha?"

The Judge knew it'd be a good story. Martha had a flair for the dramatic.

"It was about eleven Friday night, Judge. Jerry came in with this buxom blonde, kind of short but built. And it was all on display." Martha rolled her eyes.

"The girl was pretty and all, don't get me wrong, in a passing sort of way. All bubbly. Very young. And all over Jerry like he wasn't married and she hadn't had any for a month. They sat at the table in the corner." Martha nodded to the far corner of the room. "Jerry was lapping it up. I could tell."

"How long were they here?"

"Not quite an hour. Whispering and giggling, heads together, close, thigh to thigh under the table. Course Jerry was higher than a kite, as he usually is that time of night."

"You think they knew each other well, Martha?"

"I'd say very well, Judge." Martha winked.

"So, how'd the excitement start?"

"This other guy comes in about eleven-forty-five, takes his ski jacket off and stashes it on a chair, kind of glares around the room at the crowd. He spots Jerry and the girl in the corner. Stalks over toward their table. The blonde looks up, sees him. Terror's written across her face, see. So, she jumps up, rushes over, throws her arms around this new guy, calls him 'Honey.' "

"Go on."

"The new guy's not having any of it. He brusquely pushes her aside. New guy marches over to the table, stands over Jerry, points a finger down at him, says some stuff in a low, guttural voice; couldn't hear what."

"What'd Jerry do?"

"Jerry turns beet red. Angry. Kind of jumps up from his chair, which falls backwards onto the floor. Crash! The whole bar's startled, see. Everyone turns to look. Turns out this stranger is short. Powerfully built, but short. When Jerry stands up, he towers over the guy. This seems to make the guy even madder."

"And the girl?"

"She dashes for the door, disappears outside. Poof, like that. Gone. Probably the smartest thing she could do."

"What happened next?"

"The guy says in a loud voice so's the whole bar could hear, 'Step outside now and we'll settle this, motherfucker. I'm going to kick your ass out your ears.' Jerry just looks at him for maybe ten seconds, not scared, just cold, letting the silence drag. Then Jerry says in his own menacing voice, never heard him like that before. Says, 'You've got ten seconds to get the fuck off out of here or I'm calling the police. Have you arrested for assault. Your friends won't like that.'"

"Then what happened?"

"It's the guy's turn to get red in the face, like he's going to explode or something. Glaring at Jerry. Death in his eyes. He slides one hand under his sweater. I was afraid he might pull a knife or something. Then he takes a big breath, looks around, sees everybody's watching. He slowly pulls his hand down out of the sweater, controlling himself, but with great difficulty. He turns, grabs his jacket off the chair, and stomps out. He's clenching and unclenching his fists all the way."

"What'd Jerry do?"

"What he always does, honey. He walked over to the bar and ordered himself a single malt Scotch, neat."

"Did Jerry stick around long after that?"

"Perhaps a half hour."

"So, Jerry left around midnight?"

"Yeah, maybe twelve-fifteen, something like that."

"What'd this short guy look like?

"Shorter than you and Jerry, Judge. But powerfully built, muscular arms and shoulders, squat compact body of a wrestler. Expensive designer jeans, blue pinstriped shirt showing at the collar above a cashmere sweater, caramel. Looked rough and ready despite his fancy clothes, primitive face. Perhaps early-thirties, short cropped hair, blond, dark eyes. Not the kind of guy you want to meet in a dark alley."

"How'd Jerry look when he left?"

"Same as always, high and happy."

The Judge thanked Martha, promised to get back soon, and turned, winding his way around four early birds making their way across to the bar. He looked to his left at the corner of the room, at the table where Jerry had sat four nights earlier with an unknown woman. Had that woman been Cindy? Had she been the 'C', whose nickname Marie overheard Jerry use on his cell phone? Was she the 'special friend' Jerry'd had up to his house for a weekend visit, the girl Jackson had seen?

The Judge had a suspicion now it might have been all of the above. But on the other hand, short and well-endowed reminded him of his new old friend, Claire. Could it have been Claire hanging with Jerry Friday evening, trying to add him to her retinue? Each step forward seemed to lead not to answers, but to more questions.

CHAPTER 19
Tuesday Afternoon 4:45 p.m.

The Judge left Papagayos, hopped in his car, and drove west along the Lake, to Blue Jay. Blue Jay was too small to be called a town, just a few blocks of strip commercial, boasting one of the Lake's two big supermarkets, a gas station, a drug store, one major restaurant, and a raft of small business establishments and fast food outlets. The architecture firm of Hambro and James was located upstairs in a small office structure clustered with Smitty Harper's law office, an insurance office, and the de rigueur real estate office. The Judge suspected there were more real estate offices than people around the Lake, all competing to survive.

The Judge pushed the frosted glass door open and stepped into a pleasant office, pastel Easter egg colors, with pictures of past projects on the walls and two cardboard models on display under glass cases labeled 'Don't touch'. One was of a magnificent chateau the size of a small hotel, too expensive and too fancy for the Lake. The Judge was guessing Aspen or Vail. The other was of a modest A-frame more appropriate for Arrowhead; what it lacked in frills it made up for in pure bulk. The model was at least three feet high, reminding the Judge of a doll house.

There was a reception desk but no receptionist. However, a bell had gone off when the

Judge entered, and an elder man tottered out from an office hidden down a long hall to greet the Judge, extending a gnarled hand and introducing himself as Don James, the managing partner.

"I was looking for Juan," said the Judge.

"Sit down, sit down, I'll get him." James pointed to a small table and three chairs in a corner of the room, solid furniture from mid-century, chipped and worn but still serviceable, even comfortable. Not awkward looking and uncomfortable like some abominations they called modern furniture now. You could sell the human animal anything… if you used enough hype.

James hustled back down the long hall to its end. There was a brief murmur of voices. Then a tall young man came striding down the hall and out to meet the Judge, an ingratiating smile on his face, his hands clenched together in anticipation and hope. *A new client!*

Juan was tall and thin, as evident by the tight blue jeans he wore, displaying rather more of his anatomy than the Judge thought appropriate. He had on a traditional powder blue dress shirt under a beautiful burgundy cashmere sweater-vest that suggested money and style. The Judge wondered if Juan truly had either.

"So, what sort of project do we have, Mr. Judge?" Juan was all smiles, almost aglow with anticipation.

"It's just Judge, Juan. And the project is 'Murder.' "

There was a thudding silence while Juan digested this information, his smile sliding from his face like cracked wheat to the mill floor.

"I'm investigating the murder of Jerry Stone. You know, the wife of Marie Stone. Your paramour at the... Social Club."

Juan flushed, and lowered his voice immediately to almost a whisper. "I take it you have no legal authority, Judge. Why would I talk to you?"

"You don't have to. I can talk to Mr. James, your managing partner if you prefer," said the Judge in a deliberately booming voice.

"No. No." Juan cringed. "That won't be necessary. I'm happy to talk about what I know. If I can contribute in some small way to catching a murderer, of course I want to help."

"Marie tells me she was at the swing club party at Sharon Langley 's house the night Jerry Stone was murdered. Friday night."

"You mean our social club. Please, Judge." Juan had his hands out flat in front of him, pushing downward, pleading in his eyes.

"Yes, I mean your Social Club," said the Judge.

"Si. We were both there. But it's not that kind of club, Judge. It's a social club for people who take a more expansive view of their independence and freedom of action than most."

"You mean people who are loose, sexually."

"I mean people who are not bound by three hundred years of Protestant propaganda like most Americans." Juan was hissing now. "We Europeans take a much more relaxed view of our sexuality. God made us physically to be sexual creatures. We believe we should enjoy all aspects of our physical body and our psyche. Unbound by outdated religious notions of coupling, mating, and children begetting."

"So, it's okay to screw married women and jeopardize their marriages?"

"Women are freer now than they've ever been, Judge. They are asserting their individual rights, including their right to have sex when and with whom they choose, regardless of marital ties, just as males have for thousands of years. And, Judge, and... a fling now and then by a married woman is often just the tonic needed to save a rusty old marriage that is failing. You've heard of the seven-year itch?"

"I've been married for seven years and I have no urge to go sow wild oats."

"Ah, but what about your wife, Judge? In this new world for women, she has rights too. Have you asked her?"

"No, and I don't need to. She's happy with our relationship just the way it is." The Judge folded his arms across his chest.

"She may be, Judge. But then again, maybe not. You've probably never asked her."

The Judge was sputtering now, flustered by this young Spanish pop-in-jay.

But Juan held up his hands in front of the Judge. "I apologize, Judge. I didn't mean to antagonize you. Or maybe I did; and for that I'm doubly sorry. But there's no use debating these issues. In the end the female mind is a continual mystery to us males. How can I help on your inquiry into Jerry Stone's demise?"

Gritting his teeth, the Judge composed himself, then asked, "You and Marie were an item at your... social club?"

"Si. When we were both in attendance, we usually paired up for at least half the time. Marie is a wild lover, frantic really, like a desert which once watered, blooms in a panoply of vivid colors, cries and thrusts. A truly passionate woman in every sense."

"When did Marie leave?"

"About twelve-thirty. She didn't seem herself that evening I have to admit. Her body was filled with tension even I couldn't relieve. She only stayed for half the evening, long enough for us to articulate our desires and fulfill some of them. Then she left."

"Did she pair up with anyone else?"

"No."

"Where'd she go after she left the party?"

"I don't know. I assume back home. "

"What time did you leave the party?"

"I walked out about a half hour after Marie. There was no one else of interest for me at the party."

"You left alone, not with Marie?"

"Yes."

"And where'd you go when you left?"

"I went home."

"Where's that?"

"I rent a little suite in the Arrowhead Resort. It's nice and I have none of the duties of a homeowner or a tenant."

"So you drove back to the Village?"

"Yes. Well, next door, to the Resort."

"Can anyone vouch for where you were between one and one-forty-five a.m., early Saturday morning?"

"No. Guess you'll just have to trust me."

"Did you ever meet Jerry Stone?'

"Si. Once."

"During the period you were screwing his wife?"

Juan nodded.

"Did Jerry know?"

"No. At least I don't think so."

"How'd you get on with Jerry?"

"He seemed friendly enough. But I felt sorry for him."

"Why?"

"I see people the way they really are."

"And how did you see Jerry, Juan?"

"A sad man, tired, hiding behind a goofy smile and filtered layers of alcohol. I don't understand what Marie saw in him."

"Did you tell Marie that?"

"Once. She said I didn't see the side of Jerry she saw. Guess I didn't."

"You're originally from Granada, aren't you?"

"Si, from Spain. Do you know Granada, Judge?"

"Yes. I'm particularly fond of the Alhambra, and its Court of the Lions."

"You have good taste, Judge. One of the most magnificent palaces in the world."

"Tell me, Juan, do you know the Spanish town of Melilla?"

Juan looked startled. "Of course," he said, carefully, "A Spanish protectorate of ours across the water on the coast of Africa."

"Right across from Granada."

"Si."

"Ever been there?" asked the Judge.

"Yes, many times. My uncle lives there. Why?"

"You own a corporation based in Melilla? Called the Melilla Investments Company?"

Juan's face tightened. "No. I don't own stock in anything. I don't believe in stocks. Worthless pieces of paper; used to play games… like Monopoly, except the insiders always win."

"How about your uncle?"

"I wouldn't know."

"Know anyone who'd want to kill Jerry Stone?"

"No. I've assumed it was some disgruntled legal client."

"It might have been. Or… it might have been you, Juan."

"Me?"

"Sure. It clears the way now to go after Marie, now that she's a widow. And a very rich widow, if local gossip is to be believed."

"You damn Americans. All you think about is money. Don't you ever contemplate the richness of just living… experiencing life? Everything doesn't have to be about money you know. And sure, I like Marie. I'll continue to like her. She's a wonderful lover. But for Christ sake, Judge, she's ten years my senior. We don't have a lot in common beyond the sex. Hardly a candidate for a long-term relationship. Are we done here?"

"Yes, Juan. I think we're done."

The Judge stood up and headed for the door, then stopped, turning back to look at Juan. "Was there anyone else in your 'Social Club' who was really into Marie, Juan?"

"Si. There is another guy. Marie said they coupled a few times before Marie and I got tight. A guy her age, an engineer or something. Nice enough looking. But Marie couldn't stand him. She told me he was mean with her, rough. Made her do unnatural things, hurt her. Forced lots of power-play stuff on her. Dominance games and fantasies. Some women like that, but not Marie. She said he used to follow her around, try to jump in behind after she was with someone who was spent. Made himself a real pest."

"What's his name?'

"Larry… Larry Shankman."

"Does he live up here? Work up here?"

"Don't know. I think he was a pet of Sharon Langley's. She invited him probably to add a little spice. Talk to Sharon. She'll know about him."

The Judge nodded and walked out the door into the crisp cold air, feeling cleaner again.

Chapter 20
Tuesday 5:15 p.m.

On returning to his cabin, the Judge found only Annie the Dog in residence. No Katy. She must have come, dropped the dog, and left again. A note in the kitchen said Annie had been fed. He grabbed Annie's leash and they left to take a last walk along the edge of the Lake. It was close to sundown, a favorite time for both.

They said a man and his dog grew to look like each other over the years. The Judge didn't think he looked like the golden retriever, nor did the quadruped look like him, but she was a magnificent animal. A show dog, with family lines going back to champions. Beautiful, spoilt, strong willed, and demanding; a typical female for sure. She nosed along the shoreline like a vacuum cleaner, sniffing up the scents, her tail up in a tight curl, her feathers, as her fine fur at the back was called, flying in the slight breeze rippling across the Lake.

The Judge and Annie scrambled along a trail that followed the shoreline. The trail dipped in and out of mini-coves and across tiny peninsulas that gerrymandered the Lake's circumference, exposing new and refreshing vistas around each turn. The light was disappearing now. A mist was rising across the Lake, obscuring the distant shore. But this side of the Lake was clear, mirroring the deepening blue sky above and the standing green of the pines along its edges. The Lake seemed almost a living thing unto itself. Sitting quietly all puddled here, its surface disturbed periodically by a jumping bass and the slight breeze, content just to be. Humans could take a lesson from its serenity, the Judge thought.

The dog and man were walking east, toward the man-made dam and the docks, gas pumps, Association offices, and Lake Patrol Dock. But they were still some distance off. As they rounded another tiny peninsula, the mini cove it created nestled a Harbor Patrol boat. It was anchored close into shore, almost out of sight from the Lake proper. There was something odd about it.

For one it wasn't where the Harbor Patrol boats were supposed to be docked. For another, there was no one in the cockpit. It was just anchored there. The shift for the Harbor Patrol was done for the day; there would be one boat making a last pass around the Lake exactly at sunset. Apparently not this boat.

But that's not what had caught the Judge's eye. It was the ripples the boat was making in the water. The boat was rocking vigorously back and forth, as though possessed by a devil. Someone, or someones, must be in the small cuddy cabin in the bow, doing God knows what. Well, God knew, of course. And the Judge had a pretty firm idea. Two people were squeezed into the forward compartment and engaging in some physical fun.

Annie the Dog noticed it too, letting out a terrific growl as they got opposite the craft, some twenty feet from the shore. Her growl had an immediate effect. All motion on the boat stopped. They were listening. Then, suddenly, there was erratic motion aboard, the boat's hull sending out cross currents in all directions. Putting clothes on, mused the Judge. He stopped now to watch, amused.

Soon a head popped up above the side isinglass to have a look, and then a second smaller head. It was Pete Campbell, the young sheriff who'd joined Jack Chapman the night Jerry died. And Ally Monroe, the senior officer on the Lake Patrol. Ally's face went beet red as she spotted the Judge; Pete Campbell gave the Judge his customary scowl.

The Judge waved a friendly hand, then continued around the mini cove as their heads quickly disappeared again below. Whatever problem had existed between the two the fateful night Jerry died, seemed now to have been worked out.

Chapter 21
Tuesday Evening 7:00 p.m.

The Judge and Annie the Dog returned to the cabin to find Katy there, sitting on the sofa, staring out at the Lake in the darkening light. She turned in her seat to look at them as they came into the cabin's living room, Annie rushing up to demand a pet. And to see if Katy had anything to eat.

"I wondered where you two were, Judge." Katy said, a soft smile on her face.

"And we wondered about you, Katy. Did you have a nice afternoon?"

"I did, Judge. I had a late lunch with Marie. She didn't eat much, but she drank me under the table."

"How's she doing?"

"Okay. Actually, much better than I expected. I guess she and Jerry weren't as close as I thought the last six months. It was a very interesting lunch."

"Oh?"

"Yes. I told her, in confidence of course, about my disillusionment with my life. Not your fault, Judge. But there just is. She understood. It's easier to talk to another woman about it."

"You mean your seven-year itch."

"I wish you wouldn't call it that, Judge." Katy sat up straighter on the sofa. "It belittles what I'm trying to say, what I'm trying to communicate. These are powerful feelings swirling around in my head, Judge. Real feelings. Emotions. Doubts even. I don't know. I'm confused and uncertain. Not quite unhappy. But I feel like my youth is slipping away."

"It sounds like depression, Katy. Do you want to see somebody?"

"That's what I thought too, Judge. But it sort of begs the question, doesn't it? Why am I depressed? And what can I do about it? Marie went through a similar thing last year. What she had to say helped a little. It helped me make a little more sense out of it."

"I guess that's good," said the Judge, uncertainty in his voice.

"Of course it's goods, Judge. Clarity is always better."

"I love you dearly, Katy. I just want you to be happy."

"And I love you, Judge. But perhaps I need a little slack from this harness we call marriage. I don't know. I'm still thinking about it."

"Alright," said the Judge. Not knowing what else to say. Frightened now. He turned back to the kitchen to fix himself the serious drink he suddenly needed.

"Fix me one too, would you, Judge. A gin and tonic just like the one I know you're about to fix yourself. After seven years, I know your habits well. I knew you'd flee from the cabin, seek solace in a bottle somewhere, as soon as I started talking about feelings. Business, money, politics, international affairs, law, sports, even neighborhood gossip; you can handle enthusiastic conversations on all these topics. But bring up feelings and emotions. You bolt for the door every time."

"Oh, come on, Katy. Give me a break. You know that's not true."

The Judge settled into a chair across from her, cradling his drink in his hand. Trying to make light of her criticism.

"Okay, Judge," said Katy, her aqua eyes pinning his now, "What do you think about an 'open' marriage?"

"Shit," he muttered as his full drink sloshed across his lap, startled by the question. He watched a mouthful of gin spread unevenly around the zipper in his light tan slacks. Shit… Shit… Shit… he should have just stayed in the kitchen or run for the bedroom or something. She'd neatly bushwhacked him.

"What the hell, Katy? You want an open marriage?" asked the Judge, brushing gin from his groin, wondering if he was now sitting in a puddle.

"No, I was just asking, Judge."

"Why?"

"Marie Stone says she and Jerry had an open marriage and it worked very well. So, I just wondered what you thought?"

"That'd mean I could go chase and screw around, but we'd still stay married?"

"I guess so, if that's really your interest."

"And you'd be okay with that?"

"Well, from what Marie said, it wasn't like that. She joined a club."

"A club?" The Judge feigned innocence. It was the last thing he wanted to talk about.

"Yes. A club of friends, where they shared intimacy and stuff."

"You mean a swingers' club?"

"That's such an old-fashioned term, Judge. Just a social club with benefits."

"Sexual benefits."

"Well… yes."

"So, I'd have sex with someone else's wife. And you'd have sex with someone else's husband?"

"Yes. I guess so. Like that. Sort of a closed group."

"Is that something you want to do, Katy?" He couldn't cover the disapproval in his question.

"Well, I hadn't ever thought of it until Marie brought it up. But I just wondered what you thought?"

"I think fitting our bodies together in a sexual embrace is a special thing, part physical, part emotional, like our souls are touching. I don't think having sex with someone else's wife would be the same."

"Oh, of course not, Judge."

"Are you tired of me, Katy? I know I'm twenty years your senior and getting older by the minute. Maybe you need a younger man. One with more sexual energy. Or maybe it's boredom. Maybe you just need a change."

"Don't go all insecure on me Judge. You're a wonderful lover. I didn't say I wanted to try it. I just wondered what you thought."

"What about a mistress, Katy? Sort of a half step. You could find a pool boy or something. And I could take on a mistress."

"You want a mistress, Judge?" Katy's eyes widened, then narrowed as her face flushed.

"Well, wouldn't that be better than screwing a bunch of different friends' wives?"

"No... No, Judge. A mistress, a mistress... why that's a real relationship. I'm not going to compete with a mistress. That would destroy our relationship, Judge."

"So, it'd be okay for us to each have sexual relations with a set of coupled friends, but I can't have a mistress?"

"Yes. No.... I mean... I'm not saying I want to. I'm just asking what you thought. And no, you can't have a mistress."

"Women and men see sex very differently, I think, Katy."

"But people do cheat, Judge. In recent studies, twenty percent of men and thirteen percent of women report they've had sex outside their marriage. And even more interesting, research at the University of New Mexico suggests women's sex fantasies of 'other' men nearly double during their days of peak fertility."

"Do you have sexual fantasies about other men, Katy?"

"Judge. You can't ask that. That's private."

"Oh."

"Well, I had an open marriage briefly, Katy."

"What? You? No way."

"Yes, with my first wife, so many years ago."

"Damn, Judge, you just continually amaze me. What else don't I know about you?"

The Judge gave her a soft smile.

"So, Judge, how did your open arrangement work out?"

"Not so well, Katy."

"Tell me."

"Well, for me, there was a little casual playing around. Guys are mostly like that, I think. We can enjoy sex for sex's sake, without commitment or continuity. We can accept the excitement, the energy and the release of a climax, without getting seriously bound to the partner."

"And for your wife? Did she mess around too?"

"I think it was harder for her. She needed to feel some emotional commitment before she relaxed and agreed to partner up for sex."

"Of course, she did. Did she actually couple up with someone under your open arrangement?"

"Yes.

"With whom?"

"With her boss."

"What? Her boss? No way. She took her frustration to the office, Judge?"

"You might put it that way."

"Wow, that's a double problem, Judge. You've got stress with your husband at home, and then stress surrounding you and your lover at work. That's a no-win deal."

"We were very young."

"And were you both comfortable with your open arrangement?"

"She ended up leaving me for him."

"Oh my God, Judge. Really? It broke the marriage?"

"Lots of issues broke the marriage, Katy, but it was a final straw."

"How'd you feel about it, Judge?"

"Stunned, Katy… Stunned."

"Aw… come here honey, give me a hug. I'll always love you. There's only you in my universe." Katy reached for him then, her arms wide.

Chapter 22
Wednesday Morning 8:00 a.m.

The next morning the Judge stepped out of the cabin to the smell of the pines, their green canopy surrounding the cabin, blocking the sky. He took in deep gasps of the mountain air, feeling alive and refreshed, his spirits rising. He made his way up the thousand steps from his cabin to the road above. Despite stopping for breath twice along the converse, he was certain he was on the verge of cardiac arrest as he crossed the final step and put his foot onto the solid asphalt of the road. Adding to his distress, there was a car parked there, half blocking the top of his steps. It was one of those stupid Coopers the Judge considered ridiculous, perhaps because he knew he'd never fit. A Mini painted in an obnoxious candy-apple red, as if sport paint could somehow turn a small toad into a sporty car.

As he glowered at it, the driver's door on the other side was flung open with abandon, and a guy unwound himself from the vehicle and got out. He was short and stout; of course, he was short, he'd have to be to fit. A real man wouldn't fit in a car like that.

He was mid-forties, with a greying beard, clipped short but running into sideburns up his cheeks. He wore a tweed jacket in autumn browns over a pale blue shirt, no tie, tan slacks, and brown loafers sans socks, despite the brisk morning air. Bright brown eyes stared out at the Judge through Coke-like glasses with intelligence and… Oh, no!... recognition.

Shit! It was Bradford Jones, the obnoxious little newspaper reporter who had given the Judge so much trouble and public notoriety in his last case involving The Strand. A miserable weasel that fancied himself an investigative reporter, but preferred to go to print with rumors, innuendo and character assassination. Rather than digging up new, true full facts for a story. The Judge felt his good-morning spirits crumble just looking at Jones, and the artificially broad smile pasted on his mean little face as he hopped around his ridiculously small car to shake the Judge's hand.

"There you are, Judge. Heard this was your place. Good morning, good morning. How you be?" He pumped the Judge's hand vigorously. The Judge experienced an immediate need to wash it.

"What brings you up to Lake Arrowhead, Jones, and to the top of my steps so early in the morning?"

"Jerry Stone, of course. I was doing a story on The Foundation lawsuit. But now I've changed my focus to cover Mr. Stone's murder, much more exciting don't you think?"

"His widow won't think so."

"Yes, well, crime sells newspapers, Judge. It increases circulation and makes the advertisers happy. We of the press, particularly us investigative reporters, have to hold up our end and get the facts out, it's our constitutional duty, the First Amendment and all that."

"That doesn't explain why you're on my front step at eight a.m. in the damn morning."

"Well, I heard you were looking into Jerry Stone's murder yourself, Judge. Personally, him being a friend and all. And since we almost kind of worked together on that Strand story…. That was a fun one wasn't it? I thought we could, well, collaborate." Jones' artificial smile returned. He was fairly beaming at the Judge now.

The Judge snorted. "You're the one who smeared my name and reputation all over your bloody newspaper without a shred of evidence I'd done anything wrong. Knowing full well you were engaging in character assassination just to sell more newspapers."

"Tsk, tsk. Surely you don't hold a grudge, Judge. That's just business. We should let bygones be bygones. This is a brand-new case. And now we're on the same side. We can work together on this one. We can be a dynamic duo."

"You mean like Abbott and Costello," said the Judge. "Absolutely not, Jones. I want nothing to do with you. Get back into that toy car of yours and vanish from my steps… *now!*"

Jones looked hurt. He turned and dejectedly walked back around to the driver's side of his car and opened its door. Looking across the roof of the Mini before twisting his body to squirm in, he pointed a finger at the Judge.

"You'll be sorry you didn't accept my offer to collaborate, Judge. It will reflect poorly on you. I know a lot more about this case than even you do. Jerry Stone and I had been in communication for some days. I know about the Larry Shankman connection and the dog community. I know a lot. I even had a meeting scheduled with Stone to get the full scoop on The

Foundation on Saturday morning. But of course, they got to him first. I don't need any help from you, old man. You've just shot yourself in the foot."

Jones crawled into the Mini, slammed his door, and sputtered off in a cloud of exhaust, leaving the
Here is the final trailer for THE LAKE. It's got a shocking opening I think you'll enjoy.

Chapter 23
Wednesday Morning 10:30 a.m.

Later in the morning the Judge started down the hill in his Mercedes convertible, his Silver Bullet as he liked to think of it, with its top down. It was an exhilarating ride under orange sunshine and crisp fall air, the greens and greys of the foliage flying by, intermittently punctuated by the yellows and oranges of deciduous trees. He'd made an appointment to meet the mysterious David Branden at The Foundation Director's office in San Bernardino. Or San-Ber-Do as the natives liked to call it.

Thoughts about Jerry Stone were buzzing around his head as he drove around the tight curves of the upper two-lane Rim of The World Highway, a dangerous road constructed in 1934, when times were simpler and cars were slower. A thousands-of-feet drop on one side, and hewn rock face on the other, divided by a single white line defining up and down traffic. The lanes were really too small for the big trucks slamming up the road with their provisions for the mountain. He periodically dodged closer to the rock face, within inches really, as the large trailers roared past, rattling his car with their noise and dancing his tires closer to eternity with the wind of their passage.

If he'd been more alert, he might have noticed the slight mushiness of the brake pedal, growing softer with each application of his heel-and-toe brake-ballet down the mountain. But he hadn't. Not until on a particularly sharp jack-knife turn he slammed his foot into the brake hard, a penalty for not paying closer attention. And nothing happened. To his horror, his brake foot went all the way to the floor. There were no brakes.

OH SHIT!!

His car made a screeching, tearing sound all drivers loathe, as the side-view mirror snapped off, and then the facing rock began a long grinding run down the side of Silver Bullet to its taillight. There was an indelible trail etched down the side of his car. He was sick at the thought.

He instinctively jerked the wheel to the right, too far, crossing the white center line in the process and into the path of an on-coming truck. Suddenly everything was desperate, all screeching wheels and smoking brakes as the other driver tried to simultaneously break and swing the truck and trailer to the edge of the outside precipice. The truck made grinding noises of its own, matched by hissing of air-brakes, as it bucked and lurched to the right, coming to rest at the outer rim of the road in a cloud of pungent asbestos.

The Judge with extraordinary strength forced his gear lever into low to the tune of grinding shrieks under his car, testimony to what his transmission thought of this action. He jammed his left foot to the floor on the parking brake, more mush, no resistance, no stopping.

His car careened back to his side of the road in low gear now, the torque of the engine slowing his speed some. He barely negotiated the hairpin and spun into a small turn-out cut into the rock face, spraying gravel and churning dust. His car came to a smashing stop against the granite wall at the back of the turnout, accompanied by sounds of the crunching front bumper. It threw him forward, into airbags exploding into his face, nearly suffocating him, smacking into his prominent nose.

He sat there for a moment, stunned, then moved his neck experimentally. His head still seemed strapped on. The tip of his nose was sore. He looked around at what was left of the Silver Bullet and thought again about being sick.

Shit!.. Shit!... Shit. How could two separate brake systems, pedal brake and parking brake, fail simultaneously?

The Judge pushed the airbags away in disgust, and unsteadily got out of the wreck that was his car, shaken, not merely stirred. The truck driver came running back down the road to see if he was hurt, face white and worried. The Judge waved at him, gave him a thumbs up, and shooed the driver with his hands back toward his truck, which was blocking the uphill lane. Then he got out his cell phone and called 9-1-1 and Triple A.

While the Judge waited for help to arrive he pried open the now accordioned hood of the car and looked at the empty brake fluid container. He examined the hose leading out the bottom toward the brake cylinders, and the small puncture hole in its side near the top, as though someone had jammed an ice pick into it. Calculated to leak out slowly so the brakes would fail mid-trip down the mountain.

Chapter 24
Wednesday Noon

The Foundation's office occupied the entire penthouse floor of the newest high rise in Riverside. The lobby had sweeping views across the University of California- Riverside campus, framed by the San Bernardino Mountains. Expensive white leather sofas, Italian in design, made its comfortable reception lounge feel like a Fortune 500 lobby. A hint of vanilla coffee drifted from the espresso machine around the corner in a utility niche. Off-white walls were lavished with large Mark Rothko paintings which popped off the wall at visitors, adding excitement.

The pretty receptionist sitting behind the antique table desk in one corner was kitted out in a soft faun-colored tweed jacket and matching skirt. The skirt was short, displaying a glamorous set of legs encased in black pantyhose. She looked all of twenty, perky, with soft brown hair tied back with a lavender ribbon matching her manicured lavender nails. It was only her nose ring that added a jarring note, reminding the Judge how old and out of touch he really was.

The Judge presented himself and was immediately logged in on the freestanding computer screen at her desk, efficiently catalogued as being present and ready to meet. She offered coffee and water, but only after the Judge gave up his email, telephone number and address. He was relieved she didn't want his DNA too.

"Are you an animal rights activist?" the Judge asked.

The girl looked up at the Judge, puzzled. "Not particularly."

"But The Foundation is an animal rights group," said the Judge.

"Oh. I guess so. I'm not sure. But I know it makes lots of money and pays well." She gave the Judge a big smile, displaying perfect teeth. "Mr. Branden will be out to get you shortly."

The Judge declined the offered drinks and retreated to the opposite corner, settling into the soft leather sofa and picking up the morning's Wall Street Journal from the coffee table.

Ten minutes later his focus on the future of solar energy was interrupted by a deep voice from above. He looked up over the top of his Journal to find a tall, distinguished looking man staring down at him. The man looked mid-sixties. He wore his black and silver hair long, slicked back at the sides. His fraternity tie of blues and golds was carefully knotted and tucked inside an expensive looking suit, likely a Brioni. His smile conveyed warmth and sincerity, the kind calculated to cause people to drop their guard and open up.

"I'm David Branden, the Director," he said, extending a hand over the top of the Journal to give the Judge's hand a vigorous shake. The Judge put his paper down and stood up, noting the receptionist now sitting tall on the edge of her seat behind her desk, an adoring expression on her face as she gazed at Branden. Apparently she was a fan.

Branden escorted the Judge down a long wide hall hung with more Rothkos, and into a corner conference room which looked out over downtown Riverside, busy with pedestrians and lunch traffic.

"It's nice to meet you Judge. I've heard a lot about you, of course. And with this tragic loss of Jerry Stone, Tim McCarthy suggested you might step in and take over our defense. We, The Foundation, think you'd be a good choice."

"Thanks, David. But I can't make that commitment right now. Perhaps later, after I find out who's responsible for Jerry's death."

"Of course, I understand. I guess I misunderstood the purpose of your visit. How can I help you? I have about a half hour before my next meeting."

Branden gave the Judge a classic patrician's smile. But the Judge sensed concern behind his eyes.

"Tell me about The Foundation, David. How did you happen to become its Director?"

"Scott Kindle was the original founder of our organization, Judge. He had my job; he was our first Director. He asked me to come on to the Board of Directors. He was trying to staff the Board with prominent people, such as myself. He hoped to get more traction in the community for our goals, the protection of animals and their native rights. And the education of the public about inhumane animal treatment by industry and government. It's a noble cause.

Unfortunately, poor Scott wasn't very good at his job. He had no accounting experience, couldn't keep track of where The Foundation spent its money, was lousy at fundraising, lousy at grant writing, and lousy at presenting a cohesive image of what The Foundation was about."

"How did he leave being Director?"

"I talked off the record with the other Board members, laid out the mess Scott had created, and proposed a concrete plan for fundraising and endowment for The Foundation. We got our heads together and decided what to do."

"And what did you do?"

"We called a surprise Board meeting, terminated Scott as Director and as an employee of The Foundation. Then I reluctantly accepted the unanimous request of the Board to take over the Directorship and implement my plan to bail us out."

"Sort of a palace coup?"

"I wouldn't characterize it that way. It was just common sense."

"And have you bailed The Foundation out?"

"Oh, yes. Last fiscal year we've raised over fifteen million dollars to fund The Foundation's work. This year is not up yet, but we've already exceeded that sum."

"What is The Foundation's work exactly?"

"To promote laws to protect animals, to discourage their inhumane use for testing and consumption, and to educate the public on the responsibility we have on this planet to treat all life forms with dignity and respect."

"You're against harvesting animals for food?"

"Oh no. But the animals must be raised, and put down, in painless and kind ways, and with a certain dignity. We must recognize that we are all animals on this planet; we all share a common kinship."

"And now there is this lawsuit?"

"Yes. This rogue, Wildman, worked in our accounting department for a while, accounts payable. His personnel record while with us is littered with comments about his angry disposition, insubordination. A classic malcontent."

"Where'd he work? Physically, I mean."

"Oh, at one of our facilities not too far from here. His physical location is irrelevant. Anyway, he was trouble from the start. But then late last year he went over the deep end."

"What happened?"

"He began making wild charges."

"Like what?"

"Wildman claimed we were misapplying Foundation funds. He said The Foundation should not be paying fees to the board members who serve on The Foundation Board."

"He claimed no one should be paid?"

"Well… he claimed we were overpaying people on the board. But these are important and busy people. They make the world go around. Without them we'd find it difficult to raise serious money for our programs."

"Did Wildman claim you were paid too much as Director, David?"

"Well, yes. Crazy, don't you think? This is a full-time job, being the Director. I have lots of other opportunities. People want my skill set. So, I gave those options up when I took over as Director. It's only fair to compensate me.

"How much does The Foundation pay you as director?

"Well, let's just say it's a reasonable salary for a man of my skills and experience."

"How much, David?" The Judge put a slight burr in his voice, a technique that worked well when he used to sit on the bench and wanted to get to the truth of a matter.

"It's in the public records, Judge. 187,500 a quarter… But I have to pay a lot of my own expenses."

"So, you're drawing 750,000 a year."

"If you want to count it that way."

"And the board gets?"

"Twenty-five thousand a quarter for their quarterly meeting. As I said, these are important people, Judge."

"That's one hundred grand for attending four meetings a year. Is that right?"

"Well, yes."

"How many directors?"

"Five."

"So, one and a quarter million dollars raised in charitable contributions goes out each year to senior management salaries."

"I suppose. We like to think of it on a quarterly basis, Judge. Besides, we raise a lot more than that a year, so executive compensation is only ten or fifteen percent of our budget."

"Do you work full time as the Director?"

"My contract is for three-quarter time."

"What happened next?"

"With Wildman?"

"Yes."

"The board formally looked at Wildman's complaints and determined they had no merit."

"Isn't that like asking the fox to determine who's been eating the chickens?"

"I don't much like your attitude, Judge. Wildman literally tried to blackmail us. Threatened to go to the press, to the California Attorney-General's office, to the IRS, if we didn't pay him off. Of course, we said no. We fired him, instead."

"What reasons did you give?"

'Tardiness, poor performance, the usual stuff."

"And now Mr. Wildman claims he was fired in retaliation for whistleblowing."

"Yes."

"So why not just settle with him and be done? You've got plenty of money."

"It's not quite so simple."

"How's that?"

"Well, and this is privileged and off the record, Arthur's suit alleges we are misapplying Foundation funds in other ways too."

"How so?"

"He claims we aren't really interested in protecting animals. Claims The Foundation is a fraud. An empty shell designed to raise tax-deductible contributions and funnel the money to profit-making activities that actually degrade and then kill animals. Mr. Wildman has shot his mouth off to fellow employees, to neighbors surrounding our... facility. To the press. Telling folks that The Foundation isn't really a non-profit. That people might get a tax audit if they try to deduct their contributions. Says the story about how The Foundation is protecting animals is hogwash.

You can understand why we're upset. It jeopardizes our ability to raise money from our constituency. I can't afford to settle his suit and leave doubt about the integrity of The Foundation's activities. We're going to bury Wildman's ass in the ground on this."

"Is that what you do?"

"What?"

"Do you solicit tax-deductible charitable contributions, and then slide the money over to fund 'for-profit' business activities?"

"No. Of course not." Color spread across Branden's face now. He was getting angry. The public smile slipped from his face, leaving his lips in a thin line.

"Are there other allegations Arthur makes in his lawsuit?"

"Just some wild and crazy claims that have no substance."

"Like what?"

"I don't think you want to go into those, Judge. Arthur Wildman is just a disturbed and delusionary individual. His other allegations make no sense."

"Tell me."

"It's just ridiculous. Wildman claims in his lawsuit that The Foundation is conducting illegal testing on animals, mistreating the animals in the process, and then slaughtering the animals to sell their body parts. It's all craziness."

"You're sure?"

"I'm the Director. You think I don't know what's going on? Not a shred of truth in any of it."

"What about Replace/Repair Corporation?"

There was a silence then. Branden's eyes narrowed, calculating, considering what the Judge knew and what he didn't. Considering what he should say, and what he shouldn't. The Judge felt himself being scrutinized, the way a spider scrutinizes a fly.

Finally, Branden spoke, carefully, "That's a public company I inherited from my dad. It has nothing to do with The Foundation."

"But it does sell animal body parts as I understand. Does Replace/Repair share facilities and staff with The Foundation?"

"This isn't a deposition. I'm not under investigation here. I don't have to answer any more of your questions."

"David. I can go to the records which are public, but why don't you save me the trouble and answer one additional question about The Foundation's finances."

"What?"

"What percent of gross foundation revenues goes to overhead, as opposed to helping save animals?"

"That's a difficult question. Capable of several interpretations."

"Don't bullshit me, David. How much goes to overhead?"

Branden looked down at his fingernails, as though they might need a clean. Then he glared back the Judge. "About seventy-five percent," he muttered in a voice so low, it was almost unintelligible.

"I thought so," said the Judge. "Why did Jerry Stone become disillusioned and seek to withdraw as The Foundation's defense counsel?"

"I don't know. And that's two questions."

"He must have had a significant reason. He must have said something to you. Explained why he was unhappy. Why he felt he could no longer represent The Foundation."

"I don't know why, Judge. And right now, I don't care. Stone's dead. I've still got a lawsuit to defend. Now if you'll excuse me, you've run through your half hour and I have other things I must attend to. Good day."

David Branden stood and marched from the conference room, stiff necked, not looking back.

Chapter 25
Wednesday Afternoon 3:00 p.m.

The Judge retraced his steps through the lavish Foundation Suite, down the elevator, and out to his rental car in the parking lot. The car was a gutless wonder called a Chevy Cruze. He sorely missed the Silver Bullet as he started back up the mountain. He supposed he was going through the five stages of grief over losing his car, being somewhere between anger and bargaining. His rational mind told him it was just a car, but his emotional Id was in turmoil over the death of the hunk of metal he'd so identified with over so many seamless miles.

He pondered what to do next as he drove. David Branden had been very cagey. And given little away beyond what was already in the public record.

The Judge decided he next needed to know more about Marie's social club, and her relationship with Juan, the young architect. The logical next step was to talk to the social club's hostess, Sharon Langley. He pulled over and used Google to locate her telephone number, placed a call, and was met with the warm tones of what sounded like a very sexy woman. He supposed she should sound sexy, given her hobby. They chatted briefly and she agreed to meet him at her home in Rainbow Point.

Rainbow Point was a newer gated community of mansions on Lake Arrowhead's western shore. The residences mostly served as second homes for the very affluent downhill crowd. Sharon had invited the Judge for tea. He'd have preferred Scotch, but life didn't always provide what you wanted. You just had to make do. He'd make do with tea. He made a grimace into his rear-view mirror at himself with that thought.

He arrived at the guard-gate for Rainbow Point about three in the afternoon and pulled to a stop to talk to an overweight guard in an ill-fitting uniform who stepped out of the little gatehouse. The guard looked doubtful at the Judge's little white Chevy, then dutifully consulted his list. Sharon had left the Judge's name so he could be admitted, and the guard reluctantly passed him through.

He drove down a newer winding road toward the Lake, passing recently built houses that were architectural showpieces of ten to twenty thousand square feet, nestled on several acre lots extending down toward the Lake's edge. It was a ten-million-dollar ticket and up to live here; so exclusive one was in danger of getting a nosebleed. He wound the car around wide paved streets and then down the circular driveway leading to the Langley estate.

Sharon Langley's house --it was way too big to call a cabin-- sat at the water's edge, and looked to be three stories high, with dormers on the upper story. It was perched atop a rock- faced platform of concrete overhanging the Lake. The front side, facing the forest, had a large circular driveway, sweeping up to the entry. Sixteen thousand square feet of intricate craftsmanship, with granite, slate, marble and exotic woods, boasting six-bedroom suites, ten bathrooms, two elevators, a boat house and a ten-car garage for the de rigueur car collection. The Judge had looked it up on

Zillow. The natural place for a social club party, mused the Judge, plenty of bedrooms, no neighbors, restricted access.

The Judge pushed the button beside the massive doors, setting off a crescendo of bells that sounded like the Bells of St Mary's. A maid opened the door and showed the Judge into a large foyer three stories high. This led into a 'great' great room with two-story wood trusses and a floor-to-ceiling marble fireplace big enough to sit in.

Sharon Langley was there, standing against the window, looking out over the blue lake for effect, a willowy woman, late-forties, platinum blond hair, pale white skin, and alert blue eyes. She was wearing an aqua silk pantsuit that scented of money. She turned with a dramatic swish to greet the Judge, all charming smile and twinkly eyes, extending a small hand to be taken and delicately shaken. Then she showed the Judge to a sofa facing the Lake and sat down at its other end, a discreet distance apart.

"So, you're the famous Judge. So nice to meet you. I've heard good things about you, Judge. Such a shame the voters failed to re-elect you a third time to the bench." Sharon had clearly done her homework.

"Likely for the best, Sharon. I spent many years sealed inside my window-less courtroom every day, trying to dispense justice as best I could. It's a relief to be free and about now, practicing law for my own clients."

"And dabbling in murder investigations I understand."

"Yes. Sometimes."

"Well what you see here looks pretty impressive, I guess, all this house and stuff, but it's just that Judge. Just stuff. Gerald, my husband who died, cherished all this stuff. He was a sweet man, and he left me well off. But this stuff..." She waved her hands around the room. "This stuff isn't me."

"Tell me about you, Sharon?" asked the Judge, picking up his cue.

"I started off as a dancer in a club on Olvera Street, downtown L.A. Gerald was Los Angeles City Attorney back then, hired me to be his secretary at City Hall. Later, after his first wife died, well, things sort of happened. We got married, despite a twenty-year age difference. Gerald left the City Attorney's office and formed a construction company with a couple of USC fraternity brothers. He provided the city connections and they provided the money. They became very, very successful. Real estate, Judge. It's always been the key to great wealth in Southern California. They built a quarter of the sky rises of the new downtown.

I wish I'd ended up with less money and more time with Gerald. But you can't go back. Life sets you on a course, everything speeds up, and suddenly your ride's over, no chance to do things differently. You just hang on till the ride ends."

"How long have you been a widow?" Asked the Judge.

"Almost four years now. I occupy my time with charitable and community causes, try to keep busy."

"And your social club."

"Oh, you know about that?" She gave the Judge a soft smile. "Would you like to come? We have another function tomorrow night. Looking at you, I expect you'd really enjoy yourself."

"No. No. I'm happily married."

"That doesn't matter. Bring your wife. She'd have fun too. Come and just watch on your first visit, sort of as voyeurs. See if it's something you two want to try. It can give some real zip to your marriage."

"I think we've got plenty of zip, Sharon. Perhaps more than we need. But thanks."

"Well good for you then, Judge. How long you been married?"

"Going on seven years."

"That's when it becomes important to focus on the zip, Judge. The seven-year itch and all. Have to be careful not to let the excitement drift away."

"Yes… well… I really came to talk about Jerry and Marie Stone, Sharon."

"Oh. Okay. Talk away."

"You know Jerry Stone was murdered?"

"Yes. I heard. It's just ghastly. To think something like that could happen up here, to one of our own."

"Tell me about Marie. She was at your gathering on Friday night?"

"Yes."

"With Juan Fernández?'

"Why yes. You do get around, Judge. The two make a dynamite couple. Very passionate. Fun to watch."

"What time did Marie leave?"

"About twelve-thirty in the morning."

"What time did Juan leave?"

"They left together."

"Together?"

"Yes. I saw them going hand in hand down the driveway like a couple of love birds. Marie's really into him."

"And Juan? Is he really into Marie?"

Sharon looked at the Judge with a quizzical smile. "You're asking me questions you already know the answer to, Judge. Juan is European, young, enthusiastic, romantic, but not very practical. There's an age difference that will grow more pronounced as time goes on. Men like younger women. I've found the older the man, the younger the women they like. Marie won't keep Juan attracted for long. He'll go off in another direction one of these days, leaving her to sort things out. Marie will have to adopt a more realistic strategy then, find an older but more permanent replacement. But it's all fun and games right now."

"Where does Jerry Stone fit into this picture?"

"He doesn't. He's dead."

"Yes, but if he were still alive?"

"From what I understand, Marie and Jerry were pretty much over. Marie saw a divorce lawyer, they were directing their sexual energy in different directions, I think it was just a matter of time."

"You don't see your social club as a catalyst for the destruction of a marital relationship here?"

"Hell no. We are all adults, Judge. Individuals all. Our bodies are our own. Our emotions are our own. The emotional attachments we choose to make, or not to make, or to unmake, are our own. Women and men are both liberated in this new age. If a relationship is not serving both parties, it needs to be supplemented, or unwound. That's nature's way. It's the way we're built.

It's the way it should be. Life is so short. It needs to be enjoyed, savored, stretched to the limits of interest and satisfaction. You can let no one relationship hold you back."

"Wow. Glad you have firm views, Sharon."

She smiled. "You're pretty cute, Judge, pretty smooth. I'll bet it's not only your views that are firm. You should give our club a try."

"I heard there was someone else in your club interested in Marie Stone. A Larry somebody?"

"Larry Shankman. Yes. Poor little Larry. He's an engineer, aeronautical or something, quite brilliant. But like many engineers, he's a bit shy. He has a crush on Marie. Follows her around like a puppy."

"You called him Little Larry. Is that because he's short?"

"Yes, my dear Judge. Very short... and small in other ways too." Sharon smirked.

"Who invited him to the club originally?"

"I did, dear. Known him for four years now. He's harmless of course, just a bit quiet, and… you know, underequipped for the job."

"He lives up here?"

"Oh no. South Pas. But he comes up for our club gatherings. Not married, but always brings a hot date who likes to play. I don't know where he finds them. It's a new one every time, each one hotter than the last. But he abandons them immediately once he spots Marie. He proceeds to follow her around."

"And she's not... 'into him.' "

"No. I'd say not. She usually runs the other way."

"Has Shankman ever brought the same girl more than once to one of the parties?"

"Yes, back a year ago. He had a cute little blonde, not too tall, but with a big chest, really peppy. She was a lot of fun. Everybody liked her. He brought her twice, and then that was it. I asked him what happened to her. Larry said it just didn't work out, he couldn't afford her."

"You remember her name?"

"Dedra or something. But shit, Judge, we all use false names. That's part of the fun of it."

"You wouldn't happen to have a telephone number and address, and perhaps even a picture of Larry Shankman."

"I have all of those, Judge." Sharon walked over to a small drop-leaf desk, antique for sure, opened it, and rummaged around in one of its drawers. She produced a business card, which she handed to the Judge, and a picture, which she held up for him to see. It was a collection of about twenty people having a party here, in her great room. They were all smiling, drinks in hand, obviously having a good time. Marie was in the middle of the back, standing next to Juan Fernández.

Sharon pointed to a small man off to the right, mid-thirties, buff build, sandy hair worn a little long, blue eyes hiding behind steel-rimmed glasses, dressed in an ill-fitting sport coat and beige slacks, the same uniform the Judge preferred. He stood next to a young black lady who towered over him, long legs and short pink skirt. She had a glazed look, the kind one gets when they've overindulged in alcohol.

"That's Larry Shankman, Judge. Mostly a nice guy, but a little rough around the edges when it comes to making love."

"Did you know Jerry Stone very well, Sharon?"

"No. Met him perhaps four times at social gatherings, here, elsewhere around the Lake. Seemed a likable sort of bloke. Always smiling, always happy, seemed well liked. I understand he hit the sauce a lot though."

"He was involved defending a big case against The Foundation, David Branden's non-profit."

"Oh, I know of David Branden. Met him twice, I think. Seems a clever little monkey. Likable. Could charm a charitable contribution out of a stone. My broker suggested I invest in Branden's public company. What's it called, ah… Replacement… something. And so I did. When I met Branden the second time, he said his company was going to save the world."

"What's his private company about?"

"Something to do with the collection of blood from dogs for sale to veterinarians in their dog surgeries. But he's working on other stuff. Hush-hush stuff. Says he'll keep me going in my old age."

"Sounds exciting."

"Oh, it is. It's going to be really big. Branden assured me. You should invest, Judge."

The Judge thanked Sharon for her time, set his teacup down and stood, gazing again at the enthralling sight of the Lake just outside the widow. She hustled alongside him to the door, finding it difficult to keep up with his long strides, and then lingered in the door frame, affecting an Ava Gardner sort of silhouette as she watched him depart down the steps to his ugly rental car.

Chapter 26
Wednesday Afternoon 4:30 p.m.

The Judge had agreed to meet Barney Malone, his co-defense counsel on The Strand case, for a drink late in the afternoon at The Grill in Arrowhead Village. It was a long narrow place, defined by a long bar down one side and a stone wall down the other, pitched under an A-frame roof with views out over the Lake. It was known for its steaks. Barney Malone was already there, having cornered a small table overlooking the water below.

Barney was a charming yet tough criminal lawyer the Judge had watched from the bench when he was pinch hitting on the criminal calendar. Last year they'd worked closely together as counsel representing co-defendants in The Strand Pre-School molestation case. As a result, the Judge and Barney had become fast friends. Barney was in Lake Arrowhead for the weekend at the Bruin Woods UCLA Conference Center with his bride, Wendy. Barney and Wendy had been kids fresh out of high school when they'd married so many years before. Somehow, they'd gotten it right where so many others had failed.

Barney was late forties, a short rotund figure with a toothy grin and friendly blue eyes fixed on the Judge as he swung the door open and stepped into The Grill. He was dressed in country clothes: blue jeans and Pendleton shirt in a blue plaid that picked out the blue of his eyes. His face broke into a boyish smile, real warmth surging out as he rose to shake the Judge's hand and bang him on the shoulder, enveloping the Judge in a feeling of goodwill. This was the magic of Barney.

They settled into an easy conversation of catching up the way old friends do, speaking of their current cases, trading stories of past victories and defeats, Barney reporting on the status of his three daughters, two in college and one still in high school, and the Judge sharing stories of Ralphie and Annie the Dog.

Somewhere over their third single malt Scotch the Judge broached the subject troubling him. "You've been married a long time, Barney."

"Coming up on twenty-one years, Judge."

"Katy and I are in our seventh year. Do you think there's such a thing as a seven-year itch?"

"Shit, Judge. I itch all the time. But I'm Catholic, not a dirty 'Prody' like you." Barney smiled, his eyes dancing now, taking the sting out of his words.

Seeing the Judge was serious in his question, Barney changed to a more serious tone and spoke again.

"Judge, there are restrictions on us that go beyond what others may face. If we divorce, we couldn't get married again in the Catholic church without an annulment, difficult to obtain, and carrying all sorts of penalties and requirements. Besides, if I left Wendy, she'd bankrupt me in a heartbeat, particularly if another female were involved. But friends speak of it, Judge. For some, it was the time to end their marriage. For others, they muddled through it and are happy they did."

"So, Barney, you think there is really something to this seven-year itch thing?"

"Tell me true, Judge. Are you playing around? You thinking about leaving Katy? She seems a real dish to me. I'd be real careful about doing anything that might lose her."

"It's not me, Barney. It's her. Last night she asked me how I'd feel about having an open marriage."

"Wow, Judge." Barney let out a low whistle. "Now that's a problem."

"I know. Right? I did some research online, Barney. The results were a mixed bag. Some commentators say that nothing in empirical science supports the idea of a seventh-year risk period. Others find links supporting the idea of a seven-year itch."

"I was on a divorce matter at the beginning of the year, Judge. The other side brought in an expert that testified on the seven-year itch thing."

"What'd he say?"

"Well, their expert pointed out that only about three percent of mammals form a monogamous bond to rear their young. Whereas about ninety percent of the avian species create such bonds. He speculates that for birds, the bird that sits on the eggs until they hatch will starve unless fed by a mate, so they have to be monogamous to survive and perpetuate the species. A few mammals are in the same predicament. The Vixen fox, for instance, produces very thin milk and must feed her young almost constantly. So, she relies on her partner to bring her food while she stays in the den to nurse."

"So they bond for life?"

"Well… no. They bond long enough to rear their young through infancy and early toddlerhood. When juvenile robins fly away from the nest and maturing foxes leave the den for the last time, their parents part ways as well."

"But we're not birds or foxes, Barney."

"We aren't. But some cultural anthropologists contend that humans retain traces of similar reproductive patterns. In hunter-gatherer societies, women tended to bear their children about four years apart. So, children were often weaned at four and sent off to play in a group or be cared for by others in the tribe. This structure allowed unhappy couples to break up and find more suitable partners. And serial mating produced offspring with greater genetic variety, a distinct advantage."

"Did the guy talk about statistics on this seven-year itch thing?"

"Yes. He said some studies showed the likelihood of a couple divorcing before their next anniversary increased steadily during the early years of marriage and peaked at 3.25 percent around a couple's seventh anniversary. The likelihood of divorce as a percentage gradually decreased after the seventh year was concluded. Seven years seemed to be the average amount of time it took for the honeymoon period to end and the real emotional needs of each partner to emerge."

"But it's all really conjecture, isn't it Barney?"

"I don't know, Judge. I'd be very worried if my wife were talking to me about an open marriage."

"Swell. You're not helping at all. I am really worried, Barney. I just don't know what to do. So, you never experienced a seven-year itch?"

"Off the record, we did have some tense time at one point around that time. Wendy dragged me to a marriage counselor, kicking and screaming. Best thing I ever did."

"How so?"

"It gave me a different perspective on how Wendy thinks. She was needing more communication, more intimacy, more verbal acknowledgment that I was committed to her happiness. The counselor said women are like tropical plants and men are like cacti. Men like to talk where power and influence are at stake. Women like to talk about sustaining relationships, for instance in their families, and with friends. I just needed to get on Wendy's bandwidth.."

"But it's not so easy to change your nature, Barney."

"I agree, Judge. The counselor had a one on one with me and gave me some stock things to say."

"No way."

"Way. And they actually worked on Wendy. She perked right up when I used them."

"Tell me."

"Well, like 'I'm so glad we ended up together.' And 'I understand how important this is to you.' And, 'Let's talk about our daughter's grades tomorrow, tonight should just be about us.' Oh, and, 'I adore your turned-up nose,' or your legs, or whatever you think is cute about her, Judge."

"What else, Barney?"

"When you tell her about your day, try to frame some of what you say in terms of your emotional reactions. They love to hear you talk about your feelings, Judge. I know, I know, it's not how we think. But you can work at it a little. They judge the health and the intimacy of their relationship in part based on your willingness to share your emotions and your feelings. At least according to my counselor."

The Judge put his hands to his head and shook it, rolling his eyes in a classic *that's so nuts* expression.

Barney just shrugged. "You asked me Judge. I usually charge for my marriage counseling advice. Oh, and here's one more tip. Time your sexual encounters to her menstrual cycle. It turns out ovulation raises testosterone levels on average twenty-four percent, making Katy much more horny during her fertile days, that's the six days leading up to ovulation."

"Jesus, Barney, that's a lot more information than I wanted. You're a God Damn walking sex book."

Barney smiled, taking it as a compliment.

"Anyway, Judge, on this open marriage issue, I wouldn't do anything about it head on. Just relax and let the discussion run its course. We both know Katy deeply loves you. She's not going to do anything stupid. Just stay non-committal and let the idea die of its own weight."

The Judge looked doubtful, reaching for the check, accepting financial responsibility for the free advice he'd just gotten, wanted or not.

Chapter 27
Thursday Morning 11:00 a.m.

The Judge had escaped from Katy's supervision and snuck into Cedar Glen Malt Shop for an early lunch. The Malt Shop was hidden back in the recesses of Cedar Glen, in the middle of nowhere. But locals knew it well. It was said you go through a whole roll of paper towels eating their Low Rider Burger and still need your face hosed down after you were through. The Judge licked his lips in anticipation, glad Katy wasn't along to rattle off the calories and educate him again about lactose intolerance. She would have even forbidden the caramel shake he was going to order… extra thick. Katy had technically put him on the 'Whole30' diet, eliminating bread, pasta, milk, sugar, and everything and anything else that was actually tasty to eat. He was beginning to feel like a damn rabbit.

Opened in 1946, the Cedar Glen Malt S hop was an original American diner of its time and still true to its roots. It had a classic soda fountain interior with red spinning stools along the front counter and tables for two to ten strung along its length. A flamboyant jukebox graced one end of the long narrow restaurant, sporting a collection of old 45s from the fifties and sixties. There were posters of cars and motorcycles from the era mounted on its walls. Two bright red doors for the restrooms had life-size cutouts of a young Elvis, and a sexy Marylin Monroe, the picture with her skirt billowing up over the air vent in New York. There was even an autographed photo of Gene Autry and his horse, Champion.

The menu offered fifteen types of burgers, each named after a classic fifties car. The Judge had a particular fondness for the Low Rider, a cheeseburger of gargantuan proportions with a thick beef patty, Ortega chili, bacon, grilled onions, Swiss cheese, tomatoes and guacamole, topped off with a jalapeno pepper and stuck together by a long toothpick. It was a two-hander meal.

The Judge settled in at the counter next to Carol Ann Martin, the manager of the supermarket in Blue Jay. They were old friends. As kids Carol Ann had been a year-rounder and the Judge had been mostly summers, but they'd met and played together many an afternoon on the Lake, splashing and laughing and drinking sodas at the Lake's private beach club on its North Shore. That was so very long ago, mused the Judge. It seemed like twenty lifetimes ago, so much had changed.

Carol Ann knew everybody and everything that went on in Lake Arrowhead. She'd married a local fireman who two years into the marriage decided he was gay and left for more rainbowed pastures. She'd never remarried, and had thrown her energy into her job, working her way up from box boy to general manager at the market. She'd put on significant weight over the years, as we all seem to do, but was careful to keep her hair color blond and her makeup perfect on her round face. She always had a ready smile and a kind word for the Judge.

"How are you Carol Ann?" asked the Judge.

"I'm doing, Judge. How about you?"

"Busy, but always scrambling for work. It's not like being a Judge where they just troop the work in for you every morning."

"I guess not. You working on the Jerry Stone case?"

"How'd you know?

"Village gossip, Judge. You find anything out yet?"

"Not much. You know if Jerry Stone had any enemies up here?"

"Everybody loved Jerry... Well, almost everybody," Carol Ann said. "There was one altercation. But it was nothing. Just two males blowing off steam."

"Tell me."

"Well, it was with Pete Campbell, that young sheriff we got. Seems a nice enough guy, but he really got steamed this day."

"When?"

"The week before Jerry's death. Pete was off duty and in his civvies. Came into the store to get some wine. Jerry came in behind him, slightly smashed. Well, you know, it was four-thirty in the afternoon. That was Jerry. One stocker was out so I was stocking booze on the opposite side of the liquor aisle. So, I heard everything. I could see through the bottles too. It was ugly."

"What happened?"

"Jerry comes around the end of the aisle, sees Pete, stops, looks at him. Pete turns and stares back at Jerry, marches over to him, says, '*I understand you tried to assault Ally last night behind McDonald's. You ever try that again with her, or anyone, I'll personally cut it off.*'

Jerry's face gets red. His chin comes up. I can see he's angry. He fires back at Pete, '*You're just bent because we've shared the same mistress.*'

Pete says, '*What? What are you talking about?*

Jerry says, '*Ally Monroe. I was her first.. Doesn't get any better than that. How's it feel to have sloppy seconds?*'

Now Pete turns bright red, '*You son of a bitch,*' he spits out. Steps toward Jerry, his hands clenched. Jerry quickly backs up, putting his hands up in front of him. Back steps his way to the endcap and disappears around it. Pete just stands by the chardonnay, clenching and unclenching his hands, then mutters, '*I'm going to kill you, you drunken son of a bitch.*' Then Pete stomps off too. Didn't buy any chardonnay."

"You know what they were talking about?"

"Not officially. Sounds to me like Ally Monroe gets around. I know Pete is stuck on her. They've been going together for about two months."

"You think Pete Campbell was angry enough to do something to Jerry?"

"Shit, I don't know Judge. You guys often get your panties in a twist about a girl's past lovers. We females are more practical. We just keep our mouths shut and hope for the best."

"You ever attend any of these swing parties I hear go on occasionally up here, Carol Ann?"

Carol Ann giggled. "Is that an invitation, Judge?"

"No. Come on Carol Ann. I'm just trying to figure out why Jerry got killed."

"I haven't Judge. Never invited. I understand Sharon Langley and David Branden throw parties like that sometimes. Up on her big estate behind the gates, Rainbow Point."

"David Branden's involved too?"

"So I've heard, Judge. Kind of her partner in sin. But I don't really know for sure. Did Jerry go to those?"

"I don't think so, Carol Ann, but there might be some connection."

"It's a puzzle. Jerry hasn't been himself lately. Drinking more and more. Out at pubs more, and staying out later, till they close. Never seems to go home. But he may have been changing all that. I ran into him at the market Friday afternoon. He sounded happy. Said he'd just had a blowup with a senior partner over lunch at the Saddleback Grill. Some disagreement about a client. Anyway, said he was leaving to start his own practice. Sounded elated about it. I wished him luck."

"Did he go anywhere else that you know? Besides the bars?"

"Well, I heard he rents a cabin over at The Pine Tree Lodge on a monthly basis, sleeps there some nights."

"That's the motor motel kind of place with the little cabins up the highway from the entrance to the Village?"

"That's it. But new owners really fixed it up. Nice gardens, updated pool in the middle. Anyway... " Carol Ann leaned closer to the Judge now, to whisper, "I even heard Jerry had a hot blonde stashed up there a couple of times. Sounded to me like Jerry and Marie were having difficulties."

"That may be right, Carol Ann. Anyway, thanks for the scuttlebutt. It may help in identifying a murderer."

Carol Ann puffed up, sitting straighter in her chair, pleased with herself. "I'll keep my ears open, Judge, let you know if I hear anything else." She hefted her bulk from the counter stool and toddled over to the register to pay her bill, turning to smile back at the Judge with fond eyes.

Chapter 28
Thursday Afternoon 1:30 p.m.

The Judge waddled away from the Malt Shop with a full tummy. He fiddled in his glove compartment as he wound his way back out of Outback Cedar Glen and down along the Lake Road to the Village, desperate for the two Rolaids he knew were there… somewhere. He decided to pick up the mail in his PO box in the Village before he got diverted again. The mail was disappointing, all bills, not even a magazine. He tucked the bills in his back pocket and headed back toward the parking lot and his car. He took a shortcut, whizzing around the back corner of the McDonald's building and down the little alley behind the store, almost colliding with Ally Monroe, the pretty Lake Patrol officer who was whizzing in the other direction. He reached out, catching her before they could collide.

"Judge." Monroe gasped, regaining her balance.

"Guess we're both in a hurry," said the Judge.

"I kind of am, but actually I do need to talk to you for a moment."

"Okay. Can I buy you a Whopper?"

"You mean a Big Mac, Judge. A Whopper is at Burger King."

"Okay. Then it's a Big Mac I'll buy."

"How about just a cup of coffee?"

"Okay."

They walked around to the front of McDonald's and entered, the smell of brewed coffee and greasy fries perfuming the air. They dutifully stood in a three-person line to order. The lady in front of the Judge was as broad as she was wide, and didn't seem to need the double cheese, double fries and large shake she ordered. Each to his own, mused the Judge, feeling superior because of the Malt Shop burger he'd enjoyed. He looked around at the people in McDonalds, hoping he would see nobody he knew. He suspected people judged you by where you ate. He didn't want to be judged a patron of McDonald's.

Ally ordered a coffee. The Judge supplemented his coffee with a pastry, since Katy wasn't around, and also because it might settle the burning still in the pit of his stomach. They settled into a quiet corner looking out over the community dock, the Lake, and the ducks trolling for food from young children waving brown paper bags of seed along the shore.

"So, Judge. Our Lake engineer looked at your dock. It's a total wipeout. It was pretty old to start. Then there was the impact of Jerry's boat, and the burning fuel on the water melting some of the floats. And besides the deck flooring and understructure at the end, which is entirely gone, there's structural damage all the way back to the ramp. You're going to have to haul your wreck away and put in a new dock. And soon, before it pollutes our Lake.

The Judge sighed. Another expense he didn't need. "Where were you when Jerry hit my dock, Ally?"

"What?" Ally looked startled. She hadn't expected the question.

"I was out… out on the Lake, doing a routine patrol."

"After sundown? I thought your team didn't patrol the Lake after dark, particularly in the off season."

"Sometimes we go out to check things. Boats get untied and drift, drunken boaters try to be Spider-man on the way home from bars, kids sneak out on docks and do drugs, booze and sex. That sort of thing."

She sounded defensive.

"It was one-thirty in the morning, Ally."

"I know. Sometimes on my shift, when I draw a late night, I like to just go out and putt around in the dark; sometimes just drift. It's very soothing."

"Whereabouts on the Lake were you?"

"North Shore.

"Did you see Jerry Stone's boat?"

"No. Jerry's boat is pretty distinctive, with those red flames licking down the sides and over the engine compartment."

"Yes, almost prophetic, weren't they?"

"Did you see any other boats out on the Lake, or perhaps hear an engine running, tied at a dock?"

"No. It was all quiet until the explosion at your dock."

"You didn't hear the loud pipes on Jerry's boat echoing across the Lake around one-fifteen?"

"I don't remember that. In truth, I had ear buds on and was listening to music while I drifted."

"You know anyone who had a grudge against Jerry Stone?"

"Me for one, Judge. The guy was a real jerk."

"Why do you say that?"

"He was three sheets to the wind when he came out of Papagayos last week. He ran into me cutting through the alley behind here, like we just did. He kind of blocked the alley, put his arms out, grabbed me, and gave me a heavy hug, contouring his body to mine, pressing against my chest. I told him to knock it off, but he ignored me, blabbering away about how he loved me and wanted to start a serious relationship.

He scared the shit out of me if you must know, Judge. I couldn't get him to let go. Finally, I told him I would scream bloody murder if he didn't release me. That worked. He stepped back and I bolted through the alley and out the other end. Pete says I could have Jerry arrested for assault and battery. I thought about it but decided not to make a fuss."

"Pete? That's the young sheriff?"

"Yes, Judge You met him the other night at your dock. Pete Campbell. He was the second patrol car that pulled up behind the first one, came down your steps a little after Jack Prentis arrived."

"And Pete is your boyfriend?"

"Yes. For about two months. But we have issues."

"What issues, Ally?"

"It's personal."

"What else happened between you and Jerry Stone?"

"Nothing… What do you mean?"

The Judge just looked at her with old eyes. He'd been a Judge long enough to know when he was only getting half the story. And he also had the gossip from Carol Ann. The silence dragged on. Ally visibly reddened, her gaze shifting over his shoulder to the puddled Lake through the window. Finally, her eyes moved back to his.

"Aw shit, Judge. Jerry and I had a brief affair over the summer."

"You and Jerry Stone?"

"Yes, damn it. On a whim I put my name on one of those dating sites, and Jerry contacted me through the site. We went out only four times. He made lots of fancy promises about leaving his wife and looking for a serious relationship. He knew all my buttons, and he pushed every single one."

"How far did it go?"

"I slept with him on the first date and then we spent three weekends together when his wife was out of town. And that was all there was. He'd got what he wanted. Another notch on his dick. Emailed me after our third weekend that the chemistry wasn't right, he was looking for someone a little older, that kind of crap."

"Apparently he changed his mind last week."

"Jerry Stone was an asshole. A lot of people aren't sorry he's dead."

"Does Pete know about your history with Jerry?"

"Oh no. I met Pete after. Pete must never find out."

"Pete didn't seem happy with you that night on by my dock, the night Jerry died."

"Pete and I have issues."

"What kind of issues?"

"It's personal, Judge."

"Was Jerry Stone ever arrested for driving his boat under the influence?"

"No. We never arrested him. He's a fixture up here; politically connected. But we had to warn him frequently. He liked to get plowed and then drive out on the Lake."

"Are you working on the investigation into his death?"

"No. Not my job. Pete's involved though. I hear bits and pieces."

"Like what? Anything juicy?"

"They think someone hit Jerry over the head down on his dock. Used his own paddle in his boat. Then they propped him up in his helm seat semi-unconscious, pointed the boat across the lake, opened the throttles wide, and jumped off. Intended for it to look like a boating accident."

"They find the paddle?"

"Yeah. It was floating by your dock in the wreckage. Had a big notch out of the blade and some strands of Jerry's hair stuck in the wood. No fingerprints, though. The paddle'd been wiped clean and thrown back into the boat."

"They have any persons of interest?"

"I don't think so. They're trying to track down everyone who was in the vicinity of Jerrys' dock between eleven p.m. and two a.m. Friday night."

"That would include you and Pete, wouldn't it?" The Judge played one of his hunches.

"What?"

"Weren't you on the North Shore Friday night with Pete?"

Ally looked down at her coffee. Then back up at the Judge, defiance in her eyes. Quiet now.

"Ally, you claim you didn't hear Jerry's boat out on the Lake around one-fifteen. But I sure as hell heard it, all the way across the Lake. You couldn't have missed it. Pete Campbell said he was patrolling the North Shore area from the land at the same time you were patrolling the North Shore from the Lake. Doesn't that sound a little too coincidental?"

Ally just shook her head, suddenly unable to speak, panic spreading across her face. She jumped up, spilling her coffee, and darted for the door.

Chapter 29
Thursday Afternoon 4:00 p.m.

Back at his cabin in his office loft, the Judge went online to LinkedIn, searching for an aeronautical engineer named Larry Shankman who lived in South Pasadena. His name came up at once, along with a smiling face framed by steel-rimmed glasses and long sandy hair. It was the guy Sharon Langley had pointed to in her group shot of her social club gang. Pale blue eyes stared out from the page at the Judge, making him feel creepy. And he hadn't even met the guy. Shankman had started as an engineer for Northrop Grumman but was now on his own as an engineering consultant. The Judge wondered if he'd been fired, and if so, why?

Sharon had given the Judge a telephone number, which he used in a reverse director, to look up Shankman's address. But the address wasn't in South Pasadena. It was for a cabin on Yellowstone Drive, high on the hill overlooking Lake Arrowhead, right above Shelter Cove where Jerry and Marie Stone lived.

The Judge took his car out and around the Lake to the east, passing the dam, heading toward Shelter Cove. But when he reached Yellowstone Drive, he turned right, up into the steep hills above the Lake. Shankman's cabin was built on an access road high up at the back of a lot filled with scrub oak. The Judge turned right on Banff Drive, right again on Mammoth Drive, and cut down an access road fronting the top of Shankman's lot.

A very expensive looking Aston Martin convertible, metallic blue, sat in front of Shankman's cabin, top down, its swept-back lines making it look like it was in motion even when it was parked. The views down-hill from the cabin's porch were stunning, the entire Lake laid out below like some giant puddle, its placid blue splotch ringed with forest green.

The man who came to the door when the Judge rang the bell was shorter than the Judge expected. Buff though, with broad shoulders and muscular arms rippling under his t-shirt. The pale blue eyes held even more of a glint in person, complemented by the shiny silver of his metal-rimmed glasses. The Judge could see how women would be attracted to him, in a 'short' sort of way. Mid-thirties, sandy hair, physical, smart with his Aeronautical Degree, and apparently a lucrative career.

After introducing himself, the Judge explained he'd been asked by Marie Stone to privately investigate her husband's murder.

"So. What's that got to do with me, Judge?"

"I understand you know Mrs. Stone, through Sharon Langley's social club. And you were at their function Friday evening here on the Lake, the evening Jerry Stone was murdered."

"What if I was?"

Aside from Shankman's defensiveness, the Judge sensed an underlying anger, as if a volcano lay somewhere beneath, ready to explode. The Judge suspected getting along with the guy would be like walking around on eggshells, stepping very lightly.

"Sharon told me you're quite fond of Marie Stone."

Shankman's face softened then, changing from dislike and distrust to something else, anguish perhaps.

"Marie is a beautiful woman, Judge. Physically, emotionally and intellectually, one of a kind. Smart, charming, warm, giving, she's a class act. Deserved better than that drunk lout of a husband. I'm glad Jerry Stone is dead. Glad for Marie. Maybe glad for me too; you never know how things work out. But I had nothing to do with Jerry Stone's death."

"You saw Marie at the party?"

"Sure. She was wasting time with that Juan something or other. Nasty little Spaniard, a real pencil dick."

"Did you see Marie leave?"

He nodded. "About twelve-thirty."

"She leave alone?"

"No. With the pencil dick, as usual."

"When did you leave?"

"Shortly after. Wasn't much of interest there after Marie left."

"Come straight home?"

"Yeah. What else I'm going to do at twelve-forty-five in Lake Arrowhead?"

"Bring anyone with you?"

"That's none of your business."

"It could provide you an alibi."

Shankman just smiled, silent, watching the Judge like a cat watches another cat, measuring for a leap.

The Judge said, "That's a nice car you've got here. Must have come into some money to buy a car like that. Looks brand new."

"It is. Twenty-nineteen Aston Martin Vanquish S Volante, over three hundred thousand on the hoof. Sold a small business I inherited from my dad and took the plunge. Life can be short, Judge One day you're here. Next day, poof, you're gone. Have to enjoy it while you can. You should think about that. Everyone's life, even yours, can be shortened in the blink of an eye. Look at old Jerry Stone. Had it coming of course, but poof, now he's gone."

"Going to give Marie a ride in your new toy?"

"Going to try. Like to give her more than that in my car." Shankman's eyes suddenly had a faraway look, glinting even more now.

"What sort of business did you sell?"

"An ugly business. Was my dad's business. A dog colony."

"A what?"

"A dog colony. It's one of the handful of state-licensed dog colonies in California. One hundred dogs, caged up in little steel cages set on concrete pads twenty-three hours a day, hosed down once a day, automatic feeder and water,
mostly Greyhounds because of their docile temperament and their 'universal' blood type. Bled every ten days."

"Bled?"

"Yeah."

"Why?"

"You got a dog, Judge?"

"Yes. A Golden."

"Suppose your Golden gets hurt, hit by a car or something. You rush him to the veterinarian. The vet has to operate. He pulls out a clear bag of dog's blood and hooks your Golden up so he won't bleed to death on the operating table. Where do you think that clear bag of dog's blood comes from?"

"I don't know."

"From a dog colony, like the one I sold. Dogs don't just wander into a mobile clinic and donate blood. Someone has to provide the blood. That's what dog colonies are for. The animals are kept under nasty conditions and bled every seven to fourteen days, to create a blood bank for veterinarians."

"Who'd you sell the dog colony to?"

"An outfit called Replace/Repair Corp."

Chapter 30
Thursday Evening 6:00 p.m.

The Judge returned to the cabin and looked for Katy. She was off somewhere; who knew where. He headed to his fourth-floor office loft, his escape chamber of choice, and dove into an appellate brief he was supposed to have sent out two days before. He heard Katy come in around 6:30, but there was no hearty 'Hallo, Judge, I'm home' from her. She headed for the bedroom. It sounded like a nap was in the offing. Good for her. He wished he were that lucky.

His head was buried four layers down in an appellate brief, trying to make the precedent cases fit his facts and produce an appropriate result. Interesting work but challenging. When he finally looked up again, it was dark outside, and the clock had turned to almost nine. He sniffed the air, hoping for the scent of cooking in the kitchen, but there was none.

He lifted himself out of his computer chair, stretched once, almost touching the rafters of the attic, then ambled downstairs to see what Katy was up to.

It wasn't good. She was sitting listlessly in the living room in front of the open windows, with all the lights off. She was staring out at the black lake. Just sitting and staring. It looked like she'd been there awhile.

"Hi, Katy. How's the good life?" He put his best jolly into the question, his booming voice echoing around the almost empty living room. Katy made no response.

He tried again. "Why don't we bundle up and go down to the Arrowhead Resort for drinks and then dinner? Watch the hoi polloi and get lit?"

She slowly turned then, as though just noticing him, sad eyes focusing on his. "Not hungry, Judge."

"Did you have lunch?"

"Wasn't hungry then either."

"You need to eat, Katy."

"Do I? I look out at that black lake, but I don't see it, Judge. All I see is an endless flat plain of snow, reaching to the horizon. No structures, no hills, no mountains, no people. Just an empty white plain. It's as though I'm in Siberia."

"Aw, Katy. How can I help?"

"I'm not sure you can, Judge. My life is boring, predictable, insufferable. The day to day monotony has gotten me down. I keep asking myself, is this all there is?

We've become comfortable, Judge – maybe too comfortable. We've stopped dating each other. We've stopped appreciating the little things about each other we used to find endearing. Your habits have can become predictable, Judge. Too predictable, even annoying."

"But Katy…"

"No, Judge. Stop. Just listen for a change. Just listen."

"I think about our sex life, Judge. It's become routine and release-centric, instead of intimate and pleasurable like in the beginning."

"I admit we've become a little disconnected, Katy. I think part of it is all the focus on our child. We've stopped being partners and gotten too busy being parents."

"I sometimes wonder if I married the right person for me, Judge. Have you ever fantasized about being with someone else?"

"No… Well, maybe… Hell, I'm a male, Katy, I look at beautiful women. It's how we're built. It doesn't mean I do anything about it. I'm committed to you. Have you fantasized like that?"

"Sometimes, Judge. Sometimes… I always feel guilty after."

"Is this part of this seven-year itch thing, Katy? You sound very depressed."

"I don't know. Perhaps." Katy gave a soft smile. "But Judge, face it. Your tone of voice has changed when you speak to me. You easily lose patience with me now. And then you do that infuriating roll your eyes thing you do. I hate you when you do that."

"Okay, Katy. Okay. I swear, I'll never roll my eyes again."

"And worst of all is your indifference. Judge. You just have no interest in the things I say or do. You just sit there, mutter something unintelligible when I ask a question or make a comment and go on with what you're doing on that damn laptop of yours. We may not be screaming or yelling at each other, but that doesn't mean we're connected, or happy. You're just indifferent. Our relationship doesn't seem to matter anymore."

"It matters terribly to me Katy. And I'm not indifferent. I'm always attuned to you, even in the middle of the thorniest issues of a case on my maligned laptop. I love you dearly."

"I know you love me, Judge, in your own way. But it just feels so lonely sometimes in this relationship of ours. Is this what love is supposed to feel like?"

"I think most people mistake love for a noun, Katy. But in actuality, it's a verb. It's an ever-evolving process that's dynamic, constantly in flux. It's not a static thing."

"What the fuck does that mean, Judge?"

"Love is like a long and winding river that meanders its way down to the valley below. There are parts that have rapids, and things speed up. There are slow bits where you barely paddle along. And parts with rocky shoals that can easily up-end you and dump you out by yourself on the bank. But it's all part of a seamless adventure we call love. An exhilarating adventure that gives life meaning and depth."

"I wish I believed that, Judge. I used to. But now… I don't know." Katy sighed. "Anyway, I didn't make any dinner. You'll have to go out. But I want to stay here for a while… by myself. Go now, Judge. No more talking. Just go."

The Judge physically sagged, picked his coat off the coat tree by the front door, opened the door and looked out into the void. At least it seemed like a void. His world had suddenly turned terribly uncertain. He felt helpless, lost, unable to suss any direction that might stem the flow of this… this… whatever it was, that Katy had.

Katy called out then. "All right Judge. Hold on, I'll come. You look so damn forlorn. Like a small boy whose ice cream just flipped out of his cone onto the pavement. Wait a minute while I get my coat."

Chapter 31
Thursday Evening 8:00 p.m.

The Judge walked into the Arrowhead Resort, Katy behind him. It was a magnificent lobby, soaring three stories high with the check-in desk to the left, a big fireplace at the other end, a second fireplace anchoring a seated bar area, and a long bar behind. The lobby was crowded, clutches of threes and fours and fives hanging at the furniture groupings around the lobby, and the bar area packed, the bar itself stacked three-deep with people holding drinks or vying for attention from the three overworked bartenders. The place was rumbling with noise.

He wondered if Jerry's killer hid in the herd, watching him. He could almost feel the killer's glittering eyes, making the hair stand up on the back of his neck. But who? Who was the killer? Or perhaps, who were the killers?

He swung around, surveying the scene. He saw many people he knew. The Arrowhead Resort was the place to be on a Thursday night on the Lake. Marie Stone, Jerry's now widow, sat at one table near the fireplace, chatting up Juan Fernández. They sat beside each other, thigh to thigh.

Ally Monroe was seated at a table across the room in a corner, huddled with Pete Campbell. She looked fearful as she spotted the Judge striding in. Campbell had a territorial arm around her shoulders. He wore his trademark scowl. The Judge wondered if he ever smiled.

The Judge spotted Claire Henderson at the left end of the bar, all smiles, batting eyelashes at him over the shoulder of her friend, Tony, the little mob-guy from Chicago. Katy's presence didn't seem to faze Claire. Mob-guy was oblivious to Claire's flirting, focused on the dining room beyond with its Lake views. The Judge smiled politely, trying not to be caught out flirting by his bride steps behind, ever cognizant of what he was doing, every little nuance.

Larry Shankman was standing in the middle of the bar, nursing some sort of pastel-flavored martini and staring at Marie with large eyes behind his silver rimmed glasses. The way he looked at Marie made the Judge uncomfortable. It was a predator's look, as though she were an ice cream cone he would lick all over, and then crunch down on... hard. Marie's husband was gone, the field was wide open in Larry's mind. Looking at Shankman, the Judge could believe the violence inside could drive him to murder.

Jerry's law partner, Tim McCarthy, was seated on a bar stool at the right end of the bar, looking smug and well fed, almost beefy, casually assessing the Judge as he walked across the room, careful not to be overt about it. He looked the caricature of a lawyer, all smiles and wiles, just a tad too obvious about his self-serving center of interest. He was snuggled up to a tall blond in tight black ski pants and a white fluffy sweater, the kind that gets fluff all over you if you get close. McCarthy was close. But she seemed more interested than he did. The

Judge caught McCarthy throwing a look at Claire, sizing her up. She was the most vivacious female in the bar. Other heads were turning to admire her as well.

Unfortunately for McCarthy, Mob-guy spotted McCarthy looking at Claire. Suddenly up on the balls of his feet and reaching almost five foot five, Mob-guy jabbed an angry finger in McCarthy's direction down the bar, then patted the bulge in the breast of his fancy corduroy jacket, implying he had a gun. McCarthy's face looked like that of a rabbit discovered beyond its hole. He immediately brought his gaze down to study the bottom of his martini glass with great interest, and kept it there, edging closer to the tall blonde for protection.

Katy stepped around the Judge and led the way across the room toward Marie's table. Oblivious to the swirling undercurrents. Juan looked up, say Katy coming with the Judge in tow, and suddenly found a reason to leave Marie and slipped away, avoiding an introduction to Katy and further interaction with the Judge.

Claire turned to watch Katy across the room, calculating, with… what? … professional interest? She gave the Judge a silent *'aww'* with her lips over the shoulder of Mob-guy, who was still glaring down the bar at McCarthy. Mob-guy, sensing something in the ether, all smiles now to cover his intent, put his hand territorially on Claire's bare shoulder, then squeezed hard, making Claire wince. He removed his hand leaving an angry red mark on her ivory flesh. Payback for public flirting.

Marie's ex-maid, Jackson, was scrunched between two older white guys with bright colored ski jackets at a small table toward the front of the lounge. Jackson was chatting away with animation. Jackson swung her eyes around the bar as the Judge watched, her gaze lingering for a moment with venom on Marie.

David Branden was there too, huddled over a Scotch on the rocks at a dining table just beyond the bar, in the Resort's restaurant. He was with a Chinese gentleman of lingering years who sported an expensive looking suit, Italian, tailored to perfection. Everything about the Chinese gentleman bespoke money, including the Director's attentiveness and demeanor, his hands carefully buried under the table where their likely sweaty condition couldn't be seen.

Branden was ignoring Sharon Langley, who was seated beside him, leaning forward and listening intently, a Cosmo in hand. The Judge noted Branden's and Langley's comfort zone was very tight. They knew each other much better than Sharon had implied in the Judge's conversation with her. Interesting.

The Judge caught up with Katy and Marie at their table and settled into the third chair there, only to be abandoned as the girls split for the powder room. To tidy their makeup and no doubt have a private conversation. The Judge was beginning to wonder if Marie was a good influence on his bride.

He turned his attention back to Claire at the far end of the bar, wondering how he could get close enough to ask her if Jerry Stone had been her third boyfriend that died. Close, without being overheard by Tony, her Mob-guy. But Mob-guy was there, tight with her, protective and suspicious. It wasn't an auspicious time.

As the Judge turned back to the bar, he felt a light touch on his shoulder. He turned to see a small Asian man there, perhaps of Philippine descent, five-two, mid-fifties like him. Soft intelligent eyes peered out at the Judge through thick glasses. He was dressed in jeans and a Tommy Bahama shirt, preferred fare for aging gen-Xers. And he felt American, not a transplant.

"You're the Judge?"

"Yes."

"Nice to meet you. I'm Henry, Henry Banner. I'd like to talk to you for a moment if I might. May I sit down?"

"Of course."

"I was contacted by Jerry Stone, who wanted me to be an expert witness in a case he was handling. Concerning The Foundation."

"Dr. Henry Banner." The Judge remembered the name from one of the pleadings in the case, a list of potential expert witnesses.

"Yes. I have a PhD in Global Health and also in Global Disease Epidemiology from UCLA."

"Well, I won't hold UCLA against you Henry. It's a pleasure to meet you," said the Judge, softening his barb with a warm smile. "Sit down. Sit down."

"You are SC I presume?" asked Banner.

"Yes."

"You know what they say, Judge."

"What?"

"Put one idiot in a room and he'll go 'Duh!' Put two idiots in a room and they'll go, 'Duh… Duh…!' But put a whole bunch of idiots in a room, and they'll go, 'Dah dah, da da da dahhh. Dah dot Da da da dahhh. Dah dah da dump de da. Dah da… de dump da daaaa. Da dump de da, De dump de da."' It was the USC fight song.

The Judge chuckled and waved over a cocktail waitress. "I like you, Dr. Henry. Let me buy you a drink."

They sat in silence for a while, sipping drinks and watching the crowd. Neither was in a hurry to speak. Finally, the Judge broke the ice.

"Were you fully briefed on Jerry's Foundation case and the defense he was mounting?"

"I wasn't, Judge. Jerry and I talk briefly about a month ago, and he added me to his witness list as an expert. Then he called me on Thursday of last week and said he was desperate to meet with me and get my advice."

"I wondered about your selection as an expert, Henry, since your degrees are in public health. Jerry's Foundation case appears to be about animal cruelty, misuse of charitable donations, and perhaps illegal research on animals. Kind of far afield from public health and epidemiology. Do you know why Jerry wanted you as an expert, or why he withdrew as counsel?"

"No, and no, Judge. I don't. We were going to meet on Saturday over coffee up here and go over things. But of course, he died that night before."

"He was murdered."

"Yes. So I heard, Judge. Do you think there's a connection between his murder and his Foundation case.?"

"I don't know, Henry. Could be. There's a ton of money involved in The Foundation and its business. You live in Arrowhead, Henry?"

"No, Judge. I came up to the Lake to see you."

"How'd you get my name?"

"I called the Sheriff's office, spoke to a Sergeant Jack Prentis. He said you were investigating the murder as a private citizen and perhaps I should talk to you."

"Where are you staying, Henry?"

"Here, at the Arrowhead Resort."

"Can we meet tomorrow where it's quiet and we can talk more privately?"

"I've got some business I have to attend to down the hill, Judge. But I could come back. How about Monday for lunch.?"

"Perfect. I'll give you a call, Henry, to firm up the time and place."

Henry offered his hand in a firm handshake, slid his chair back, stood up, and wound his way back through the crowd and out of the bar.

The Judge turned back to the crowd at the bar, looking for Claire. But she and Mob-guy were gone. Two one hundred-dollar bills lay on the bar marking where they'd been.

Chapter 32
Friday Morning 7:00 a.m.

The Judge's cell phone went off with the USC fight song. The damn phone played whatever it liked when someone called.

"Hello," said the Judge.

"It's Claire, Judge. Claire Henderson. You know. Your special friend."

"Oh. Hi Claire."

"I'm in an awful jam, Judge. Anything I tell you; it's privileged. Right? You're a lawyer."

"Yes, that's right."

"I need someone to help me figure out what to do. I'm desperate. I trust you. You're a good man, principled. I can tell."

"Well, thank you, Claire. What's the problem?"

"Not on the phone, Judge. I'm still here, at the Arrowhead Resort, room 308. I badly need your advice. Can you come here? Please… Oh please."

"When?... Now? You want me to come over now? It's seven in the morning, Claire. I haven't even shaved."

"Please, Judge. I'm so scared."

The Judge could hear Claire softly crying now. It wasn't a setup, not another pitch to sell the Judge her intimate services. He could tell. Claire was scared.

"Okay, Claire. Give me a half hour. I'll jump in the shower and then scoot to the Resort. Room 308 you said?"

"Yes, Judge. God, please hurry."

Forty-minutes later the Judge walked down the corridor at the Arrowhead Resort and knocked on the door to room 308. For some reason the door wasn't closed tight. His knock sprung the door open perhaps four inches. He pushed lightly, saying, "Hello… Hello… Claire?" in a loud voice. The door swung out into the room.

The room was dark, all the lights off and black-out curtains drawn, leaving only streaks of grey light seeping in around their edges from the grey morning outside. He flipped on the light switch by the entry door, bathing the room in stark light from the ceiling, then wished he hadn't.

Claire was in an overstuffed leather chair by the bed. She was dressed in a delicious pink negligee, sheer, showing off her beautiful breasts and the expanse of her alabaster hips and thighs. She was beautiful in life… and she was beautiful in death.

Her head with its long blond curls was slumped back and to one side in the chair, her large brown eyes directed toward the ceiling, vacant, her mouth wide open in surprise. It was the top of her head that was in distress. In fact, the top of her head wasn't there. It'd gone missing. Blood and bone and grey matter surrounded the gaping hole as a bullet transcended her upper jaw and ripped up and out the top of her skull, spreading its contents far and wide across the ceiling, the lamp shade, the walls and curtains behind. The Judge felt sick.

The gun that had been in her mouth, a Beretta M9, had fallen to the floor beside her, still partially wrapped in the monogrammed towel used to muffle its use. Beside the gun was an empty gin bottle, Tanqueray, and a glass on its side.

He saw Claire's pen on the nightstand beside the bed, resting on a hotel pad. He leaned over to have a look. Nothing was written on the pad. But there were indentations, as though an earlier top sheet had been written on, and then torn off. The Judge took his pencil and carefully dusted lead on the sheet to bring up the markings. He could just barely make out two telephone numbers. One, on top, perhaps the last one called, was his. The other one looked familiar, but he couldn't quite place it. He grabbed one of his business cards and wrote the second number down.

He stepped backward, easing himself out of the room, startled at the bloody scream of the young cleaning lady passing behind him in the hall. He turned to watch her abandon her cart and go sobbing back toward the elevator at a panicky trot. It was going to be a long morning.

Chapter 33
Friday Morning 8:00 a.m.

The scream of the sirens, the hustle of the paramedics, the plod of Officer Jack Prentis and the scowl of Pete Campbell, the body whisked away under a covered sheet, the endless repeat of his story; it all was so damn familiar. It had been only six days since they hauled away Jerry Stone's body from the Judge's dock. Now another friend, or at least a semi-friend, was gone. Murdered. The Judge felt drained and depressed. It hadn't helped that Pete Campbell had volunteered, "Gee, Judge... bodies just seem to follow you around. Are you some kind of Jonah or something?"

Claire had been a beautiful and sparkling young woman. If she was going to kill herself, why call him first? Did she want legal advice, or just an audience for her curtain call? It made no sense. Perhaps she knew Jerry's killer, had stumbled onto something, or seen something. What was her 'jam' she couldn't speak about over the phone? *Christ.* He wished it wasn't too early to have a drink... but it was, way too early. The morning wore on, and finally at 11:00 a.m. the police were done with him and he could leave.

As the Judge walked to the parking lot, he took out his cell phone and dialed the other number he saw on the nightstand's pad. The one he couldn't quite place.

He heard the ring on the other end of his cell, then it stopped as the phone was picked up. A voice came on, a man's voice, "Larry Shankman."

The Judge hung up. He trudged to his car and drove slowly toward Cedar Glen, then turned down Palisades Drive to the Lake front and the refuge of his cabin. Trying to remove the image of the hole in the top of Claire's head.

Katy had slept in and was just getting up as he walked into his bedroom, looking radiant and glamorous in her white silk pajamas. She sat at the edge of the bed and stretched her arms over her head, arching her back, like a cat. Her scent, mixed with cinnamon and violet, filled the bedroom. She seemed happy and relaxed. That was good. It wasn't the time to tell her about Claire.

That's when his cell went off again, this time playing Silent Night. How damn appropriate. It was a client with an emergency, needing the Judge's presence in an immediate meeting to plan strategy. The Judge put his cell phone down with a sigh.

"I've got to go down the hill, Katy. I've got a meeting I can't change in the South Bay today. It's starting late in the afternoon and is going to run late. I think I'll just crash in Palos Verdes tonight. Come back up tomorrow morning."

"I can go down with you, Judge. Just drop me at the house."

"No, Katy. You're on sabbatical. You're supposed to be enjoying yourself. Relax up here and chill. It'll be good for you."

"You sure that's all right, Judge?"

"I am."

"Okay. I would like to kick back a little longer. It's so very relaxing. It's all the trees, and air, and water. Besides, Marie asked us to dinner tonight. Since you're going down the hill, I guess it'll just be me."

"Sounds right, Katy. Your friend will want to talk to someone. Better if it's you two alone. Just be careful if she starts giving advice."

The Judge sailed out the door and started up the thousand steps.

Katy could hear him panting near the top, his sounds fading into a door slam; then his car roared off.

Chapter 34
Friday Evening 7:30 p.m.

Much later, as the sun disappeared behind the cabin, bathing the tops of the trees across the Lake in a last yellowy glow, Katy awoke from a long nap, showered, and dressed in a favorite white dress, a low-cut summery number that buttoned down the front. She splashed some light makeup on, put on a warm coat, and headed out for Shelter Cove and her dinner at Marie's house.

They sat together in the big dining room under candlelight, Katy and Marie, two friends at one corner of a table for twelve, feasting on fresh flown-in salmon Marie had snapped up at the market. There was rice, a Chinese sauce on the side, a homemade Cobb salad, and three bottles of Babich Hawkes Bay Unoaked Chardonnay, chilled to just the right temperature.

They traded stories about the Jerry Stone they knew, Marie doing most of the talking. Because Marie had more stories, of course, and because she needed to tell them. There were funny stories, tragic stories, hard-done-to stories, and lucky break stories. A collection of vignettes that was all that was left of Jerry's life, revisited by a woman who had once been his loving bride and his best friend.

Is that all we are? wondered Katy. *Just a collection of short stories vaguely remembered occasionally by the people close to us?* Lines from the Bard from centuries before drifted into her mind: *(A) walking shadow, a poor player that struts and frets his hour upon the stage… And then is heard no more.*

After a time, and the opening of the third Babich Hawkes bottle, Katy turned to Marie and asked softly, "Tell my about your 'open' marriage with Jerry?"

"Well, you need some background first, Katy. It's happening on both Coasts more than you might imagine. People call them polyamorous relationships. One researcher has concluded that more than five percent of existing relationships between sexes characterized themselves as non-monogamous."

"I don't know what that means, Marie."

"A polyamorous relationships is not completely about sex, as contrasted to an 'open' relationship, Katy. Polyamory is having multiple relationships, where love and emotional connections are the driving force.

"And that's what you and Jerry did?"

"That's what I thought we were doing. We started about eight months ago, Katy."

"Why?"

"I don't know. Boredom, I guess. Jerry was always busy with his clients, didn't seem to have any time for me. No kids, nothing to divert my energies. We'd shared each other's stories out of our past more than once, exchanged our thoughts on political and moral issues often enough so we knew which opinions to keep to ourselves. We didn't seem to have anything left to talk about. Meals and evenings consisted of long drawn out silences, punctuated by too much alcohol. We'd often get smashed together, but Katy, it was like drinking alone. There was nothing there. And the sex was… well, awful."

"How so?"

"Jesus, Katy. Jerry'd just jump on my bones, last about two minutes, sweaty and panting, then roll off and go to sleep. No romantic conversation, no touching, no kissing, no petting. I may as well have been a Goddamn wall socket."

"So, how'd your 'polyamorous marriage work out?"

"I thought it was great. Jerry wasn't happy about it at first. He stormed out of here and got himself a younger mistress right away, last summer."

"Who?"

"I wasn't supposed to know who. That was our deal. But I knew full well. It was that boat patrol lady, Ally something."

"Ally Monroe?"

"That's her. The cheap little bitch. She sensed Jerry was available, so she started wiggling her ass around him till he got the idea. Jerry'd often come home smelling of her perfume. And of their sex."

"So, they are... were... still seeing each other when… you know."

"No, Katy. They had a falling out after several weeks from what I've heard. Jerry found someone else to screw. I don't know who. But she wore him out big time. He'd come home exhausted, his dick dragging between his legs." Marie sounded bitter now.

"And how'd it work for you, Marie?"

"It's really cool, Katy. It's the best of both worlds. You have the security of a husband, and the excitement of a new lover. It matches the way we're made It's the way we're programmed. The way we're supposed to be."

Marie's face was aglow now, a smile on her face.

"Do you have a lover now, Marie?"

"I do, Katy. He's a wonderful man, younger than me. And Spanish. The Europeans know how to treat their women. How to make me tingle all over and give me multiple orgasms."

"Wow, Marie. That sounds awesome."

"His name is Juan. In fact, in about an hour I'm going to see him at a late cocktail party this evening on the other end of the Lake. Just a handful of people, all old friends. You said you wanted to meet more people up here. And you said the Judge is stuck back in L.A. tonight. You should come."

"I'd just be a third wheel, Marie. I don't want to mess you up."

"Oh, you wouldn't mess me up at this party. I assure you. Come along with me, we can take my car. They're all interesting local people. Nice people. Flamboyant people. It's at Sharon Langley's mansion out on Totem Pole Ridge. Have you seen her house? It's spectacular."

"I haven't."

"Well okay then. And you'll get a chance to meet Juan."

"You sure it'd be okay?"

"Absolutely. Let's have dessert and some more wine; then we'll go."

Chapter 35
Friday Evening 10:30 p.m.

After dessert was finished, Marie disappeared to change, reemerging in a tight yellow skirt displaying her crisp figure, hourglass but slim, emphasizing her flat stomach. She wore patterned stockings and a white silk blouse, topped with a violet silk scarf for fun. They both slipped into their ski jackets and headed out, climbing into Marie's Aston Martin, a Rapide AMR, and roaring off. A girls' night out, mused Katy. Good clean fun for a change. Marie drove fast, efficiently, enjoying the power of her Rapide, which Katy envied for its flair. Around the Lake road, through the private guard station, and down to the mansions of Rainbow Point.

Cars were parked in the driveway of the Langley house, and so Marie parked on the street outside its big gates. They hoofed it up toward the bright lights of the estate and its large front doors... Katy paused in her stride half-way up the long driveway swooping up in a half circle to the chateau above and looked back at Marie. She wished she'd brought a change of clothes, something more elegant than her white dress with the buttons down the front. Marie looked so... sophisticated, and... sexy.

The house had stained cedar wood and bright windows overlooking the driveway and the grounds on this side, and no doubt the Lake on its other side. It was a magnificent mansion. But now as they walked past the expensive cars lining the driveway, Katy wasn't so sure of the wisdom of her decision to join Marie; go socializing with a lot of late-night jayhawkers and party. She'd had an awful lot of wine over dinner and she was feeling it. She turned to Marie with mild panic in her eyes, "I don't know about this, Marie. I'm pretty tired and a tad smashed from all the wine. Perhaps I should give this group a rain check."

"Oh, come on, Katy. Relax. You'll like these people. They're a collection of local folks and people from down the hill. You don't have to entertain anyone, just kick back and enjoy the camaraderie until you get the lay of the land." Marie giggled for some reason at her words.

"Besides, we're already here, Katy. Just come in for a few minutes and meet my friends. And I want you to meet Juan. Then if you're tired, you can call an Uber and go home. Get your car from my place tomorrow."

"Well... okay."

"But Katy, I have a confession to make."

"A what?"

"A confession."

Katy came to attention, focused on Marie now, sensing there was something more here than she'd originally understood.

"Well, you see, Katy, this party, this… well it's more like a club. Anyway, this group of people… this function… it's something a bit more than a cocktail party. In the old days you'd have called it a swingers party."

Katy's eyes got big and round. Her jaw dropped open, allowing for the whoosh of air as she gasped. "You don't mean…"

"Yes. I do. It's how I met Juan, who is already here. That's his BMW over there."

"You've brought me to a swingers party?" Katy's voice had lowered to a whisper. "Marie, I can't go in there. I just can't."

"It's not what you think, Katy. The first hour of the evening is just an innocent cocktail party. It's just good conversation and good fun. Like any other. Then, a bell is rung, and some people who aren't into this sort of thing say goodnight and go home."

"And the rest? They… they shack up?"

"If they want to. Some just like to watch. Or they just continue to flirt and party and have a good time in the great room and don't do anything else. There's no pressure to do anything, just have fun."

"And you? Marie, do you… shack up?"

"I will tonight, mostly with Juan. But that's later. Come on. Let's just join the party now and have some fun. You said you wanted to meet new people. And these people, many of them, have 'open' or 'poly' arrangements with their spouses. You said you were curious about open relations earlier. Well here's your chance to ask questions of people who know firsthand about it. And they'll talk freely about it I know."

"I don't know, Marie. I'm not sure an open marriage is what I want. I mean, it sounded like an intriguing idea when we talked about it earlier in the week, but now, now..."

"Now you're not ready to get so close to it."

"Something like that."

"It's a natural thing, Katy. Sex is a natural human thing. It's what we're built to do. It's satisfying and relaxing and fun. And no one need ever know that you visited. Just come meet my friends. You can leave when the bell rings. You're not obligated in any way to stay or to do anything. And understand that in some rooms what might look like a sea of swirling bodies is actually a handful of triads or couples getting it on with their usual partners."

"You're sure there's no pressure."

"Absolutely not. Oh. But you need to decide on a name. "

"A name?"

"Yes. We all adopt a fantasy name. Just for fun. It's a game. Part of the game of the party. It can be any name you'd like."

"And you'll introduce me under my made-up name?"

"Yes."

"What's your made-up name, Marie?"

"Tasha."

"Tasha?" Katy giggled. "You don't look like a Tasha, Marie."

Marie smiled. "You'd be surprised. But anyway, you can't make fun of anyone's name. It's not polite. It's their personal fantasy and must be respected."

"Oh. I'm sorry, Marie. But do you wear masks too? Is this like a masquerade party?"

"Sometimes, but not tonight. You'd be surprised how pleasant it can be to have a mask and your fantasy name, and just leave your old identity at home for a night. It can be a real turn on."

"I see. I think."

"So, what's your name, Katy?"

Katy thought for ten seconds, then smiled.

"I'll be Lucy, Marie. Short for Lucifer; the devil in me that's brought me
this far." Katy giggled. The wine was going to her head, but it seemed there wasn't much she could do about it.

"Great."

"The Judge must never know."

"Of course not, Katy. This group is very discreet."

"The Judge's old fashioned, you know. He'd be very upset."

"That's why he'll never find out, Katy. Trust me on this."

Marie put her arm around Katy and gave a little tug, starting her up the steps and across the large tiled patio that served as the entry. Marie pushed the doorbell beside one of the huge carved front doors, setting off Notre Dame chimes rumbling through the house. Katy could feel her blood pressure rising, her pulse fluttering, as she tried to look calm, collected, worldly… and reasonably sober despite the wine.

The door swung in and their hostess was there to greet them, a middle-aged woman, pushing fifty, but well preserved, angular and erect, with pale skin and platinum blond hair. She had what appeared to be an honest smile, reflected in soft brown eyes which only exposed a few crinkles around the edges. The mark of a good Beverly Hills plastic surgeon. She wore a black silk pantsuit that set off her hair and skin, and she looked relaxed.

"Come in, come in, Tasha," she said to Marie. "Welcome, welcome. Everyone's here already;

but we're all looking forward to partying with you. And I see you've brought a new friend."

Katy hesitantly stepped in behind Marie, blinking from the blast of brightness from all the light thrown by a large chandelier made out of antlers, and numerous wall sconces adorning the entry hall and the adjoining great room. The Theme from Somewhere in Time was playing in the background through expensive speakers, barely audible over multiple animated conversations conducted by eighteen guests, ten guys and eight women. With Katy and Marie and the hostess, it made ten men and eleven women.

The hostess introduced herself as Carmel, like the town, which seemed silly since they all knew she was Sharon Langley. Katy supposed it made it more fun for her too. Carmel volunteered she and her husband had built the place years before, overseeing every detail to assure it suited them perfectly. Katy could see off the living room a formal dining room with a large dining table made out of a single piece of tree, twenty chairs tucked around it. Beyond, a door led to the kitchen, showing a sliver of quartz counter, wood pegged floor, and a Viking Tuscany range.

The people in the room turned to greet Marie and be introduced to 'Lucy'. They all seemed friendly, although two of the men stared a tad too long at the top of Katy's dress and the cleavage bolstered by her uplifting bra. Licking their chops already, she thought, feeling repelled.

Marie went over and snatched a younger man, European, perhaps Castilian, dragging him over and introducing him as 'Alfonso'. Alfonso took her hand

and bent over to kiss its top, saying shyly, "Alfonso means noble, and ready, in my country."

"His name's really Juan." Marie whispered, her eyes dancing. "He's my special Juan. We're going to slide down the hall for a little bit, kind of jumping the gun, but I'll be back."

Katy watched them disappear down a long side wall, trying to put aside feelings of being abandoned to a pool of sharks.

Carmel handed Katy a glass of punch, shimmering all red in cut crystal, whispering, "It's not very strong but it's really good."

Katy took an exploratory sip. It tasted of cherries and pomegranate, with hints of strawberry. Carmel was right. It was good.

She took Katy by the hand and introduced her around to the other people. They were all polite, the men looking non-committal, the women sizing Katy up the way women instinctively do. They were a gregarious lot and knew each other well…. Well of course they did!

They made Katy feel welcome and comfortable. There must have been something more in the punch than Carmel had let on, as Katy felt a slight blush rising in her cheeks and a warm glow invading her belly. She could feel her stress evaporating, replaced by a relaxed devil-may-care attitude. It was an hour of conversation on politics, the new fashions, the stock market, the real estate prices in Lake Arrowhead, and the latest fad diets.

A sandy haired man came over, sporting honest good looks, a square jaw, soft blue eyes, and hair worn a bit long. He moved under his tan slacks and blue sport court like a tennis pro. He wasn't very tall, but clearly buff; Katy could tell the way he moved in his clothes. He rested his eyes on Katy with a soft twinkle that bespoke friendship and perhaps a touch of humorous partners in crime.

"Hi Lucy. I'm Nate." He extended a hand to shake, firm, soft and white, his fingers long and aristocratic

"What do you do for a living, Lucy?" asked Nate.

"I am a high school counselor. I deal with lots of teenagers struggling their way through puberty. It's a challenge, but it's very interesting. And I think I make a difference."

"That's an important job," said Nate, watching Katy puff up a little at the praise. "I'm an aeronautical engineer, myself. More scientist than engineer really. Also, a challenging job, but interesting, rewarding, and most important, lucrative."

As they both took another sip of punch, Carmel moved to the center of the room and rang a small bell. Apparently, this was 'The Bell', the signal for more serious horseplay.

Several people coupled up and wandered to the back of the room and down a long hallway where Marie and Alfonso had disappeared. Katy could see doors on either side down its length, apparently bedrooms. Some couples joined making a foursome as they squeezed into the hall, laughing and chatting animatedly.

Katy turned nervously, wishing Marie was beside her for mutual support. But Marie hadn't returned. Katy's elbow bumped into someone's hand behind her, and she turned to see Nate there again, watching her with amused eyes.

"First time?"

"Yes. I came for just the pre-party." Katy muttered, blushing now, feeling self-conscious.

"That's the way to proceed," Nate said. "Take it slow and only do what you feel comfortable doing."

Katy nodded, silently damning Marie for fluttering off like a moth in heat.

"So, let's watch, Lucy. It's allowed, and quite interesting."

"I don't think I want..."

"Oh, come on. You may never have another chance to see what goes on at these things."

Nate put his arm around her waist and guided her down the hall like a dancing partner. Katy was regretting the punch she'd drunk, which had left her mind cloudy, decision making difficult.

Nate stopped at the first door and opened it a crack to peek in. "Not much to see in there yet. Let's try the next one." He took several more steps, reaching the next door, and quietly opened it, ushering Katy into the half-light beyond.

White walls and white painted furniture, a large four-poster bed, a bureau of drawers, and a white leather sofa along one wall. Four people were on the bed, already out of their clothes and rubbing their bodies together in a sort of daisy chain. There were soft grunts, ohs and sighs, building in tempo and volume. The pheromones of sex and passion were spilling off the four-poster and filling the room.

Katy's breath caught in her throat, her cheeks hot now. She felt damp in places where she shouldn't be, certain Nate could sense it. As Katy watched, the two couples each joined with one another and then the two couples mingled into an almost single throbbing orgasm, locked together internally by their sexual structures, carrying out an instinctive dance that made them move in coordination and noisy desperation, seeking mutual release. Suddenly, there were cries and then a mutual collapse as they fell apart. Spent, exhausted.

Katy shuddered. She wasn't sure why. Then she looked at Nate, who somehow seemed more appealing now, his arms casually sliding across her back in soft strokes. He took a slight step backward, reaching across her back with one hand and around to cup one of her breasts through her dress. Warm. Sensual. Alive. Then he bent his head to nibble at the nape of her neck. "Let's go find Marie, shall we?" Katy said, gently removing his hands, desperately stalling for time now, trying to clear her head, to think.

"Sure. I think she's in the last bedroom. Come on."

They returned to the hall. Various noises of foreplay and climax seeped in from under closed doors as they made their way to the last door on the end. Nate opened it just enough for Katy to squeeze in, then disappeared back down the hall, saying he was getting more punch. Katy placed her back flat against the wall beside the door, perhaps for support, her knees suddenly weak.

Marie was there, naked, straddling the hips of Alfonso, or Juan, or whatever his name was, in a reverse cowgirl. Marie bounced up and down with abandon, fully engaged. Suddenly, her partner pulled away and they both collapsed onto their backs, laying there for some seconds, savoring the petite death that was climax.

Marie turned her head and spotted Katy.

"Katy. Katy. I mean Lucy. This is so much fun. I never feel as alive as I do at these parties. You need to give it a try." Then she rolled over to cuddle Alfonso's head in her breasts.

"I agree," said Nate, suddenly behind Katy in the now open doorway, two more glasses of punch in hand. He leaned over to give Katy a soft peck on the cheek.

Katy's head was spinning now. Was it all the excitement? Or something in that damned punch? As if in a daze she felt herself being led by Nate out of the room, across the hall, and into an empty bedroom on the other side, where Nate sat her down on the bed. He sat beside her and reached over to give her a big smoochy kiss, his fingers fumbling with the top buttons of her dress.

Suddenly her breasts were free, lifted out of the push up bra and unbuttoned dress. Nate's mouth moved to suck one nipple and then the other. His tongue then teased around each nipple with short tight strokes. She could feel hormones coursing through her body. She wanted this. Damn she wanted this. She smelled his body, watched with fascination as his organ raised against the material of his pants, looked down at his hands on her white breasts, gently massaging them, sending electric sparks of hormones through her body.

Christ. Oh, Christ. But… these weren't the Judge's hands. These younger hands didn't belong to the Judge. What was she doing? God damn it. She couldn't do this. This wasn't her man. She belonged to the Judge. The Judge belonged to her. She was committed, forever. She loved her Judge. She would not do something that would hurt him.

"No," she said, and "No!" again, louder, pushing his hands away, hard, rising from the bed as she got back into her dress.

She rose and fled for the door, fumbling with the buttons. He didn't follow. That was a relief. No one was in the living room. They were all back down the hall. She grabbed her ski jacket and purse and tumbled out the front door and down the driveway, gasping great heaps of cold mountain air into her lungs, trying to clear her head. At the bottom she dialed an Uber and hoped no one would come outside before it arrived.

She wasn't sure what had just happened to her, but she was glad to be away. She never wanted to go back.

Chapter 36
Saturday Morning 10:00 a.m.

As the Judge drove up the hill Saturday morning, he decided to explore the cabin Jerry Stone was said to have kept on the side. The Pine Tree Lodge was a cross between a bed-and-breakfast and a motel, with one large main building containing reception, dining room lounge, and upstairs bedrooms; and a series of small cabins built down a gully around a pool, each with a private entrance and parking, perfect for an assignation. And only a few hundred yards from the bars and nightlife of Arrowhead Village. The cabins were small, quaint, and discreet, plenty of space separating each cabin from the next. Back in the forties when the Lake was the playground for the Hollywood crowd, many an affair had been consummated here among the pines. It was just as well the cabin walls couldn't talk.

The Judge walked into the small manager's office and asked for Jerry Stone's cabin number. The teenager behind the desk, interrupted in the middle of his video game, gave up the number twelve quickly so he could return to *Call of Duty: Black Ops 4*.

The Judge meandered down the little path among the cabins, to cabin twelve, and knocked on the door. Not surprisingly, there was no answer. The Judge tried the door. It was locked. He wandered around to the back and tried the back door, also locked. Cabin eleven had all of its doors and windows open, the flurry of the cleaning lady flapping sheets visible through the window. The Judge walked back up the hill to eleven and looked at the cleaning cart on the walk in front of its porch. He casually walked over and lifted the pass key hanging from the end of the cart, moved back down to cabin twelve, unlocked its door, then back uphill and replaced the key.

He gave his best boyish smile to the cleaning lady, who suddenly appeared at the front door of eleven, eyeing him suspiciously. But the key was back where it belonged, and all seemed in place. "Just visiting Mr. Stone in twelve," said the Judge, waving his hand in the air as he turned and retraced his steps downhill.

He pretended to knock again on twelve, then casually opened the unlocked door and stepped in. The cabin was small, a single room plus a bathroom. It had a stone fireplace at one end. The decor was Ralph Lauren Western, dark leather upholstered furniture, gaily colored Indian blankets over the wood floor, a small antler chandelier over a distressed dining bench, and a bed comforter of dark green plaid with a faux fur folded across its bottom.

There was an old ski jacket thrown over one chair, and the drawer in the distressed nightstand next to the bed contained the Bible and a half-used pack of condoms, Trojans. *Would a USC man use anything less?* smirked the Judge.

There wasn't much else indicative of the cabin's occupant, except for the cardboard file box tucked neatly under the wooden bench. The Judge slid it out, noting the title sprawled in crayon on its side: Extra Docu Set. He peeled off its top to display a collection of brown folders. Each was labeled: The Foundation for the Advancement of Animal Rights vs Wildman; with a second caption for the contents of each file. There was the complaint, the answer, various motion documents, a set of documents about The Foundation, delivered in response to interrogatories, transcripts of the depositions of Larry Wildman and David Branden, and an unsigned contract contemplating the retention of one Dr. Henry Banner as a consultant for the defense.

The Judge took the box to the bed and spread out its contents on the plaid comforter, opening the first file and reading. A half hour later there was a rattle on the cabin's front door, as the cleaning lady prepared to enter. "Don't need cleaning today," the Judge yelled in a hoarse voice. The rattling stopped and the Judge heard the squeak of the wheels as the cleaning cart moved further downhill.

Larry Wildman's allegations were fleshed out in far more detail in his deposition. He claimed the non-profit Foundation was merely a front to illegally raise tax deductible money for Replace/Repair Corp and its research. He claimed Replace/Repair was violating ethical and scientific rules and protocol, extending its research far beyond the businesses of dog colonies for blood production and pig valve harvesting for human valve replacement. But Wildman was vague on what this new research was about.

The twin corporations had been careful to compartmentalize what they were doing on a need to know basis. Apparently, Wildman wasn't high enough in the organization to know the whole story. He did claim that whatever experiments Replace/Repair Corp was doing were unethical and unsafe, utilizing unproven and unregulated methods. Unfortunately, his opinion wasn't worth much since he didn't know what the research involved, and he couldn't point to specific practices or procedures that were unsafe.

He was more specific about the way the pigs and other animals were kept. He described the squalor of the dogs and pigs kept in their small metal pens with hardly room to turn around, no exercise, minimal water and food. He contended their mistreatment made a mockery of The Foundation's name and constituted a fraud upon those who'd made generous tax-free contributions to what they understood to be a charitable organization dedicated to protecting animals.

Wildman said that when he tried to protest about these practices to management, he was immediately fired. And further, he was threatened with litigation if he made any public outcry or released any information about what he'd observed at The Foundation's ranch.

The second file contained Director David Branden's deposition transcript. Branden's testimony was peppered with objections from his legal counsel, Leonard Black, who continually asserted privileged information and a right not to answer. Wildman's attorney doing the questioning sounded young and inexperienced, his questions often fuzzy, seemed to miss the point. He failed to follow up on inviting openings created by Branden's answers. The Judge would have burrowed in with a plethora of follow-ups each time a probing question touched a defense nerve.

And Branden was a master of evasiveness, turning questions to shift their meaning and answer something else. He'd also give vague answers that weren't capable of verification. Rambling on with nonsense unrelated to the case, dragging the deposition out, chewing up time and everybody's energy until Wildman's counsel often got tired and just gave up on a particular line of questioning.

Still, much information emerged from the Branden deposition. Branden controlled The Foundation and Replace/Repair Corp and spent time working for both. There was one other shareholder who owned over ten percent of Replace/Repair Corp's stock, who Branden could not or would not identify. Replace/Repair had booked over thirty million dollars in 'brokerage' transaction revenues over its prior fiscal year, but Branden refused to elaborate on what sort of brokerage was involved.

Replace/Repair Corp was using animal DNA for research, but Branden refused to disclose the nature of the research. There was a secret Foundation ranch in the mountains above Lake Arrowhead where research was conducted. There was no independent scientific oversight of the research.

There was also an invoice for $5,000 from Henry Banner. Scribbled across the bottom was a note in Jerry Stone's scrawl*: Meeting with Banner confirmed for Saturday at 10:00 a.m.*, *Bradford Jones at noon.*

Jerry had been murdered the evening before.

At the bottom of the file a small diagram fell out; actually more of a hastily scribbled map. The Judge picked it up and looked closely. It was in Jerry's hand, directions from Lake Arrowhead Village to the Foundation's ranch.

The Judge sat back in his chair, muttering, "What the hell had Jerry gotten himself into?"

Chapter 37
Saturday Afternoon 2:00 p.m.

The Judge followed the rough-hewn map on the scrap of paper he'd found in Jerry's cabin, turning left on State Highway 173, winding his way around the Lake and out of Arrowhead, up into the wilderness above the Lake. He stayed on Highway 173 for a time, finally turning left on Lake Arrowhead Road, left again on Saddle Dike Embankment, and then right on Deep Creek Road. From there he turned left on Happy Valley Road, taking it almost to its end, stopping just before it made a hard turn toward Glenmill Road. There was supposed to be a side road here cutting off to The Foundation's ranch.

But there was nothing. He got out of his car and looked around. He'd expected to see a fancy circular drive to a grand ranch house, as was the custom with ranches in these parts. There was no raised curb on the narrow road, just dirt and then grass. As he looked, he spotted one place where tires had briefly scrunched the grass down in their passage off the road and through the adjoining meadow, leaving faint marks. He pulled off the road and bumped his way across the meadow, following the faint tracks, glad he was still driving the rental car.

On the other side of the meadow the tracks turned into an uneven dirt road, rutted with potholes and gulley's. He reluctantly turned his car on to the dirt road, actually more trail than road, and crept along, stirring up a sizable dust cloud behind him

He traveled about half a mile, down a winding embankment, hoping there would be room to turn around at the bottom, very uncertain about his decision to proceed. But at the bottom there was a circular turnaround. A chain link fence ten feet high, with barbed wire strung along its top, stretched off into the distance in both directions. There was a gate set in the fence, made of steel panels. Out twenty feet in front of the gate a small box rose from the ground and extended up window high, with a built-in intercom for calling the gate keeper. There was no sign identifying the property as The Foundation's Ranch. He leaned out his window to the box and pushed the button. Above a small camera's aperture built into the panel, a light suddenly flashed red, and then a disembodied voice said, "Yes."

The Judge gave his name into the box, and said, "I'm visiting at the request of Director David Branden and undertaking an inspection visit. I may become a new Foundation Board Member."

"Come ahead," said the voice. The gate swung open eerily. On the other side was a reasonably new asphalt road which led across a pasture, over a small bridge with fish jumping in the pond underneath, and then disappeared into a strand of old sycamore trees.

The Judge climbed back into his now dusty car and set off. On the other side of the trees was a large fenced paddock with two thoroughbreds enjoying the fresh green grass, and beyond a circular drive that brought the Judge up in front of a colonial house that, but for its smaller scale, could have been out of Gone with the Wind. A very large, long and very weathered barn, its doors shut, stood off to the left and behind the house.

A young man all of twenty stood on the porch waiting for Judge in fresh-pressed tan slacks and a white shirt, open at the collar. Soft brown eyes watched the Judge approach. He nervously stepped down from the porch extending his hand to pump the Judge's.

"I'm Bobby, the Foundation's intern. Nice to meet you. Sam, the foreman is on the back quarter, but he's coming right in. I'm to leave you hear on the porch and call the Director immediately to confirm…ah… to let the Director know you're here."

Bobby turned and bolted back up the porch and through its front door, closing it behind him.

The Judge counted to ten, then stepped off the porch and ambled around Gone with the Wind to the left, down its side, and across to the doors of the barn behind it. The barn doors weren't locked, so the Judge pushed one open, stepped inside, and closed it behind him.

Outside the barn had looked old and beat up, but inside it was new. Stainless steel supports and rails, new lights that blazed from the ceiling, skylights set periodically in a new roof, and the hum of air conditioning somewhere in the background. It was also considerably larger than it looked from the front of the house, perhaps fifty feet across, and running off at least a seventy-five feet he could see, where it stopped short by some roof-to-floor divider, with something looking much like an airlock door at its center. It was lined with steel cages and pens down the middle. Food supplies and assorted equipment lined either side.

The Judge wandered down the long corridor beside the cages, passing cage after cage of dogs, all confined in tiny squat conditions on concrete pads, serviced by automatic water and feeding equipment . IV equipment was hooked to each cage rail, as was a high-powered hose to wash feces off into a covered drain that ran down the middle of the building. This was the dog colony business that Larry Shankman had sold to Replace/Repair. A dirty business, Shankman had called it, and the Judge could see it was.

These were the caged dogs whose blood was periodically drawn to provide dogs' blood for veterinarians across the country. The dogs looked lethargic, barely noticing the Judge's passing, no barking, no seeking of attention, no interest in their dull eyes. Heavily sedated was the Judge's guess. The Judge felt sorry for them.

The Judge came to the dividing sectional with its floor-to-ceiling wall that cut across the width of the barn. At its center was a glass-enclosed chamber with two doors at each end, functioning as an airlock.

The Judge pushed through the first door, which automatically and noiselessly closed behind him, sealing him in. There was a blast of cold air blown across his body, rippling his hair back over his forehead, a buzzer sounded, and then a green light went on above the second door. He stepped forward and pushed the door open, entering the second segment of the barn.

It was as large as the first. But it was entirely different. It looked like the inside of a hospital laboratory. There were still the cages down the middle, stainless steel, somewhat larger, with concrete pads underneath. But these cages contained what looked to be young pigs. They made no movement as the Judge passed, but their mournful eyes registered his presence as he walked by, several giving him accusatory looks. The place smelt of heavy disinfectant. It almost hid the animal smells of their limited existence in cages where again there was hardly room to turn around.

On the outside of the center aisle on both sides were metal tables, butcher saws, and large freezer units, the kind used on fishing boats to quick freeze a catch. Under the tables were drains, colored with permanent red stains no amount of washing could remove.

A man came around from a freezer further up, spotted the Judge, and came toward him, smiling. He was mid-thirties, already bald, and wore horn-rimmed glasses that partially hid watery brown eyes. He wore the white coat of a lab technician over a flamboyant knotted tie of purple and red, protruding from a brown cashmere sweater. The Judge realized it was very cold here; full-on air conditioning.

"I'm Gene Armstrong," the man said, offering a hand which the Judge took to shake.

The Judge said, "Pleased to meet you, Gene. Branden's been after me to invest in your operation, but I don't like to put money into something I can't see."

"Wish someone had given me a heads up. But I'd be happy to show you around and answer any questions you might have"

"What is it you do here, Gene?"

"We manufacture and harvest biological heart valves from genetically engineered pigs. Up here in the middle of nowhere we're pushing back the barriers of science."

"Science is very noble and all, son, but I want to know if there's a future in… pig hearts."

"Well, 250,000 heart valves are replaced worldwide each year in humans with valvular heart disease. A cadaveric valve comes from a human donor. Bovine valves are recovered from cows. And porcine valves come from pigs. Like ours here. The valve may be an actual valve recovered from one of our donors, or it may be manufactured from our donor tissue such as the pericardium, the sac that surrounds the heart."

"Okay, but why would I want to invest in your pig hearts, as opposed to cow hearts… or somebody else's pig hearts?"

Gene was practically bursting with professional pride. " We've taken it a big step forward by creating our genetically-engineered pigs. Pigs that do not express Gal and NeuGc, pigs transgenic for human complement-regulatory proteins and coagulation-regulatory proteins and/or anti-inflammatory proteins."

"Okay," said the Judge, nodding wisely, covering the fact he hadn't the least idea what the guy was talking about.

"Here, I'll show you." Armstrong led the Judge over to a large walk-in freezer and together they entered. It was half filled with small, frozen plastic packages. Armstrong pulled one out and handed it to the Judge. It was a small organ, a pig's organ. A heart valve.

"We ship these all over the world. Guaranteed that the human recipient's body will not reject the replacement."

"And The Foundation is in this business?"

"Yes. Well, no. Its sister corporation is. The Foundation supplied the capital to get started, and continues to provide money when we need it, but the business is conducted by Replace/Repair."

"And who owns Replace/Repair?"

"Well, I'm not in management. But I think because The Foundation is a not- for-profit, you know, it can't own this business. So, I think David and his partner actually own most of the operating Company. But it's technically a public company with lots of small shareholders. I even own a few shares."

"But you use The Foundation's money?"

"Oh yes. We have quite an ongoing research program. I thought they would have briefed you on all this."

"Who's David Branden's partner?"

"I don't know. He's a mystery man. Off-shore or something I think."

"What's over there?" asked the Judge, pointing to an enclosed office halfway up the room. Floor-to-ceiling glass defined the space, which contained four desks with computers, fax machines, and file cabinets. The glass room was empty, but then it was Saturday.

"That's hush… hush. I'm not supposed to talk about it."

"I'm not going to say anything."

"Well, I think it's our department which brokers the sale of replacement organs for people. Human kidneys, livers, skin, human parts from all over the world are sourced and then sold on a commission basis to those who need them. Drop shipped from the source directly to the surgeon. I'm not involved in that business. but I understand it's extremely profitable."

"Where's the profit go?"

"Not my wheelhouse, but I hear it's an all cash business. If you need a kidney, you're in a hurry and you've got plenty of money, well I suppose you'll pay any price. Rumor is the cash generated by that little room, and the cash generated by The Foundation's contributions, fund our entire research program and give everyone here a very generous living."

"What's up there?" The Judge pointed to the end of the cavernous space, where another sectional wall ran floor to ceiling and another airlock door was positioned in its middle.

"That's the future."

"How so?"

"We're genetically modifying pigs to grow transplant organs to the size and scale of their human counterparts. And even more amazing, we're growing the parts inside units we've modified using actual DNA elements which match our human volunteers. So, each of the units is growing replacement organs to function, size and operation, with compatible DNA. Each unit is a walking, living inventory of spare body parts for its designated human recipient."

The Judge was stunned. "Say it again, more slowly, Gene. I want to be sure I understand."

"Let me put it this way, Judge. If we create a unit matched to you, the unit would have human sized organs that contain your DNA, eliminating the risk of rejection. You would have a living inventory of spare organs to keep you going almost indefinitely. You could live forever."

"And when you say 'unit', you're talking about a live pig?"

"Yes."

"What sort of parts?"

"Oh, you know. Hearts, lungs, livers, kidneys, gallbladders, pancreas, ureters, skin, even the lens of the eye."

"So, everyone will have their own pig?"

"Exactly. I have my own pig in there. We all do."

"We all who?"

"The Board of Directors, David and the other directors, some employees, even our legal counsel."

"Jerry Stone has a pig in there?"

"Yes, he does. We all do."

"Can I see?"

"Sure." Armstrong led the way through the last airlock, bringing them into a final segmented area of the barn.

"That's Mr. Stone's animal over there," said Armstrong, pointing to a larger pen with a very large pig in it.

There was a name plaque on the front of the cage. It read:… *CINDY*!

Chapter 38
Saturday Afternoon 4:00 p.m.

Jerry Stone's name was emblazoned underneath Cindy's name on the brass plaque, designating his DNA kinship. Cindy the pig was big, full grown, and looked lonely and unhappy. She had deep-set blue eyes that almost looked human. She was penned up like everyone else in a cage too small, with metal floor and rails, barely enough room to turn around. Small beads of moisture glistened around Cindy's nose, and streams of mucus ran from the corners of each bloodshot eye.

The animal stared at the Judge with tired, sad eyes. Then she gave a pitiful bark at the Judge, and then another. It was a soft bark, akin to a human cough. There was corn in the trough behind her, apparently untouched. Cindy had little appetite. The sags here and there in Cindy's skin suggested she'd been losing weight at an alarming rate. Cindy looked very, very, sick.

"She has lungs, liver, heart and kidneys the size and structure of a human," said Armstrong proudly. "And of course, much of her DNA matches Mr. Stone's. She's a living Porcine-DNA Replacement Part Inventory Unit, or as we like to call her, a "PRPU". Specific in her DNA to Mr. Stone."

"Does it help to call her a 'Unit' or a 'PRPU', Gene?" asked the Judge. "Does it dehumanize her enough so you don't feel sympathy for her condition?"

"She's not human, Judge. She's just a pig."

"She's a living creature."

"She's an artificial construct we've created here in the lab, Judge. Her only purpose is to provide spare parts."

"Her lungs match Jerry Stone's?"

"Yes. She's got a true replica of Mr. Stone's lungs, through modification of her DNA combined with Jerry's DNA. If and when Jerry needs a new lung, it will be ready for him."

"I don't think Jerry Stone will be in to pick it up anytime soon, Gene."

"You're right of course. Mr. Stone may never need it. But it's reassuring for Mr. Stone, and for all of us, to know these parts are here if we need them."

"Cindy looks sick."

"Naw. That's just a little allergy she has. Her stats are great, pulse, blood pressure, temperature, all within norms."

"How often do you check her vitals?"

"Every forty-eight hours, like clock-work."

"Don't you think she'd be happier if she had a larger pen, and maybe a place to go outside and exercise, sniff the wind, see the sky and trees?"

"Are you kidding Mr. Judge? This is a very expensive facility to build and to run. It's designed for maximum efficiency and economy. Cindy's a lot easier to feed and to check up on in her cage. It takes fewer staff. And Cindy's used to it. Doesn't know any other way. It's difficult enough getting around to feed and check on each of the units as it is. It'd be impossible if we had to expand the storage space and periodically move the units outside. That's a ridiculous idea." Armstrong smiled to soften his criticism, satisfied he'd convinced the Judge.

The Judge shook his head in disbelief, then thanked Armstrong for the tour, turned and made his way back through the segmented barn and out into the sunlight, thankfully breathing in gulps of fresh air after he stepped through the barn entrance doors. The Judge walked back around to the front of Gone with the Wind, to find another man leaning against his car and looking grim. He wore scuffed blue jeans, a blue work shirt, and had a disreputable Stetson sitting on the back of his head. Mid-forties, with bright, keen blue eyes in a weathered face, he frowned as he watched the Judge approached, as though he knew exactly who the Judge was.

"I'm Sam, the ranch foreman."

"Hello, Sam." said the Judge. You lied to us, buster. No one invited you here. I checked. And you had no right to go into our barn and poke around. You've been trespassing for the last ten minutes. I've a mind to call the police and have you arrested for trespassing."

"Oh well," said the Judge, stepping behind the man and sliding into his car. "Somehow I suspect the powers-that-be won't want the police sniffing around. Good day."

The Judge heard the car doors automatically lock as he quickly started the engine and swung the car around the circle and a way, speeding up as he hit the trees.

Chapter 39
Saturday Afternoon 5:00 p.m.

The images of Cindy haunted the Judge as he maneuvered his rental car back across the dirt trail, up onto the highway, and wound his way back down into the Arrowhead Valley. And he thought about Gene Armstrong, likely a brilliant scientist, but so blind to the suffering he was creating. He finally shook the whole experience off, turning his focus to Katy, their marriage, and what was to be done.

An hour later the Judge stepped out of the mini market in Cedar Glen, loaded to the gills with groceries. He would cook a nice dinner 'in' with Katy and they'd eat next to a roaring fire. He had fixings for steak, baked potatoes, Caesar salad, and two bottles of Jadot Pouilly Fuisse. It would be a romantic interlude. He hoped it would lead to feelings of closer intimacy. As he bounced out the market door in better spirits now, he damn near tripped over Bradford Jones, the stubby little reporter who never wore socks. The little bastard was so damn short he was hard to see.

"Hi Judge. Found our killer yet? I expect not. Perhaps you're ready now to share information and collaborate with me on this Stone homicide."

"I'm doing just fine on my own, Jones. I don't need your help."

"Well Judge, don't be out late too many nights. I hear your young bride was over at the Lake's secret social sex club last night. Solo and the life of the party is the way I heard it."

The Judge took a deep breath, willing himself not to strangle the little rodent's neck right there, in front of Jensen's Mini-Market. He just kept walking, head held high, poker faced, shoulders stiff, leaving Jones behind him still looking for some reaction.

Damn that little prick. And what the hell had Katy been up to behind his back? Shit… Shit… Shit…!

Chapter 40
Saturday Afternoon 5:45 p.m.

As the Judge pulled out of the mini market, a sheriff's car flashed by him into an adjacent space, and then the car honked. The Judge pulled back into his parking space, parallel to the sheriff's car and rolled his window down. Sheriff Jack Prentis leaned low across his seat to wave at the Judge through his open window. "Can we talk for a minute, Judge?"

"Sure," said the Judge, getting out of his car again.

"What happened to your car, Judge?" asked Prentis.

"Don't ask, Jack. You don't want to know. What's up?"

"It wasn't suicide, Judge. Claire Henderson. She didn't kill herself."

They huddled then, leaning together against the front hood of the Judge's rental car.

"I'm not surprised, Jack. It was suspicious there was no note. And then she'd called me and wanted to talk. Her actions were not those of someone who was about to take her own life. And she sounded really scared."

"Your instincts were right on, Judge. The gun was positioned to look like she shot herself, and it had her fingerprints alone. There was even lipstick on the barrel where it was jammed into her mouth. But there was no gun powder residue on either hand. The tipped over glass of gin puddled on the carpet was laced with several ground up sleeping pills, and her bloodwork confirmed she was in a very drowsy state when she was shot. The coroner says he doesn't think she'd have had the coordination to place the gun in her mouth, position it toward the top of her head for maximum effect, hold it steady, and maneuver her finger to pull the trigger."

"Did she suffer?" asked the Judge.

"I think she was pretty scared of whoever was there, Judge. Terrified. But whether she drank the gin unknowingly or it was forced upon her, she must have been pretty out of it when it happened."

"The pills weren't enough to kill her?"

"No. She'd have needed a lot more of them. It was her own prescription; we found the empty bottle. Perhaps three pills were used."

"So, the murderer was improvising."

"We think so."

"Fingerprints?"

"We're still looking, but so far the place looks wiped clean. But we may have his DNA."

"How?"

"She had sex, shortly before she was snuffed. We found semen in her vagina. No match so far on the DNA, but we'll keep looking."

"Consensual sex?"

"Looks like it. No indications of force."

"So, she'd been with her lover."

"Yes. Course that doesn't prove he's the one who did this to her, whoever he is. But, he's a serious candidate."

"We'd had a conversation at the bar at RB's Steakhouse in Cedar Glen on Sunday evening. She told me she'd been seeing three separate men on a continuous basis under a 'Friends with Benefits' arrangement. It's how she supported herself. But she'd lost one sugar daddy and was down to two."

"Were you one of the 'friends', Judge?"

"Me?... No. I'm happily married, Jack."

"We're going to want a sample of your DNA, Judge. You found the body. You know how it works."

"Not a problem. I'll come over to the station later and give one."

"Did she tell you who the three men were?"

"No. But there was a friend who showed up, a mean little guy from Detroit or somewhere, very territorial. I'm guessing he'd be one of them."

"Did you get a name?"

"Tony something… Rovelli, or Roselli. He is, or was, staying at the Arrowhead Resort. You should be able to find his name and contact info."

"We'll track him down, Judge."

"Did you find anything else of interest in the room, Jack?'

"No. But it's interesting what we didn't find."

"What?"

"Claire Henderson's cell phone. The one she used to call you!"

Chapter 41
Saturday Evening 8:00 p.m.

The Judge and Katy settled in over their steak dinner, mostly prepared by Katy since if truth be known, the Judge had only a rudimentary idea of how to cook. Blackened steaks cooked almost to charcoal and burnt baked potatoes were his standard. The Caesar salad was great, readymade, and the Judge did its tossing, thereby taking full credit for producing the entire meal. After all, everything was in the 'toss'.

Opening the Jadot Pouilly Fuisse was a different matter. The Judge had vast experience in such matters and insisted the first bottle and then the second be opened early. As cooks' wine, he said. By the time the steaks reached the table, set out on the old stone patio overhanging the Lake with lighted candles, it had become necessary to invade the wine cellar for more wine to accompany the steaks. Fortunately, too, as red wine was so much better with steak than white.

The Judge located an old Château Branaire-Ducru, St. Julien, 2010, a ninety-five pointer if ever there were, in the large closet that served as the cabin's wine cellar. It would have been gobbled down years ago, but for getting lost behind newer bottles. The Judge pulled it out with a shout of glee, dancing around and waving the bottle over his head, but always level to the ground. It tasted just as it promised: licorice, oak, truffle, black cherry and plum, soft tannins, round fruit and freshness in the finish. With a hint of dust on the tongue after the taste. Probably the best wine made at Branaire Ducru after Patrick Maroteaux bought the property in 1989.

Katy asked, "What was the ranch like you said you were going to visit, Judge?"

The Judge described how the dogs and pigs were being kept at The Foundation ranch. Katy looked appalled.

"How can they treat animals that way, Judge? And even worse, pretend to be a big non-profit that protects animals' rights. How can they miss the commonality between those animals and us? For Christ sakes, those dogs, those pigs, and us… we're all mammals, Judge, just trying to live and have a reasonable life."

"Perhaps it's part of this 'we' vs 'they' attitude that seems baked into our genes, Katy. Homo Sapiens since the beginning of time have been dividing life into the us and the them. We do it with other races, we do it with other countries. We do it with political parties. Hell, we do it with the soccer team from the neighboring town. Of course, we're going to do it with other species."

"I think you're right, Judge. One million species are threatened right now with extinction on this planet. Yet no one seems to give a damn. We need to frame the discussion not about how different animals are from us, but rather as how similar we are to other animals. Are you going to do something about this... this... this Foundation?"

"I'm going to try, Katy. I'm going to try."

"What about Jerry's murder, Judge? Are you any closer to finding out what happened? Who killed poor Jerry?"

"Perhaps, Katy. I still believe the attack was initiated at the community dock in the Village, not at Jerry's dock, and therefore involved two people, a killer and an accomplice."

"The accomplice drove around the Lake and picked up the killer, right Judge. We talked about it."

"Yes. That's what I've believed from the start. But it's not what the police think. And I may be wrong."

"So how do we analyze it, Judge?"

"The initial question is what's the motive for Jerry's untimely demise? People kill for only a few basic reasons. Out of jealous rage, for financial gain, or to protect themselves from discovery of involvement in another crime. I'm beginning to suspect we have all three motives present here."

Katy looked at him with puzzled eyes.

"Jerry was involved in this big case, Katy. But suddenly he decided to withdraw as its defense counsel. The case was about alleged animal cruelty, the misappropriation of charitable contributions to 'for-profit' activities, and maybe some illicit animal research. The animal research part was initially a little murky."

"That's this Foundation outfit, and David Branden, Judge?"

"Yes. Just before his death Jerry hired a public health expert, a guy trained in disease control and eradication. But human disease control, not animal disease. And also, Jerry calendared to meet an investigative reporter, one Bradford Jones. A gnarly little yellow press reporter, certainly not someone I would have chosen. But independent enough to get a story out without caving in to pressure from big business and well-connected people. I think Jerry was appalled, maybe even a little scared, at what he'd found out about The Foundation. He wanted out of the case, and he wanted to be sure whatever The Foundation was doing got out to the public."

"Tell me about this Foundation, Judge."

"The Foundation has a sister company, Replace/Repair Corp. Between the two companies, there's a lot of money involved, millions and millions. Replace/Repair is a public company with a high-flying stock. Branden of course is the controlling shareholder, but there's also a thirty-percent block of stock held by a mysterious offshore company."

"Do you think this David Branden, or one of his henchmen, attacked Jerry to keep him quiet?"

"It's very possible, Katy. But there's another aspect of the facts we have to consider. Jerry's domestic life was falling apart. He was drinking more and seeking solace outside his marriage. You said that Jerry and Marie had made a pact to have an open marriage. And I'd confirmed that with Marie. As a result, Jerry touched a lot of people, perhaps engendering feelings of hate and jealousy. And consider the initial assault on Jerry with a boat paddle. That sounds more like a spur of the moment act committed in a jealous rage, rather than the beginning of a premeditated murder."

"Who would be the suspects then, Judge?"

"Well, Marie was attending certain neighborhood parties put on by her friend, Sharon Langley. Swingers' parties, Katy, if you can believe it.

Katy suddenly looked guilty, covering it with a quick bluster.

"Marie's my best friend, Judge. That talk about an open marriage I'm sure is mostly talk. Perhaps she's got a small fling going on the side with someone. But she'd never take part in a plot to kill Jerry."

"Do we really know anybody that well, Katy? I mean, I know you well… know you'd never attend a swingers' party. But I'm not so sure about Marie."

Katy went silent, color rising in her face. Electing to focus suddenly over the Judge's shoulder, out to the Lake. Finally, she muttered, "Perhaps you're right, Judge. Perhaps we don't know people as well as we think."

"Well anyway, Marie met a young Spaniard at the sex party, Juan Fernández, and the two have been pursuing an intense love affair. And, Katy, Marie's marriage was falling apart. Jerry was way over stressed at work, drinking too much, working all the time. I think Marie was getting very little attention. The seven-year itch thing was real for them, tangible. I can understand how it happened. We're all human. We all need nurturing, touching, caressing, attention, confirmation that our life partner actually sees us."

Katy's eyes came back to meet the Judge's gaze. There was a sense of pleading somewhere in the far back of them.

"Consider these facts, Katy. Jerry was moving to divorce Marie and they were locked in a battle over the division of community property. Jackson, the maid, heard Marie raging to Juan on her cell about what a bastard Jerry was being. How Jerry was trying to cheat Marie out of what she was entitled to for staying in the marriage as long as she had. Jackson overheard her say, 'It'd be better if the asshole just died.' Marie even fired Jackson after she realized she'd been overheard. Perhaps Marie, and her new friend, Juan, acted together to dispose of Jerry. There was anger there, perhaps even rage.

And there may have been a lot of money at stake. I don't think Jerry had changed his will. He certainly didn't come to me to change it. And I'm the one who drafted his initial will after Jerry and Marie were married. It kept everything as separate property but gave it all to Marie on Jerry's death.

"But Judge. As I understand it, they both have alibis. They were at this social club."

"Oh. You know about that?"

Katy bit her tongue.

The Judge said, "They each claim they left the social club party separately, by themselves. But others say that was not the case. That Marie and Juan left together. At any rate, they either have no alibi, or the only alibi they have is each other. And consider this. The offshore entity that owns thirty percent of Replace/Repair's common stock is organized and headquartered in a small Spanish territory on the coast of Africa where Juan Fernández's uncle lives. Coincidence? Maybe. But it seems unlikely."

"Oh my God. You really think it was Marie? Marie and Juan?"

"I don't know. But there are other people to consider as possible suspects. I found out Jerry had a short, secret affair last summer with Ally Monroe. An affair Ally has tried to keep secret. But her current flame, Pete Campbell, the young sheriff, found out about it. He was very angry. And days before his death, Jerry tried to rekindle his affair with Ally, caging her in the alley behind McDonald's. We can image what Pete thought about that. Campbell had an altercation with Jerry in Jensen's market over it the week before Jerry's death, and threatened Jerry.

"You think Pete Campbell hit Jerry with the paddle, Judge?"

"I don't know, but I think there must have been a lot of emotion involved in the decision to strike Jerry down. Anyway, it seems Sheriff Pete was on solo patrol the night Jerry died on the North Shore, near Shelter Cove. And Ally was on patrol, solo, in her patrol boat, also along the North Shore near Shelter Cove. Personally, I think they were together. The question is, were they merely making whoopee in his car or on her boat on company time, or were they up to something more sinister? It's curious they both claim not to have heard Jerry's boat running across the Lake."

"No alibi except each other, a strong motive, and in the neighborhood, Judge."

"That's the way it lays out."

"You think Pete went into a rage and acted out his feelings at the end of a boat paddle?"

"He might have. That would mean I'm wrong about the location. Jerry may have been struck down at his dock. And perhaps a single person, no accomplice."

"Anyone else, Judge?"

"Yes, but it's a little complicated."

"Tell me, Judge."

"Well, see I ran into this girl at the RB's Steakhouse bar. This Claire Henderson."

"An old lover, Judge?" Katy sat up straighter in her chair, coming out of her cautious state, almost glad to have something to deflect attention.

"For God sakes, Katy. No. Just someone I met in my investigation last year during The Strand case. Anyway, Claire has an interesting philosophy which has led her into a unique lifestyle. She likes to set things up so she sees at least three men as their mistress, typically older men who can afford to donate generously to her lifestyle on a monthly basis. I ran into Claire on Sunday night."

"When you stormed out of here, Judge?"

"I didn't storm, Katy. I just left for some alone time."

"At a bar."

"Well, yes. Anyway, Claire said she had been maintaining affairs with three lovers. Each man thought she was exclusive for him and was donating generously to her support accordingly. That can be a dangerous game if they all happen to be at Lake Arrowhead at the same time."

"And they were?"

"Yes. This last weekend."

"Wow. That's a prescription for disaster."

"It gets even more interesting. Claire said she'd lost one of her lovers, had only two now, and was interviewing for a replacement."

"She was interviewing you, Judge."

"Yes… I mean no. I mean... we were just talking."

"Right. This is that busty broad you were making eyes with when we walked into the Arrowhead Resort Bar the other night?"

It was confirmed, thought the Judge. Katy did have eyes in the back of her head.

"Consider this, Katy," the Judge barreled on. "Jerry was in the Village before he was killed. He was at Papagayos. He had an altercation there, apparently over a woman he was sitting with. A jealous boyfriend came in and threatened Jerry."

"Who was the woman, Judge?"

"I'm not sure, but I think it was Claire."

"Whoa. You think Jerry was Claire's third lover! The one she now needs to replace. The spot she was interviewing you for?"

"I suspect so. Jackson, Jerry's maid, told me Jerry was head over heels in love, or infatuated, or at least in lust, with a girl. Jackson saw this girl when Jerry snuck her into this house for the weekend while Marie was away. A short blond girl with blue eyes and a big chest."

"And that sounds like the description of your Claire?"

"She's not my Claire, Katy. She's just a pretty girl. A 'good' girl we used to say in the old days, as opposed to a 'nice' girl."

"Bull shit, Judge. You mean a cheap tart."

"Well, yes. Anyway, the girl in Papagayos with Jerry fits the description of Claire."

"This Claire really gets around, Judge. I'm liking her less and less by the minute."

"I met one of Claire's lovers Sunday night. A Tony something or other. A ne'er do well son of a Detroit mobster. He appeared a jealous sort with a quick temper. And he fits Martha's description of the guy who threatened Jerry in Papagayos when Jerry was meeting with a short blonde. With Claire, I think."

"Oh my God, Judge. That must be it. It's this Tony guy. Of course it is. It's all clear now. Jerry's one of Claire's shared lovers. She's trying to keep all her balls in the air." Katy giggled. "So, Tony walks in and catches Claire with Jerry, Judge. Realizes what's going on, has an altercation with Jerry. Then Tony leaves. But Tony waits outside. He follows Jerry when Jerry leaves the bar to go down to the community dock to go home. Jerry's smashed of course, an easy target. Tony extracts his revenge by clobbering Jerry over the head with a boat paddle. Then this Claire helps Tony load poor Jerry in his boat. Tony drives off in the boat to set up the boating accident from Jerry's dock. And Claire picks Tony up in Shelter Cove afterwards. It all fits."

"You could be right, Katy. According to Jack Prentis, Tony says he was in his room alone at the Arrowhead Resort when this all went down. But there was no one there to give him an alibi."

"Damn, Judge. That's so suspicious. Tony wasn't with the love of this life in the middle of the night. He was just by himself in lonely hotel room. Hah."

"It does sound off. But it also highlights something else. We have the mob son, Tony, and we have Jerry Stone, now deceased, as two of Claire's lovers. But she told me she had three lovers."

"Who's the third lover?"

"I don't know, Katy."

"Well, that's easy. Let's ask her."

"That's another problem, Katy."

"What?"

"Claire is dead."

"Dead! Jesus, Judge."

"It was made to looked like suicide, but it was murder."

"And Claire didn't tell you who the third man was?"

"No. Only that he was very powerful and coming into a lot of money. He wanted to retire her number, marry her and whisk her away to a new life, or so she said. Let's call him Mr. X for now, Katy."

"So, Judge, you've got as suspects David Branden and his Foundation people; Marie, and Juan Fernández; Pete Campbell and Ally Monroe; Tony, the mob kid, and this Mr. X, Claire's third lover. And Claire, who might have been involved in Jerry's murder, has also been murdered."

"You've got it, Katy. There is one more person whose name comes up."

"Who?"

"There was a guy who was a member of Sharon Langley's social club who had a thing for Marie. Followed her around at their sexual gatherings, always trying to cut in and have sex."

"She's a beautiful woman."

"Yes. But this guy is really rough in the bed, almost a predator. Anyway, the guy's still around. Has a cabin up here. I spoke to the guy. He's glad Jerry's dead. Believes in some deluded way the road's now open for him to romance Marie. I saw the guy at the Arrowhead Resort Bar the other night, staring at Marie."

"You think he might have killed Jerry?"

"It's possible. In a misguided effort to get to Marie. And he seems to have ties to this case everywhere."

"How so?"

"He sold a dog colony business to Replace/Repair Corp for a bundle. The dog colony I saw at The Foundation's ranch."

"Replace/Repair, the public sister company to Branden's Foundation?"

"Yes. And his telephone number had been written on a pad in Claire's room the night she died. I could tell by the impression left on the under sheet. His name is Larry Shankman. And he brought a short blond girl with a big chest, who sounds a lot like Claire, to Langley's social club party a couple of times late last year."

"By God, Judge, I think it was him now, this Larry Shankman guy. Who is he? What's he do?"

"Lives in South Pasadena. Weekends up here in his cabin. Seems like a smart guy, although a little hostile. Short guy, sandy haired. He's an aeronautical engineer."

Katy, in mid-swallow of her wine, suddenly started choking, coughing sputtering. The Judge grabbed her glass and pounded her on the back.

"I'm okay, Judge," she finally gasped. "Just swallowed the wrong way."

Chapter 42
Sunday Morning 8:00 a.m.

The Judge was just finishing his omelet at the Saddleback Grill when his cell phone went off, pealing a deafening wolf-whistle, causing every eye in the restaurant to turn in his direction. He muttered under his breath about new technology and hit the accept button quickly before it could peal off a second whistle. "This is the Judge."

"This is your favorite reporter, Bradford Jones, Judge."

The Judge sighed. "I thought we'd already had our conversation, Jones."

"Yes, but I've run across some new information about The Foundation that will blow you out of the water. It's unbelievable." There was a strain in Jones's voice now.

"If it's from another of your self-designated 'credible sources', I'm sure it's both unbelievable and untrue."

"Judge, this is real information from an inside source. It's so hot I'm a little scared of handling it."

"Okay, so tell me."

"No, Judge, it doesn't work like that. We must meet. I'll trade you the facts I've uncovered about The Foundation, for the facts you've uncovered about

Stone's death. We'll collaborate. Decide what we should do next. When I should release my story."

"You've got to give me a better idea of what you've got, Jones. I'm not going to waste my time."

"Okay, get this. I told you Jerry Stone called me that night before he died. He was anxious to meet the next morning and talk about The Foundation and what it was doing."

"Yes."

"Well I now understand why Jerry Stone was so anxious to meet me and pretty much what he was going to tell me."

"Which was?"

"Oh, no, Judge. On, no. Like I said, face to face. Somewhere private and safe. I want to know what you've found out about Stone's death. I'm pretty sure David Branden had Stone killed to shut him up. In fact, I'm certain of it. I just need more of the facts on the murder for my story. I know you have them."

"How do you know…"

"No, Judge, no," Jones interrupted. "I'm not saying anything else over the phone. If David Branden gets wind of what I know I'll be another Jerry Stone…. Dead!"

"You have real, independently verifiable information, Jones? Not like last time in The Strand case, where everything you wrote was bullshit."

"Oh yes. I do, Judge. The entire Lake Arrowhead Community is at risk. You, me, your pretty wife, everyone. Even San Bernardino, perhaps all of Southern California or the entire West Coast. I don't know where it will stop. Maybe even the world. I'm going to get the Pulitzer Prize for this story." Jones was chortling with excitement now.

"Okay, Jones. Where are you now? Where and when do you want to meet?"

"I'm hiding out at a bed and breakfast in Rim Forest. Let's meet at Billy's in two hours. I'll be there on time, Judge. I'm counting on you to come and be timely too. This is a very dangerous situation for me. You and I, we need to pull this all together and get my story out. It's the only way I'm going to be safe."

"Okay, Jones. I'll be there. But this better be good."

There was a click at the other end. Then a hurried 'bye', and Jones hung up.

Two hours later the Judge sat next to the window in Billy's, the breakfast shop in Blue Jay, nursing his third cup of coffee of the day, watching out into the highway for Jones. At 8:05, a candy-red Mini Cooper whipped off the highway and pulled into a parking spot across the street. Thirty seconds later a now very timid looking Bradford Jones squirmed himself out of the car. He looked nothing like the cocky bullshit reporter the Judge has run into the day before, coming out of Jensen's Mini-Market. This Bradford Jones looked tired, cautious, fearful even. He scanned the street in both directions, then started nervously across.

He crossed the first lane and was barely into the second lane of traffic as a lumbering dusty green SUV pulled out of the adjacent parking lot into the first lane. Suddenly the SUV cranked up speed, barreling down its lane and quickly swerving into Jones' lane, crashing into him head on, mowing him down like a scythe through dry wheat.

The Judge jumped from his table, spilling his coffee, rushing out to the street in time to glimpse paper plates pasted over the SUV's license plate, its windows heavily tinted. Just before the SUV disappeared around the corner, the driver's side window came down and an empty Jack Daniel's bottle was tossed out, smashing on the road into a million shards.

Jones wasn't moving. He wasn't ever going to move again. His head was like some large melon, split open, squashed, gushing red and grey cells into a growing pool.

The Judge put two fingers to Jones's neck. Of course. There was no pulse. *Damn… Damn… Damn!*

Chapter 43
Sunday Morning 11:00 a.m.

The Judge walked back into his cabin with a heavy step and collapsed into one of the overstuffed leather chairs in the great room facing the Lake. He watched out the tall open window as the light played through the trees and dotted the blue Lake with sparkle. But it gave him no joy this morning. He couldn't get the image of the flattened Jones out of his mind. It mingled with images of Claire, the rear part of her skill missing, and the wet and burnt face of Jerry as he lifted up with his dying effort to warn the Judge about Cindy… the pig.

Sheriff Pete Campbell had been even more sarcastic than before, suggesting the Judge take his investigations back down the hill to the flats, before the entire Arrowhead Valley was filled with bodies. Jack Prentis was more philosophic, his face long, his eyes sad, as he slowly moved through the required paperwork, taking down the Judge's statements, having him repeat his story so all facts got recorded.

"So, you think it was a drunk driver, Judge?" Jack had asked. "Pitching his whisky bottle out the window as he tore away down the road? Afraid to stop and accept the consequences of actions?"

"I don't," the Judge had replied evenly. "The driver waited in the SUV in the parking lot over there, pulled out only as Jones started across the road. Immediately accelerated to a killing speed. Swerved to hit Jones. It was premeditated. A cold-blooded killing."

The Judge stared out at the Lake now. Not seeing it. Depressed, tired, frustrated. Homo sapiens, he mused. The deadliest, ugliest creatures on the planet, willing to kill their own in a heartbeat. And for what? For stuff? For prestige? For a handful of paper money representing some mercurial store of value rapidly depreciating even as one held it in his hands?

Willing to ensconce their fellow mammals in cages of hell, cramped and tortured, without a thought to the commonalities that made them brother animals in so many ways. Self-centered, egotistical, selfish, self-destructive, and menacing to themselves and to all life around them. Creatures God gave opposable thumbs and quick minds, but so often without the gift of understanding, of compassion, of respect and empathy for the teeming life and environment of the planet, or for their fellow man.

Soft hands quietly leaned over and down each shoulder from behind and wrapped him in a clumsy embrace. Katy. She was trying to cheer him up. Thank God for Katy, and for people like her. But it reminded the Judge it was time to clear the air between them.

"They killed Bradford Jones today, Katy. Ran him down like a stray dog in the street."

"Oh, Judge. No. Are you in danger? Are they coming after you next?"

"They've already tried, Katy. With my brakes. I have no idea what's going to happen now."

Katy pressed against him, fearful. "Was this Jones a friend?"

"No, Katy. He was an arrogant little prick. A miserable newspaper reporter who was a disgrace to his profession. But he didn't deserve to die."

"Oh."

"Jones is the one who told me my wife was the hit of the sex party across the lake Thursday night!"

Katy's arm's yanked upward and away, as though scalded. There was a silence then so thick it felt like the Berlin Wall, amplifying the pink color spreading from Katy's lost smile up to her aqua eyes, now focused on the Judge… with what? Shock? Guilt? Horror? Mostly 'sick', appraised the Judge.

"Oh, Judge. I was going to tell you about that. I truly was. I just didn't have a chance." Katy's voice went up several octaves, betraying her stress.

"Well I'm here," said the Judge with a sigh, automatically folding his arms across his chest. "Perhaps you can tell me it now."

"Well, see, it was like this. Marie belongs to this social club that's a friendly group. And after our dinner, well, she knew I'd like to meet some new people. So, she invited me to their late night social. I had no idea they were doing a little swing-sex and stuff. She honest to God didn't tell me until we walked in."

"By 'swing-sex', you mean people sleeping with each other's mates."

"Errr, yes. Or friends, or dates or whoever. Not everybody. Some people just come for the social interaction."

"You mean to watch."

"Well, I guess there's that too."

"And Marie invited you?"

"Yes. Just to come and meet some new people."

"And to watch."

"Well… well… turns out it's all over the house, so it's pretty hard not to see what's going on."

"So, you watched?"

"Well, yes. A little."

"Did you participate, Katy?"

"Oh, no, Judge. I could never do that. I belong to you."

"So why did you go?"

Katy broke down then. She started to softly cry, her voice keening up to even higher octaves through tears. "I truly didn't know, Judge. I'd have never gone if I'd known it was that sort of group. So, of course Marie didn't tell me. We went, and suddenly I was just there.

When we got there, over at the Langdon Estate, I didn't really want to go in. But Marie was so insistent. Said it'd cheer me up just to meet some nice people. Nothing would happen the first half of the party, and then I could leave. She wanted to introduce me to her Juan. And I guess I was a little curious."

This all came out in a rush, leaving Katy almost hyperventilating as she gasped for breath.

"I'm so sorry, Judge. I didn't do anything, honey, honest. Some guy followed me around and tried to make out and I just pushed him away and got out of there. No one else touched me. I could never cheat on you. It was a miserable party, a miserable experience. I had to fight this stupid lug off and then I just left by myself. It was awful."

"I'm relieved you didn't have a good time. I suppose that's small of me, Katy."

"Oh, no, no, Judge. And I should have told you. I'm just so embarrassed about it. Cause I went. Cause I didn't tell you about it right away. Cause, I don't know. Just because. I'm so sorry, so ashamed, so… Oh, shit, Judge, come here and hold me."

The Judge stood up and Katy collapsed into his arms, sniffling into his shoulder, leaving a wet patch on his shirt. He didn't mind. He could feel them coming closer again, reviving the mutual chemistry that had attracted them together in the first place. It would always keep them together, so long as they could nurture that attraction. He loved her so dearly. And she loved him. He wasn't afraid of losing her anymore. They would always be together. Of that he was certain.

Chapter 44
Monday Noon

The Judge pulled into the Antler's Inn parking lot in Twin Peaks and walked over into its restaurant, The Grill. It was an ancient room, built in the log cabin style of old, the walls covered with historic pictures and memorabilia from the days when it was a small logging village one hundred years before. Henry Banner was steps ahead of him, heading for a quiet table in a corner. The Judge followed. They shook hands formally, the smaller man's slightly oriental eyes, dark and liquid, examining the Judge with interest.

"You're part Asian?" asked the Judge, preferring bluntness to diplomacy.

"Yes. Dad was English; my mother was Pilipino," said Banner. "I'm a hapa, and proud of it."

The Judge said, "And one smart guy I'd guess, given all these degrees after your name. I saw your bio in Jerry Stone's file."

"I do enjoy school, learning disciplines, exploring the frontiers of our knowledge, conducting research, collaborating with other scientists." Banner gave his soft smile to the Judge.

They ordered food, the Judge ordered a breakfast waffle, Henry a burger. Then huddled over their initial cups of coffee.

"So, Henry, what can you tell me about The Foundation, and the defense Jerry Stone was mounting in the lawsuit against it?"

"I'd just started my research, Judge. We were supposed to meet later on that Saturday morning, the morning of his death. He'd asked me to review some preliminary stuff. But I don't know what was going on with his Foundation."

"I visited the Foundation's ranch on Saturday, Henry. Most of the staff was off for the weekend, but I got a good look around."

"You did, Judge? Gosh, you got closer than I was allowed to."

"My guide pointed to a glassed-in office inside their barn, Henry. He said the people in this little glass office produced more income for their operation than anything else."

"What did they do in their glass office, Judge?"

"My guide said Replace/Repair Corp acted as a broker for the sourcing and sale of replacement organs; human kidneys, livers, skin, other human parts, from all over the world."

Banner whistled.

"Tell me about it, Henry. Is there widespread demand?"

"Oh yes, Judge. As of March of this year there were more than 113,000 candidates waiting for an organ transplant in the U.S. alone. The median wait time for heart and liver transplant is 148 days. Patients listed as Heart Status A1 wait an average of 73 days. There is a desperate worldwide shortage of organs available for these people. Demand for kidneys for example, far outstrips the supply."

"And I suppose the desperate will pay what they have to, if they have the funds. And go outside the system if necessary for that kidney or other part they need to replace?"

"You're right, Judge. There is a thriving black market for kidneys around the world. Even though commercial trade in human organs is illegal in all countries, except Iran. Despite the prohibitions, organ trafficking and so-called transplant tourism remain widespread. The question of whether to legalize and regulate the organ trade to combat illegal trafficking and organ shortage is a hot topic of debate right now."

"Why is it illegal, Henry?"

"Transplant tourism raises concerns because it involves the transfer of healthy organs in one direction, depleting the regions where organs are bought. This transfer typically occurs in trends: from South to North, from developing to developed nations, from females to males, and from people of color to whites."

"What sorts of organs get sold?"

"The kidney is the most common, Judge. It's estimated that three-quarters of the illegal organ trade involves kidneys. The liver trade is also prominent. Though livers are regenerative, there is an excruciating postoperative recovery period, making it difficult to find willing donors. Kidneys and livers can fetch from a few thousand dollars to one-hundred-and-fifty grand.

Other high-priced body parts include corneas at around twenty-four thousand each, and unfertilized human eggs at around twelve thousand. Lower-priced bodily commodities include blood, skin, sold by the square inch, and bones and ligaments."

"What about hearts?"

"While there is a high demand and hearts and lungs command a very high price, transplant tourism and organ trafficking of these parts is rarer due to the sophisticated nature of the implant procedures. They require specialized doctors and facilities."

"Is it mostly one-off transactions between individuals selling and buying, or is organized crime involved?"

"Clearly organized crime is involved, not only in the brokering of willing donors, but also in the expansion of organ supply by the coercion of people to donate, the theft of their organs, and even the out and out murder of individuals for their body parts. Non-fatal organ theft and removal is more widely reported than murder-for-organs on a worldwide basis. But criminal networks increasingly engage in kidnappings, especially of children and teenagers. Young people are taken to locations with medical equipment, murdered, and their organs harvested for the illegal organ trade."

"What countries supply the most organs to the black market, Henry?"

"It's a tossup between China and India. China is rumored to be executing Falun Gong political prisoners solely in order to sell their body parts on the black market. Reports and testimony suggest prisoners are routinely assessed for transplants and tissue typing, procedures unrelated to general patient care. Organ availability and speed of delivery of transplants within China is under two to three weeks sometimes, compared to years of waiting elsewhere.

This has led several renowned doctors in our field to speak out. Suggesting historic statistics and transplant rates would be impossible to achieve without access to a very large pool of live pre-existing donors. Donors available on short notice for on-demand organ harvesting. The Chinese government of course denies such activity."

"Jesus, Henry. That sounds like 1984 all over again."

"Doesn't it, Judge? And the organs are not distributed based on need, but rather simply sold to wealthy Chinese and foreign individuals. Knowledgeable people estimate China executed at least four thousand prisoners last year in order to supply organs to foreign buyers. China adopted new laws in response to criticism, but many non-profit organizations and international jurists are skeptical that the country has truly reformed its organ transplant industry. There's too much big money in it for everyone involved."

"And India?"

"India is also a big organ-exporting country. Organs from local donors are regularly transplanted to foreigners in illegal brokered transactions. Although the number of foreign recipients decreased after the enactment of a law banning the organ trade, the drop in foreign recipients in India was accompanied by an increase in foreign recipients in Pakistan and the Philippines. And now the India market has come roaring back."

"And there are other countries too, Henry?"

"Oh yes. In Pakistan, according to the Sindhi Institute of Urology, approximately two-thirds of transplants are performed on foreigners. In the Philippines, data obtained from the Renal Disease Control Program of the Department of Health, show that approximately a third of all kidney transplants are for patients from abroad. There is no comparable data for Egypt, but a considerable number of patients from neighboring countries are believed to undergo organ transplantation there. Bolivia, Brazil, Iraq, Israel, the Republic of Moldova, Peru, Turkey, and of course Mexico, all provide organs to the illegal trade. Recently a nephew of the head of the Knights Templar Cartel in Michoacán State, Mexico, was arrested and charged with kidnapping children, taking them to homes fitted out with specialized medical equipment, killing each child, and harvesting the child's organs for resale."

"But not here, Henry. This organ trade doesn't go on in the U.S., does it?"

Henry produced his soft smile. "A guy was arrested in New Jersey last year for buying organs from vulnerable people in Israel for ten grand a pop and selling them to desperate patients in the United States for up to a hundred-and-sixty thousand per organ. It was alleged that some of the implant operations with illegal organs were performed at one of New York's premier hospitals."

"Who are the people whose organs get sold?"

"Donors in the illegal organ trade are predominantly impoverished people in developing nations. In India, one study suggested that seventy percent of all donors fell below the poverty line. One of the primary reasons voluntary donors say they have sold an organ is to pay off debt. While some supporters of the organ trade argue that it helps lift some people out of poverty by providing compensation to donors, evidence of this claim is hotly debated. In many cases, people who sell their organs in order to pay off debt do not manage to escape this debt and remain trapped in debt cycles. And of course, donors often report weakness after surgery that leads to decreased employment opportunities, especially for those who make a living through physical labor."

"And as to outright theft of organs?"

"Poor people are more likely to fall victim of organ theft. Accounts characterize the victims as unemployed individuals, often but not always men, between the ages of twenty and forty, who are seeking work. Kidnapped and taken out of their country to an implant center, they are subjected to operations to remove their organs against their will."

"So, if Replace/Repair is brokering such parts on a world-wide basis, it could be pulling in considerable cash, Henry?"

"Oh, I'd say so. Perhaps many millions annually," said Henry. "There's lots of demand."

"Jerry Stone would never be a part of something like that, Henry."

"Well, there's your answer, Judge. That's why Mr. Stone resigned."

"I don't think so, Henry. Jerry died in my arms. His last words were about stopping 'Cindy' and... 'Thousands will be killed'. It was something even worse than brokering body parts."

Banner spread his hands out and smiled. "I don't know Judge. Don't know what that was about."

"I met Cindy, Saturday, at The Foundation ranch."

"Who is Cindy, Judge? What's she like? Is she some kind of terrorist?"

The Judge shook his head. "Cindy's a pig."

Henry's mouth dropped open, but no words came. He spread his hands, shaking his head in disbelief.

"Would you be willing to come out with me to The Foundation's ranch right now? See if we can get in? Have a look?"

"If you think you can get us in, and it's safe, let's go. I'm not liking the undertones of what I'm hearing."

"Safety is a concern, Henry. You're right. Perhaps we can line up some company." The Judge took out his cell phone and dialed Sheriff Jack Prentis. He explained the situation, what he knew, what he didn't know, and what he suspected. He explained his desire to take Henry out for a look see, and his concern that something might be terrible wrong with the things being done at the ranch.

"Doesn't sound like enough for a warrant, Judge. And our District Attorney is a namby pamby, very cautious. He won't be anxious to take on the Foundation Director. Why don't I take a ride out there with you, tag along behind in my cruiser. I'll linger in the parking lot while you ask the Director, or your foreman, or whoever is there, for another look at their lab with Henry. Maybe the color of authority will encourage them to allow a second tour."

"It's worth a shot, Jack. Can we do it now?"

"Sure. I'll meet you at the turnoff to their private road in say, twenty minutes."

Chapter 45
Monday Afternoon 1:30 p.m.

The Judge and Henry Banner rumbled over the rutted dirt road leaving a mandatory dirt storm behind them, partially obscured Jack Prentis' squad car which followed. As they approached the fenced entrance to The Foundation's ranch, they could see the gate was partially ajar. No explaining to the intercom would be required. Henry got out of the car, turned a little timidly to look for confirmation from the Judge, then swung the gate wide. They rounded through the sycamores and came up on the roundabout. There were perhaps twenty cars in a parking area off to the right. The lot had been practically empty on Saturday.

They got out of the Judge's rental car and walked up onto the porch. Jack Prentis pulled his cruiser up beside them, got a hunting magazine out of his glove compartment, got out of his cruiser, and leaned against as he flipped pages in the afternoon sun. But the Judge could feel his eyes on them, over the top of the magazine.

The Judge again rang the bell. It reverberated throughout the house. They waited. Nothing happened. They waited some more. Nothing. Anyone in the place couldn't have missed the bells. The Judge rang again, resisting an urge to put his fingers in his ears at the racket. Nothing.

Curious now, the Judge reached over and tried one of the double doors. The door was unlocked . The Judge looked at Henry, shrugged, swung the door open, and stepped in.

There was a long hall, covered with expensive oriental carpets, one a hand-knotted wool Agra in muted reds and creams, another a Herike TU from Turkey in beige and blues. Someone had a good eye for antiques.

Down the hall were stairs to the upper floor, and off to the left was an expansive front sitting room that looked like a men's club. Rich overstuffed leather sofas and chairs in browns and tans, competed with more oriental carpets, antique oils of English hunting scenes, and heavy green brocade curtains across the sweep of windows in the front and on the side facing the barn.

To the right off the hall were double doors marked *Board Room*, one of which was slightly ajar. And there was an odor in the air. A very bad odor, faintly familiar, but somehow different. What was it? Blood? Puke? Shit? Perhaps all the above.

The Judge stepped over and knocked respectfully on the Board Room door. It swung open of its own accord, revealing a Board of Directors meeting in progress. Or which had been in progress. The Judge expected to meet startled, even angry faces as he stepped into the room, interrupting their meeting uninvited.

The last thing he expected was the scene before him. The board members were slumped in their seats or lying on the table. One member, a woman, was sprawled on her face on the floor, stretched in a last desperate lunge for the doors where the Judge stood. Henry looked over the Judge's shoulder, gasped, and stumbled back out toward the front porch. The Judge heard him losing his breakfast over the porch rail.

The Judge turned back to the Board, four men and one woman. Their clothes were thick with vomit. Their chairs were stained where they'd bled out at the other end. Soft pools of red and brown were drying under their chairs. The stench was overpowering.

Their faces looked like they'd been hit by some cosmic death ray. The veins on their faces were raised out of their flesh like the straining veins of a muscle beach trainer trying to lift over his weight. But the protruding veins weren't red. They were black. Similar black veins showed on their hands, and the backs of the legs of the woman lying on the floor, as though some giant spider had covered her legs and face in black mesh.

But it was their eyes. Or lack of them. The three men whose eyes he could see had merely blank spaces in their sockets, as if the gelatin material of their eyeballs had dissolved in place. The Judge wondered if he would have to join Henry on the porch. His morning waffle was feeling very iffy.

At the head of the table sat David, straight back in his chair, head thrown up in the agony of death. The protruding veins were concentrated around his eye sockets, lending an almost macabre smile to his death mask. What had the bastard done here that had gotten so out of hand? Something had happened. Something had killed David and his entire board.

The Judge squatted down to get a look at the face of the woman lying on her stomach on the floor. It was Sharon Langley.

The Judge stood up, giving the carnage one final look. There was no need to get closer. And he didn't want to. He suspected a rogue virus that could easily clamp onto him. He backed out of the room and closed the doors tightly, pulling his cell out and calling 9-1-1. He urged them to send a HAZMAT unit.

Henry was still on the porch, wiping his mouth with his hanky, looking dazed. Jack Prentis had dropped his magazine on his hood and moved forward, sensing Henry's distress, his hand resting on his gun.

"Come on, Henry," the Judge said. "There's a lot more cars in the parking lot than there are people in there. Let's have a look in the barn."

Henry looked doubtful, but reluctantly stepped off the porch after the Judge, following him around the side of the house to the barn. Prentis brought up the rear, still uncertain what was happening. A green SUV was sitting next to the barn, dusty, dark-tinted windows, temporary plates taped over real plates. The SUV's front grill was broken, and the bumper dented, both splashed brown. Blood!

The driver's side door was open, and a man had fallen half out the door, hanging there, his head just touching the ground, his legs caught under the steering wheel. Suspended in eternity. He was covered in blood, and puke and diarrhea. His eyes were black sockets, like the others. But the Judge still recognized the features. It was Sam, the ranch foreman. "Jesus Christ", muttered Prentis.

They made a wide detour around the SUV and back to the barn doors. Both doors were unlocked. The Judge opened them wide to bring air and light into the front segment of the barn. He stood for a while, peering into the gloom.

All seemed in order. The dogs were still in their cages, looking despondent and underfed as ever. All alive. Both corridors down either side were vacant of people, as before.

The Judge plunged ahead into the barn, and back to the second door. Henry followed, slowly, cautiously, falling behind, producing his handkerchief again, this time to cover his nose and mouth despite its less than minty condition. He waived Prentis back, suggesting he call for more help.

The Judge pushed through the set of doors for the airlock and stepped into the section of the barn where the pig valve operation was housed. The pigs all came to the front of their cages and began to angrily bark. The Judge suspected they'd missed a meal, or perhaps two. They pleaded and whined at the Judge and Henry as they walked by. The pigs all looked ill, runny noses, pink around their eyes, crap-filled stalls, but they still seemed anxious to eat.

With even more trepidation the Judge approached the second set of airlock doors and eased open the first door. Henry huddled up close to the Judge now, perhaps for warmth. The plastic sheeting dividing the chambers was airtight, and opaque. The Judge could not see through. He eased the door into the last chamber open about six inches and peaked around. He gasped.

Perhaps fifteen bodies littered the hall, some slumped over desks, some sprawled back in their chairs, some on the floor. All white coated, all dead. The death agony on their faces was etched in protruding veins across their foreheads. The black veins ran down their faces to their jaws, then extended down into their necks. They'd all lost their eyes. Black holes of eternity where once there had been light and color.

Whatever had got them must have immobilized them immediately given their positions. But judging by their faces, consciousness had lingered as they'd died. Death had not come easy… or fast.

"Oh my God," muttered Henry pressing his hanky tighter against his face. "We can't go in there! It's… it's… Christ, Judge. It's like Jamestown."

"Not quite," whispered the Judge. "The Jamestown people chose to commit suicide. This is more like Goethe and his Sorcerer's Apprentice. These people tried to play God, pushing their science beyond their knowledge of safe practices."

The Judge took one last look at the lab, and then at the cages. Cindy was still there, but on her side, black veins showing through her bristly hair, not moving. She had black craters for eyes. "That's the pig I was telling you about, Henry, manufactured with human DNA."

"That's where your virus came from, Judge," said Henry. "A porcine virus. Immunities were bred into pigs by natural selection for a hundred-thousand generations against this virus. That's why the pigs in the second segment of the lab aren't dead.

But they cross-bred Cindy with human DNA, Judge. That destroyed Cindy's immunity. So, Cindy died of the virus, along with the rest of the genetically modified pigs in this section. And crossing human DNA with Cindy's created a pathway for the virus to modify itself, and to jump species. The virus has become lethal to humanity, destroying all humans within reach. This could become a worldwide pandemic. We've got to get out here, Judge. Now!"

Chapter 46
Monday 3:00 pm

The Judge bumped along the dusty road back to the highway in a metal truck, like a milk carton on its side, but bigger, no windows, one door, two long benches down the side with seat belts attached, and heavy duty air filtration routed through large scrubbers mounted on the roof, purifying the air before it was released from the carton back into the environment. He felt like he was in a cattle car.

Henry Banner and Jack Prentis sat across from the Judge on the opposite bench, looking equally uncomfortable. There hadn't been much time to talk. The HAZMAT people had suddenly appeared in their space walker suits, barely intelligible behind their glass faceplates, and bundled them into the truck almost immediately. They'd been sealed in and trundled off for some HAZMAT site where they'd be poked, prodded, needled and examined. Under quarantine. What a lousy way to spend a vacation Monday in the mountains.

"We are very lucky to be alive, Judge," said Henry Banner.

"Do you think we have it?" Asked Jack. "Are we going to die, Henry?"

"I'm hoping not. It looked from what I saw at the ranch that it comes on very suddenly, so it's hard to know. We'll have to wait and see."

An hour later the Judge sat on the edge of his hospital bed, his paunch swaddled in his hospital gown, while the nurse checked his vital signs, talking at him all the while through her N95 respirator mask. The doctor had just left after listening to the Judge's lungs, safe behind a hood that contained its own air supply.

The nurse was explaining to the Judge he was in isolation, he could not leave, and he'd be here several days. She moved on to discuss the negative pressure in the room. The pressure was lower than the pressure in adjacent areas, keeping air from flowing out of the room and into adjacent rooms and areas, preventing airborne transmissions. She explained he was under Contact Precautions, no touching the patient or items in the room. Droplet Precautions to prevent spread of tiny droplets caused by coughing and sneezing. And Airborne Precautions, hence the negative pressure maintained in the room.

"Swell," said the Judge, leaning forward so he could see his toes over his paunch, a 'lean' that seemed to get farther over every year. He wiggled his toes. At least they seemed to work.

The nurse had stuck him repeatedly in both arms, drawing blood with a vengeance, giving him a malevolent smile all the while, enjoying her work. He felt like a damn pin cushion. He hated being stuck and he hated nurses, and he hated hospitals and he hated doctors, and he hated the government most of all, with all of their regulations, and the ease with which they could eliminate your freedom and leave you locked up, trapped and helpless, without rights, in a HAZMAT facility.

Finally, the nurse was done. After she washed her hands she left, opening and closing the door with a whoosh, sagging a bit physically under the weight of the load of tubes of blood she'd extracted from her unwilling victim. It made him feel faint just to watch her depart under the weight of her load.

The Judge got up and wandered around the room, stopping to look at one wall covered in a floor-to-ceiling plastic curtain. He reached up and tugged the curtain aside, opening up a large square of glass built into the wall, exposing the adjacent hospital room. A small speaker was set in its center.

Henry Banner looked up from a book he was reading in the adjacent room, sitting up in an identical bed. He waved. The Judge waved back. Henry got out of his bed and marched over to his side of the wall, tapping his finger on the built-in speaker. It crackled on the Judge's side.

"How you doing, Judge?"

"Okay. Lonely. How about you?"

"About the same I'm afraid, Judge. I've been talking to the scientists here. Getting the full picture. They've concluded this was an attack of a new form of the African Swine Flu."

"What the hell is the African Swine Flu, Henry?"

"Oh, it's mean stuff, Judge, mean stuff. It started simply enough. A pig in Africa came down with a high fever and a loss of appetite. Its skin went flush, then purplish. There was discharge from its eyes and nose, vomiting, coughing, breathing difficulties. Then came the hemorrhages in the skin and internal organs, bloody diarrhea and quickly death.

African Swine Fever quickly became endemic in the sub-Saharan areas. But in January of last year this disease, or plague really, leaped across continents to appear in the northeastern province of Liaoning, China. And it showed up with a vengeance. Within weeks, cases were being declared in provinces hundreds of miles south. It's a highly contagious virus which can be one hundred percent lethal to domestic pigs and wild boars. No treatment or vaccine exists.

The disease has now spread to every Chinese province and region, and has also jumped the border into Cambodia, Mongolia and Vietnam. China alone has lost over two hundred million pigs in the last twelve months. Piles of pig bodies rot near villages across the Far East. It appears farmers and pork producers have been unknowingly, or knowingly, butchering and selling infected animals.

The virus lingers in all body fluids and tissues of infected domestic pigs and spreads via direct contact with infected animals or ingestion of garbage containing infected pig meat or pig meat products. It can survive in feces for several days and possibly longer in urine. The few animals that recover from the disease can carry the virus for several months. African Swine Fever can linger for weeks or months in uncooked and frozen pork.

Blood-sucking flies, ticks and other insects can spread the virus between pigs, as can contaminated premises, vehicles, equipment and clothing. The virus was detected in several Chinese processed pork products intercepted at airports from Japan to Australia. Outbreaks have spread across the EU, causing billions of Euros in losses. Outbreaks have been reported in Bulgaria, Hungary, Latvia, Poland, Romania, Russia and the Ukraine.

The plague's victims die gruesomely, but the disease attacks pigs, not humans. Or so we thought."

"And now?" asked the Judge, his voice hoarse.

"The Foundation modified pigs with human DNA to grow their spare human body parts into the animal. They didn't give a damn about the ethical considerations, nor about the scientific protocols and procedures to ensure the safety of their experiments and protection for our human community.

The African Swine Virus jumped across the DNA corridors and became a virulent human plague. It infected everybody at the ranch, immediately incapacitating them, then disposing of them in a spasm of vomiting, diarrhea, and hemorrhages of their skin and internal organs. It must have been agony and hell."

The Judge swallowed, shaken. "And do we now have this virus, Henry, you, Jack, me?"

"So far… no, Judge. They're hoping the virus has been isolated at The Foundation ranch, which they're going to raze to the ground."

"And if they're wrong?"

"Then we potentially have a pandemic so big, so deadly, it could change the course of our history, the history of the whole damn human race."

"It's that virulent, Henry?"

"Yes."

"Outbreaks like that have happened before though, right Henry? I mean we're still here. Humanity always survives."

"Consider the Black Death, Judge."

"The Plague?"

"Yes. The plague's nickname comes from the black skin spots on the sailors who travelled the Silk Road and docked in a Sicilian port, bringing with them from their Asian voyage a devastating disease, the Bubonic Plague. In the middle of the fourteenth century, from 1347 to 1351, the Black Death remade the landscape of Europe. In a time when the global population was an estimated 450 million, at least seventy-five million are believed to have perished throughout the pandemic, with some estimates as high as 200 million. As much as half of Europe may have died in a span of only four years."

"This could be that bad? This thing they created out there?"

"Yes, maybe even worse. The scientists here think what evolved at The Foundation's ranch is in many ways similar to the Spanish Flu of 1918. At the beginning of 1918, reports of an especially dangerous form of influenza began to appear around the globe. Kansas was the site of the first U.S. case in March 1918. Appearing in multiple countries around the world, the disease spread quickly, ushered along even faster due to the close living quarters of troops fighting in World War I. This first instance of an H1N1 pandemic would be dubbed The Spanish Flu, although it didn't come from Spain. It burned out suddenly in 1919. We still don't know why. But Judge, it left the global population decimated—with a mortality rate as high as one in five and an estimated one-third of the world population afflicted. As many as fifty million people are believed to have died. Approximately twenty-five million of those deaths came in the first twenty-five weeks of the outbreak."

"My God," the Judge muttered.

"Before that, in 541, there was the Plague of Justinian. Rats on Egyptian grain boats brought a pestilence to the Eastern Roman Empire that left approximately twenty-five million people dead. Modern scholars estimate at one point as many as five thousand people died each day in Constantinople. By its end, about forty percent of the city's population was dead, so many and so quickly that bodies were left in piles. It spread and killed almost a quarter of the eastern Mediterranean populace.

And the Antonine Plague began in 165 and ran through 180. About five million people died. It began in the Mesopotamian city of Seleucia, now Iraq, and was spread to Rome by soldiers returning from the city's siege. During the extended pandemic an estimated two thousand Romans died each day."

"Wow. What do they say here, Henry? Have they killed this thing for good? And if we were exposed, how come we don't seem to have come down with it?"

"They think The Foundation's virus was transmitted in the air between victims, Judge. From the altered pigs, to the research staff, to the board members, who likely did a tour of the facility. But once the virus had attacked all the humans and altered pigs available, they believe the virus just burned itself out. It had nothing else to spread too, so it stopped."

"And that happened before we came along to poke around, Henry?"

"That's what they think."

"Jesus, I hope they're right."

"They're going to keep us in isolation here for few days Judge, until they're sure…."

Chapter 47
Monday 6:00 p.m.

The Judge was dozing on his bed in his quarantined room, the events of the day having worn him down, when he felt a soft gloved hand on his forehead. He struggled to waken, his eyes semi-focusing on a yellow-gowned figure in a self-oxygenizing hood leaning over him. Jesus, the vampire nurse was back, likely for more blood. He pushed sleep from his eyes and peered up at the suited figure. He could just make out through the pane of the hood several locks of blond hair straggling down one side, and a pair of aqua eyes, watery, with tears tracing down perfectly made-up cheeks. *Katy!*

"Hi lover," he muttered, still trying to wake up.

"Oh, Judge…" Katy's voice was almost a wail, her gloved hand shaking now with emotion. "Are you okay? I thought you were going to die."

"I'm fine, Katy. Just tired, emotionally exhausted, and anemic from too much blood letting by the vampire nurse."

"I'm so sorry for our fights, Judge. I love you so much. I never want to lose you. Do you hear me? Never!" She slugged him in the shoulder with her gloved hand, anger now flaring in her voice. It was better than her sharp elbow by a long stretch. The Judge accepted it for what it was, a love pat.

"I'm surprised they let you in here."

"I had to work on them awhile, Judge. Threaten, cajole, beg, threaten some more, all the things I learned as a lawyer's wife. I wore them down and they finally let me in, 'off the record', as they said."

"God, it's good to see you." The Judge gave her a small smile, reaching up to hold both her gloved hands, wishing he could touch her flesh.

She whimpered once, then stood bolt upright, forcing herself into a calm place, determined not to let him see her weak. She dropped one hand to stroke his forehead again.

"How long, Judge. How long before they give you back to me?"

"Perhaps tomorrow, Katy."

The door whooshed open then and the dreaded masked nurse marched in, taking Katy's hand away from the Judge, and propelling her toward the door with all the style of the Nazi she was. Katy turned back once, to blow the Judge a kiss through her mask, and then whoosh again and she was gone. The Judge was alone.

Chapter 48
Wednesday Noon

Forty-eight hours later the Judge walked out of the hospital facility, a free man. Or as free as anyone can be in 21st century America. It felt good to be out of confinement. And to know he'd been given a clean bill of health. They'd said the virus had been contagious through the air for about an hour. But then the risk had subsided, leaving the primary method of contagion the touching of the dead, or their fluids. The pigs were all dead of course. What the cross-over virus had missed the Swine Flu had gotten. The dogs had all survived, apparently immune to both viruses. The dogs were under quarantine still but would eventually find their way to a pet shelter and then hopefully to new homes.

Henry Banner, Jack Prentis and the Judge were declared free of the virus, having arrived too late to catch the airborne virus, and having been careful not to touch the dead.

All the records had been removed from the structures, and the entire barn and ranch house had burned to the ground. The HAZMAT team were taking no chances. The Judge deemed himself lucky to be alive. But it had been a miserable couple of days of isolation. He'd missed Katy awfully.

As he stepped off the last step and down onto the sidewalk in front of the hospital, a silver Mercedes SUV came roaring up, hell bent for leather, screeching to a stop at the yellow drop off curb with a rattle and a shake as its brakes were applied,… hard.

Katy had arrived!

Late, but with flair, as was her style. She jumped out of the driver's side, then lounged back in to retrieve a bouquet of twelve yellow roses, which she swung over her head like a trophy, as she made a dash for the Judge, throwing herself into him like a lineman from Notre Dame, nearly bowling him over.

"Katy, Katy… I'm glad to see you too. But don't kill me in the process." She threw her arms around his neck, giving him a big smoochy kiss. Several people turned to see the old guy swarmed by the pretty young girl. He loved her so.

The Judge climbed into the passenger side, and Katy rode off, scattering kids, dogs, chickens and leaves… Or she would have if there'd been any kids, dogs or chickens around. Instead the SUV scattered leaves, pine needles and dust.

"Are we going to the cabin, Katy?"

"Yes, Judge. I want to snuggle." Katy turned and gave him a wink.

"I need a stiff drink," muttered the Judge.

"I got a bottle of your favorite single malt for you at home, Judge. Laphroaig eighteen-year old."

The Judge licked his lips, which were suddenly dry.

Much later they settled in together on their favorite love seat facing out the tall windows, wide open to the Lake. They watched the shadows grow long as the sun sank behind the cabin. It was quiet and peaceful, the Lake turning from blue to purple as the sky grew dark and stars appeared. The Judge was feeling mellow, eighteen-year-old malt mellow, his stomach warm.

"Thank you for the flowers, Katy. But, why yellow?"

She gave him a big smile. "Yellow roses send a message of appreciation and idealistic love, Judge. They tell of my joy in being with you, and our vast friendship. The color represents feelings of gaiety and delight."

"But you love me physically too, Katy, don't you? We're good forever, right? You don't need anybody else?"

Katy tried to control obvious giggles, leaving the Judge feeling uncomfortable.

"You're worried cause I talked about 'open' relationships, Judge. And because I got tricked by Marie into going to that stupid social club."

"Well… yes."

"That open marriage thing was just talk, Judge. I was teasing you, pulling your chain a little. As I consider it now, I can see it wasn't so kind. I apologize. But I don't need anyone else. You're more than enough for me to handle. You and Ralphie."

"So, you're happy?"

"It's like this, Judge. You make me feel wanted and desired when I'm around you, even when you're off playing your work games and solving your mysteries. That's a huge turn-on for a woman. An expert once said, 'For a woman, being desired is the orgasm.' I feel desired and appreciated all the time with you in my life. So, no, I have no need to go looking for someone else."

"And our sex life is good, Katy?"

"Well, now there's an interesting question. We should talk about it Judge. Is our sex life good for you?"

"You first, Katy, I'm kind of shy to talk about it."

Katy snorted. "I'm a trained counselor, Judge. A quarter of my day at the high school where I counsel kids seems spent, directly or indirectly, on sexual issues as they deal with becoming young adults. I've got no problem talking about it."

"So, how's your sex life with me, Katy?"

"It's been the very best right from the beginning, Judge. You do all the right things to please me. I love that we always sleep together naked with our skin-on-skin contact. I love our outercourse, the oral and manual stimulation, and all our kissing and rubbing. The way you give me such passionate kisses drives me up the wall with desire for you. And when you softly bite my neck, sending goosebumps down my legs and the inside of my thighs. Wow!

You know in the end, Judge, our sexuality is a kind of energy that is expressed in many ways, not just in genital performance. Our shared goal is pleasure, and the vehicle of pleasure is touch. For me, Judge, it's not so much about our plumbing working properly. It's more a state of connection with you, of relaxation with you, of feeling safe in your arms."

"What about your seven-year itch, Katy?"

"I'm sorry about that too, Judge. It was partly about my birthday coming up. Turning older. Been feeling a little sorry for myself, I guess. I just got down, maybe even a little depressed. But I'm past that now. This business with you and your Swine Flu really shook me. I was so scared. I couldn't contemplate a life without you."

"So, it wasn't a seven-year itch?"

"No, Judge. There's actually some dispute about whether a seven-year itch exists, although I believe in it.

"So, you're happy, Katy? No open marriage? No experimentation with social clubs? We're tight?"

"Yes, Judge. We're tight. You're a lusty old goat, and I'm your lusty young broad. I think we get on just fine."

Katy gave the Judge a devilish smirk as she stood, offered her hand, and led the Judge across the grand room to the stairs, leading him up to their bedroom. Again.

Chapter 49
Wednesday 5:00 p.m.

As they lay sprawled across the bed, the back of Katy's head resting on the Judge's naked chest, Katy turned her head up to look up at the Judge.

"So, Judge. You found Jerry's killers. And they're all dead. Sort of a karmic justice don't you think? You must feel good."

"Is this what they call pillow-talk, Katy? I feel good now that I'm back with you." The Judge smiled at the top of her head, admiring the slight rise and fall of her breasts from her breathing. "I feel good to be out of that damn quarantine, Katy. And out from under the clutches of Nurse Vampire.

Katy snuggled down closer into him, almost purring.

But I'm not so sure about Jerry's killers."

"What? No way. Tell me, Judge, tell me."

"Well, the green SUV at the ranch was the same one that ran down Bradford Jones. Hair and blood samples on the grill matched Jones' type and hair. We're pretty sure it was the ranch foreman, Sam, at the wheel. He's the one we found halfway fallen out of the driver side of the vehicle, dead, on my last visit to the ranch."

"So, Sam certainly got his just deserts, and so did his employers."

"I think it was also Sam in the parking garage , Katy. Shoving a gun muzzle into my spine and demanding to know what Jerry told me with his last breath. And I believe it was Sam who punctured my brake lines before I went down the mountain. As sort of a warning to stop my investigation. Sam was David Branden's go-to guy for that sort of thing."

"They killed poor Jerry, and… your Claire, Judge. And they could have killed you too with that brake stunt. You got off lucky."

"Not 'my' Claire, remember. Anyway, I'm not so sure they were responsible for Claire's death, Katy."

"You think there's still someone else out there who's involved? Who's not dead?" Katy sat up on the bed now, alert.

"I think someone was angry, enraged even, at Jerry. They hit him with abandon with that boat paddle. A split-second decision to abuse him. A nasty swing with a paddle to the back of the head, swung with... anger, jealousy, desperation, hate... I don't know. But strong emotions. Then a very cold and calculated after-effort, likely with a motive of financial gain, to finish the job and cover it up. A decision to kill Jerry to shut him up about The Foundation. And an effort to cover it up as a boating accident."

"To shut him up about what The Foundation was doing."

"Yes."

"Your hidden thirty percent stockholder."

"Yes."

"You're saying it wasn't pre-planned in advance, Judge, even though the killer had all those motives?"

"Right. It wasn't like someone on an assignment. It wasn't like Sam's sitting in a parking lot waiting, watching. Watching for an opportunity to pull out and run Jones down. Here Jerry was assaulted first. Then it occurred to his assailant how much simpler life would be if Jerry were out of the picture. Unable to spread the word about what The Foundation was doing."

"But what about Claire, Judge?"

"A different murder. But I suspect not pre-planned either. Again, committed with a lot of emotion, perhaps angst. Claire was sitting there in her very revealing negligée. She knew her guest intimately. They were drinking together. The bed covers were all askew. I think they'd just made love.

But her assailant found her sleeping pills in her luggage and mixed her a mickey. And, for whatever reason, he'd brought along a gun. But it wasn't some dry corporate hit. They were in an intimate relationship."

"Mr. X!"

"Yes. I think so. I think Mr. X caught Claire smooching with Jerry Stone down on the village dock that night, dissolved into a jealous rage, picked up the handiest thing, a boat paddle, and slugged Jerry over the head."

"And Claire was part of it."

"I don't think so. Not initially. I think it just happened. Jerry wasn't dead. He was just semi-conscious. He'd received a nasty bump. I think Mr. X probably leaned on Claire to help him put Jerry into Jerry's boat. Told her he was going to drive Jerry back to his dock and get Jerry into his house. Then he would call a doctor to see if Jerry had a concussion. I think Mr. X asked Claire to drive her car around the Lake to Shelter Cove and pick Mr. X up after he got Jerry settled."

"But who, Judge? Who is Mr. X?"

"I don't know."

"Maybe it's Miss X, Judge."

"What?"

"Maybe we're looking for the wrong sex. Maybe it was, say, Ally Monroe. She certainly had a motive. Jerry was going to screw up her romance with Pete Campbell. And she was out on the Lake alone that night. No alibi and in the vicinity."

"But what about Claire in her negligee when she was killed?"

"Two women can be lovers too, Judge. Maybe Ally and Claire were an item; Ally got jealous of Jerry and smacked him. Then she got scared Claire would talk and had to shut her up."

"The way that Claire talked about Mr. X, not to mention the semen at the crime scene, doesn't point to a woman. You don't like Ally Monroe much, do you?"

"Frankly, I don't Judge. I don't like the way she looks at you. Like a hungry cat. She has no respect for territory. For my territory." Katy's eyes flashed.

"It could have been Pete Campbell on that dock, Katy. He hated Jerry. And Pete was also in the area with no alibi."

"But why would Claire help him get Jerry into the boat, Judge? She'd have run like hell and called some other policeman for help."

"I suppose you're right, Katy, unless Pete is Mr. X. Maybe young Pete really gets around, which is why he always looks so tired and glum. Or how about Juan Fernández, Marie's new sex partner, Katy? Removing Jerry left his path to Marie clear. And if Jerry hasn't redone his will, Marie will inherit everything, making her very wealthy in her own right."

"But why would Claire help him, Judge?"

"Perhaps he's Claire's third lover, Katy. The Mr. X that Claire was seeing."

"It would make sense, Judge. It would explain Claire in her negligee. I didn't like the guy much when I met him. Too oily for me. But what about this guy that was following Marie around?"

"Larry Shankman?"

"Yes, that's him. What about Larry Shankman?"

"Possibly, Katy. He no doubt wanted to get close to Marie. That would be a motive to get rid of Jerry. But Juan told me Marie hates Shankman. Said Shankman's mean, aggressive, degrading. Forced Marie to do awful, unnatural things. Showed no respect for women or their bodies. On the other hand, Clare knew Shankman, called him that morning she was murdered. It sounded like Shankman actually brought Claire to a meeting of your social club last spring."

"It's not 'my' social club, Judge."

"No, of course not." The Judge sighed. "There's just no proof to tie any of these people to that dock that night, Katy. I think there is a Mr. X, and I think he killed them both, Jerry and Claire. But as to who he is?... We may never know. Mr. X may have gotten away with murder… twice."

"Well, some of your suspects will be gathered together on Friday, Judge. And so will we. They're going to read Jerry's will. I hear it's a new will. Guess Jerry got his law partner, Tim somebody, to prepare it for him. Marie has asked that I come, and bring you, in case she needs a little legal advice."

"What time, Katy?"

"At noon. At Marie's house. Although Marie's not sure it's her house anymore. It's Jerry's family's house. It is... was... Jerry's separate property."

"Of course, I'll come with you, Katy. It sounds to be interesting."

Chapter 50
Friday, 11 am

The Judge ambled down the thousand steps to his lake-front cabin after a long walk with Annie the Dog. The blue jays were noisily chattering away, hoping perhaps he'd put out more peanuts now he'd returned. The air off the Lake was fresh and pure. It was a tad warmer now. The snow had mostly melted.

Katy had been fluttering around him all morning like a giant moth, excited about going to hear Jerry's will read. Katy and the Judge had each gotten a belated email from lawyer Tim McCarthy, asking that they attend. Apparently, Jerry had left them a little something in the will. He was a true gentleman. But Katy had already been invited as Marie's best friend, and the Judge too, at Marie's request, lest she need independent counsel in a hurry. And the Judge, after some reflection, had arranged for Jack Prentis to 'encourage' a few other people to attend, in the hope of sorting out what had actually happened to Jerry and then to Claire.

The Judge walked in through the kitchen door. The kitchen interior was so much a part of his growing up, filled with memories of his grandmother and later his mother cooking over the small stove against one wall. Old memories that seemed particularly precious to him now. After his brush with mortality.

As he glanced around the kitchen, he spotted two pink FedEx notices stuffed behind the fruit bowl that he'd missed before. Katy'd apparently tucked them there and then forgotten in all the flap over his isolation and then return. Hardly surprising, given the turmoil the last several days. Each notice was about an effort to deliver the same package. No one had been home on both tries and the package required a signature. The Second notice said he could call for his delivery at the local FedEx store in Arrowhead Village.

"Judge, come on," Katy called. Get cleaned up. We're going to be late for this will reading. Marie specifically wanted us there early. She's as nervous as a cat on a hot pavement."

"Katy, Katy. I'm just going to wear my uniform, tan slacks, blue striped shirt, and blazer, as I always to. This isn't like a funeral or anything. I'm not required to wear black."

"Judge, it's just impossible to budge you. You're so frustrating sometimes. Your like… like… like a damn elephant."

"Look, Katy, you go on. I can see you're all dressed up. I'll be there but I have a stop in the village. I'll take my own car."

"Harrumph." Was the only response the Judge got, that and the slammed door as Katy started her way up the thousand steps. And of course, Annie's disapproving look; the damn dog was always in sync with the female perspective on events occurring in the nest. And particularly so as her tail had been stepped upon recently. She had a long memory for a dog.

The Judge screeched to a stop in front of the FedEx store, dashed in, and came out carrying a big cardboard envelope. It was addressed to him. But the sender was marked with just the initial: 'C'. He wondered idly if it was a bomb from a disgruntled client, turning it over in his hands, feeling something of small weight but some thickness inside, making the envelope bulge a little in the middle. He tore the top cardboard top off the envelope and reached in, surprised to bring his hand out holding an Apple iPhone…, in pink!

He hit the on button and it started right up. A small post-it note on the back gave him its code, 7877. He punched the code in. The main screen came on. There was a picture there… of Claire. He moved to contacts. There were a large number. He looked at recent calls. The last one was to him, on Friday, a week ago, at seven a.m. Shit, it was the call he got from Claire just before she was killed. There was another number before that looked familiar. There had been several calls to it that morning, and in each of the proceeding days.

He turned to the pictures. The setting was on video. He hit play and watched the last video recorded, a short sixty second piece. Then he stuffed the cell in his pocket and climbed back in his car, figuring he'd just make the will-reading party.

Chapter 51
Friday Noon

They were all seated in Marie's great room , its somber paneled walls matching the mood of those assembled. The Scottish plaids of the upholstery brought no gaiety to the occasion. Tim McCarthy, as Jerry's law partner and apparently most recently his personal estate planning attorney, had called them together for a traditional reading of Jerry's Last Will and Testament.

Tim had pulled a small table desk over, underneath the moose's head, and placed himself in a chair behind it, giving himself some presence, in order to ensure his control of the meeting and the maintenance of proper decorum. The Judge spotted familial similarities between McCarthy and the moose; both stuffed animals of sorts.

The Judge settled his rear end deep into the padded sofa facing across the room toward the giant picture window and the Lake. He'd be able to look out at the Lake and daydream a little while the dreary proceedings went on. True to his word, he was dressed in his standard uniform, tan slacks, blue striped dress shirt, no tie, and blue sport coat. Jerry wouldn't have expected anything more.

Katy sat next to the Judge on the sofa, scrunched in tight, looking like a doll propped up between bruisers, in a dark grey tweed skirt and jacket over a white blouse. She had nothing black to wear, a fact she told the Judge was his fault, since she had been too busy worrying about him to go shopping.

On Katy's other side was Pete Campbell, his arm territorially around Ally Monroe, who sat next to him. He was in full uniform, his gun digging occasionally into Katy's side as he squirmed around uncomfortably, a trademark sour expression on his face. Ally looked drawn and nervous. That she was there indicated she would get some sort of bequest. This hinted of juicy scandal to come upon the reading of the will. Occasionally Marie Stone looked across at Ally from the opposite sofa with its back to the Lake, daggers in her eyes.

Marie was decked out in a tight pink dress that emphasized her figure. You'd never know by looking she was recently widowed. Beside her sat her new paramour, Juan Fernández. Juan was looking uncomfortable, despite the blue corduroy jumpsuit he sported. The jumpsuit implied 'artist', 'European' and expensive, all in one outfit, of which he was obviously proud.

In the chair behind the Judge sat Larry Shankman, hauled over at the Judge's request, and next to him Sheriff Jack Prentis, who had done the hauling. On the other side of Prentis sat his other charge the Judge had asked him to bring to the meet. Mob-guy, Tony Roselli, who sat quietly with a glum look on his face, clearly wishing he was somewhere else.

In a chair behind them sprawled Jackson, the Stones' ex-maid, fired by Marie the day after Jerry's murder, looking insolent. Jackson must be included in the will, the Judge reasoned. Next to her sat Carol Ann Martin, the manager of the market; the Judge had asked her to show up as a favor to him.

Juan Fernández stood up, walked across to the Judge, and handed the Judge a small folded piece of paper, then returned to his seat. All eyes turned to the Judge, curious. The Judge opened the paper, nodded at Juan, folded it again and put it in his shirt pocket. Katy craned her neck to see what was on the paper, as everyone did. But no one was quick enough.

Tim McCarthy had set up a projector behind him on a blank portion of the wall and projected the facing page of the will he was about to read. He looked at the assemblage over the top of steel-rim glasses like a wise old owl, then banged his pen against a water glass on his small desk for attention.

"We are gathered here today to formally read the contents of Mr. Jerry Stone's will. He specified his will should be read in this fashion, and so I shall begin."

There was tension in the air now; quiet conversations stopped in mid-sentence; all heads turned to listen.

"Let me add that this is a new will, prepared by me as Jerry's personal estate planning attorney and executed by Jerry only two weeks before his untimely death. As some of you are aware, Jerry Stone and his wife, Marie Stone, had been in discussions contemplating the dissolution of their marriage. They had been in heated negotiations over property matters at the time of his death, but nothing had been agreed to or signed. So, this will constitutes the only document which disposes of Jerry's separate property. As a result of an initial marital agreement executed at the time of Jerry and Marie's marriage, there is no community property."

The Judge could hear Marie's quick intake of breath. And sense Ally Monroe stiffing on his sofa, her small hand immediately taken by Pete Campbell and squeezed hard.

Tim McCarthy then began to read the entry paragraphs of the will, droning on like a buzzing bee while everybody fidgeted, waiting for the bequest parts, which came last:

"I hereby leave my wonderful ski boat, which I know the Judge has admired, and even coveted, to my dear friends, the Judge and his wonderful wife, Katy, title to be transferred using the Judge's legal name."

Great, thought the Judge. A nice gesture to be sure. But the boat was now in a junkyard somewhere, cut up into chunks of smashed fiberglass, wood kindling, and twisted metal.

"I leave to Ally Monroe the sum of one million dollars, in recognition of the wonderful summer we secretly shared together, a summer I'll never forget."

Ally's gasp filled the room, almost covering the low guttural mutter of Marie on the opposite sofa: "Slut."

"I leave to Jackson, my faithful housekeeper who did so much to ease my pain over trying days of domestic strife, the sum of five hundred thousand dollars."

"Lordy-lou," burst from Jackson's mouth behind the Judge, accompanied by a snort from Marie across the room.

"I leave the balance of my estate to the University of Southern California, my alma mater, except for the sum of one dollar I leave to my ex-wife, Marie Stone, as a measure of how little effort she gave to our marital union, lightly abandoning her marital vows at the least temptation and opportunity."

Marie jumped to her feet at this, snarling, "No, no. You bastard, Jerry! That's unfair."

The whole room broke into a buzz then. Expressions of shock, congratulations, gossip, it was all there. Or it was until the Judge stood up and cleared his throat, using his judicial throat clearing noise so effective when he'd been on the bench. The room immediately went silent, like a room of small children when the disciplinarian headmaster suddenly walks in. Even Tim McCarthy shut up, scowling at the Judge.

"I think we should also talk about Jerry Stone's murder," said the Judge.

Everyone sat up straighter in their seats, and all heads turned to eye the Judge.

"Jerry Stone was murdered here a little over two weeks ago. I know the police, and I'm sure most of you, have concluded it was The Foundation people who did it. And now those people are mostly dead as a result of their own carelessness. But you'd be wrong. The person who killed Jerry Stone is very much alive. That person smugly believes they've gotten away with murder. The murder of Jerry Stone, and also the murder of Claire Henderson. But they're wrong."

The Judge turned to Tim McCarthy. "If I may, Tim, can I borrow your projector for a couple of minutes?"

"Of course, be my guest." One could hear a hint of envy in Tim's voice as the Judge so easily took control of his meeting.

"I'd like to marshal the facts as we know them," said the Judge. "You see, I believe Jerry Stone's murderer is someone in this very room."

Chapter 52
Friday 12:45 p.m.

The Judge paced up and down as he spoke across the alley formed in Marie's great room. Formed by Tim McCarthy's moose-sheltered desk at one end, and the two festive plaid sofas lined perpendicular to the desk and parallel to the room. The room's inhabitants were in rapt attention now, like two lines of ducks, surprise and awe on their faces.

"Our murderer, let's call him Mr. X, was in love with Claire Henderson. X and Claire planned to run away together, as soon as X's grand plan to scoop up perhaps fifty million dollars matured. Fifty million dollars in Replace/Repair's public stock. That's the sister company to The Foundation. He just needed to wait until legal restrictions came off; then he could sell his stock into the public market.

You see, our Mr. X was Replace/Repair's second largest shareholder. His other business affairs were on the rocks. He was on the verge of bankruptcy. He was desperate to obtain this one mega-hit so he could set his financial affairs aright and retire to some offshore island community with Claire.

But our Mr. X caught Claire smooching and on the verge of having sex with Jerry Stone on the Arrowhead Village Community Dock, out in the open, publicly, a week ago Friday night.

X already hated Jerry Stone. They'd had a violent argument that very afternoon after Jerry announced he was withdrawing as The Foundation's legal counsel and going public about Replace/Repair's illegal activities. Mr. X's fifty million was 'toast' once Jerry went public, and he knew it.

When X saw Jerry and Claire kissing and petting and clinging together on the dock, he was filled with jealous rage. He crept onto the dock, picked up the first thing he saw, a boat paddle, and crashed it down on the back of Jerry's head."

The assemblage gasped in unison. The Judge puffed up a little, envisioning himself practically a Hercule Poirot. Liking the feeling, increasing the speed of his back and forth pace with a bit of a flourish.

"Claire really loved X. And he was her one chance to gain the wealth and a lifestyle for which she'd always hungered. But she was a flirty girl. She'd chosen to entertain three different men on a continuing basis, as a way to cover her rent and living expenses. Jerry was one of those men. Tony Roselli over there was a second." All eyes went to Tony, who scowled back. "The third man was our Mr. X.

Now here's the thing. Jerry was unconscious from the blow, true, but he wasn't dead. He likely had a concussion, but he would have recovered. If only Mr. X had walked away right then. Taken Claire and just walked away. No one would have gotten killed."

The Judge's audience was still now, listening closely

"But as his jealous emotions receded, Mr. X began to consider his options. If Jerry publicly spoke out about Replace/Repair's illegal activities, its stock would plummet like a rock into our Lake out there. His last chance to recoup his business losses and assure his future lifestyle lost. Here was an opportunity to stop the financial disaster Jerry was going to wreak. A chance to obtain his fifty million and sail off into the sunset with Claire as he'd always planned.

Note, ladies and gentlemen, Mr. X's next actions would no longer constitute a crime of passion. He would cross a line here. His next actions would constitute premeditated murder."

People moved as one toward the edge of their seats.

"Mr. X ordered Claire to help him get Jerry into Jerry's boat. He told her he would take Jerry back to his home, or at least his dock, and call the paramedics for help. It would keep Claire out of it, he said. Claire had some instinct this wasn't right. She took a precaution we'll discuss in a minute. But she helped X load Jerry into his boat and agreed to pick X up with her car in Shelter Cove twenty minutes later.

At Jerry's dock, Mr. X, a nautical man himself, easily turned the boat around and maneuvered it backwards into Jerry's slip. Now, Jerry's boat faced outward, out into the Lake. X rigged the unconscious Jerry Stone into the helm seat in the boat, set the engine to full throttle, and sent the boat and Jerry racing out full tilt across the Lake. The boat made a fiery crash into my dock, where it exploded. Killing Jerry Stone in what appeared to be a boating accident."

The Judge waited a few beats, enjoying himself, heightening the suspense.

"Things began to unravel for Mr. X when Claire found out Jerry had died. She was now frightened of our

Mr. X. And scared the role she'd played in Jerry's death might send her to jail. So, when X met Claire for a previously planned sexual escapade in her room on that Friday morning she died, he decided to borrow some of her sleeping pills to covertly mix into her drink. Once Claire was woozy and unable to defend herself, it was easy for Mr. X to force a gun into her mouth and put a bullet through her skull in a contrived way to make it look like a self-inflicted wound. A suicide. This was Mr. X's premeditated homicide number two."

People were looking around the room at each other now, questions raising in their eyes.

"So, who is this Mr. X. Do you know him? If you think about it, I think you do. He's right here in this room."

Heads turned to survey each other again. Suspicion was thick in the air.

"Our murderer's someone who was in the Village that night. Someone with a large stake in Replace/Repair stock. Someone who knew all about Replace/Repair's illegal brokering of body parts. About its illicit research genetically altering pigs with human DNA with neither ethical approval nor adequate safeguards to protect our human community. Someone whose business had gone downhill fast, leaving them under extreme financial pressure. Someone with the nautical skills to easily maneuver Jerry's boat backward into his slip and tie Jerry to its helm.

That narrows the field considerably. Any takers?"

The Judge's audience looked puzzled now.

"There's only one person here who fits that description. Unfortunately, there's was no evidence tying him to the community dock that night. Not until now. You see, one of the last things Claire did that morning before she met her lover, and died, was to slip out to the hotel desk and put her cell phone in a FedEx envelope directed to me. I finally received her cell phone package about an hour ago."

The Judge touched the button on his laptop, and the screen under the Moose lit up.

"Claire got very worried when Mr. X hit Jerry with the paddle. She put her cell phone on video record and put it back in her breast pocket where it just ran, catching a part of the sequence on the community dock that night Jerry died, sound and all."

The video on the cell phone was running now on the big screen. All eyes were glued there. The image was shaky, all over the map. There was a brief look at a Claire's feet, open toed shoes, pink nail polish. And then a shaky landscape as the phone was positioned into a semi-stationary location, her breast pocket. The view then moved as Claire moved, recording her voice. She was whimpering. There was a man's voice now, close, snarling.

"Shut up and give me a damn hand. Grab his legs. We'll drag him over and load him into his boat."

More whimpering.

"Shut up. You're the one that agreed to come out here to the dock with him. You're a part of this thing as much as I. Besides it's your fault. I couldn't stand to see him kiss you. See him touch you like that. Christ, he was going to take you right here, out in the open, on this God damn community dock."

'I didn't know you were following us, honey. You know you're the love of my life. This was just a little side business."

"I give you enough money to be exclusive, without any side business, Claire." The man's voice rose threateningly.

"Yes, dear. Of course. It's just you only from now on. I don't want anyone to get hurt, honey." Claire was speaking through gasps, large in-takes of air, trying to control herself.

"He's not hurt much. I didn't hit him that hard with the paddle. But he deserved it. The bastard! Come on, help me get him into his boat. I'll drive him over to his dock, call 911, then leave. He can wake up there. He didn't see me, and he won't remember what happened."

The video swooped toward the surface of the dock, and a pair of small hands, well-manicured with pink nail polish, reached down to grab two shoed feet attached to dark jeans, helping larger hands at Jerry's shoulders, dragging Jerry's unconscious body a foot across the deck to the edge of a boat. There the male hands took over, hoisting Jerry into his boat.

"Listen. I need you to take my car, drive around the Lake to Shelter Cove. You know the gate code."

The video bobbed, likely along with Claire's head, a nod yes.

"Good. In fifteen minutes, I want you to drive through the gate and park in front of the house to the right of Jerry's house. Just park there and wait for me. I might be five or ten minutes late. And for God sakes turn the lights and motor off and just sit there silently in the car. You got all that?"

The video bounced again. Another nod.

"Okay, then. Here are the keys." The video showed a hand extended into the frame, holding keys.

It was only then that Claire straightened up, suddenly standing tall, even leaning backwards a bit as she was short, allowing the video to briefly capture the face of the man. There were gasps at the final frames displayed a very recognizable face.

Tim McCarthy!

Tim McCarthy's face had turned grey, the lawyer's arrogant expression gone. His eyes darted around the room now, looking for what... support? A quick exit? Suddenly he rose from his table and made a lunge for the dining room and its kitchen door beyond. But Jack Prentis had risen and positioned himself to block that exit. Pete Campbell was blocking the front door. McCarthy was trapped and he knew it. He retraced his steps to his chair under the moose head, collapsing into it.

He looked at the Judge then, his eyes watery, unfocused, seeing mostly into the past.

"Jerry and I'd had a nasty fight earlier, Judge." McCarthy said. "I'd come up the mountain Friday morning to talk sense into him. But he wouldn't listen. The bull-headed pompous son of a bitch. He was going to ruin Replace/Repair, destroy the company, destroy the value of my shares, destroy my one chance to recoup my fortune and bring my life back from the brink. The bastard didn't care about me or anybody. I was desperate to stop him. I just didn't know how.

And that evening I found Jerry and Claire together.

I loved Claire. I would have done anything for her. We were going to leave this miserable L.A. together, escape to Fiji. And Claire said she loved me. Even though she was younger. Said it made no difference. There was only me, she said.

But she lied. Oh, how she lied. I even introduced her to Jerry last summer over drinks, my own law partner. Wanted to show her off a little. But the conniving bitch snuck around behind my back and started seeing Jerry. Playing me for a fool.

I saw her and Jerry on the community dock late Friday night. About to make love. Saw the way she touched him, what she was doing for him out there on her knees! Publicly! I just snapped. I quietly walked out on that dock, grabbed that paddle and I hit the bastard... hard.

And after that… I don't know. The solution just became obvious. I saw the opportunity and took it. I made Claire help me put him in the boat. I'd never seen her so scared. Scared of me. I took him back to his dock, turned his boat around, and set him off full tilt across the lake, hoping the Lake would finish what I'd started. And it did!

Except for you, Judge. Jerry managed to blab something to you before he succumbed. But for that it was perfect.

But then Claire started coming unglued. She read Jerry had died in a boating accident on the far shore. I'd told her I was taking Jerry home in his boat and would get him a doctor. She knew then I'd lied. She got even more scared. And meanwhile I'd found out about you." McCarthy stabbed an accusing finger out at Tony Roselli. "I was beside myself. I'd been such a fool.

I met Claire in her room at the Arrowhead Inn that morning. We made love but it was strained. Then we had an enormous fight. She said I should turn myself in. Said it was the best thing for both of us. Ha! Best thing for her, perhaps. And it seemed to be all working out. My shares in Replace/Repair were about to be freed up and sold, cashed in. Jerry wasn't around to bring the

Company down. And I was over Claire for good. The bitch.

I came out of the bathroom and she was just coming back into the room. Said she'd gone for ice. But right away she started talking again. Yak yak yak yak yak. How I had to go to the police. How someone might have seen us. How, if I loved her, I'd protect her and confess. Explain she had nothing to do with it. On and on. She just wouldn't shut up.

I could see she was falling apart. She'd never keep her mouth shut. And I didn't want her anymore anyway. Not after she'd been with Jerry, and with Mr. Detroit trash."

McCarthy cast another angry glance at Tony.

"She just had to go. So, I improvised her suicide. She didn't suffer. She was out of it with the sleeping pills when I put the gun in her mouth. She didn't know what was happening until I pulled the trigger.

That was it. I'd taken some chances. But I'd won. I sent my shares into my broker to free up and sell.

But it all came crashing down again. The virus escaped at the Ranch. Everybody died. The entire facility has been razed to the ground. My Replace/Repair stock went from fifty million dollars to zero. I had to file bankruptcy yesterday. There's nothing left. Thirty years of law practice down the drain. I'm broke. I don't care anymore. My life's over."

McCarthy hung his head then, staring aimlessly at the table in front of him, his outburst complete. It indeed was over.

Tim McCarthy had lost everything, and he knew it. His law firm, his assets, his mistress, and now his freedom.

END

XXXX

SOME ADDITIONAL NOTES

For those who want to read more about the brokerage of human organs:

The Wall Street Journal: OPINION: The Nightmare of Human Organ Harvesting in China. LINK: https://www.wsj.com/articles/the-nightmare-of-human-organ-harvesting-in-china-11549411056.

WIKKPEDIA: Organ harvesting from Falun Gong practitioners in China. LINK: https://en.wikipedia.org/wiki/Organ_harvesting_from_Falun_Gong_practitioners_in_China.

Extra News Feed: New Horrors: China Harvesting Muslim Organs in Concentration Camps. LINK: https://extranewsfeed.com/new-horrors-china-harvesting-muslim-organs-in-concentration-camps-9a252d3c373e

For those who want to read more about unethical gene splicing:

THE WASHINGTON POST: We need to talk about genetically modifying animals: LINK:
https://www.washingtonpost.com/news/theworldpost/wp/2017/12/11/gmo-animals/?noredirect=on

LIVESCIENCE: Gene-Edited Babies Reportedly Born in China. What Could Go Wrong? LINK:
https://www.livescience.com/64166-first-genetically-modified-babies-risks.html

For those who want to read more about polyamory:

The New York Times:
https://www.nytimes.com/2019/08/03/style/polyamory-nonmonogamy-relationships.html

ACKNOWLEDGEMENTS

Thanks to those good friends who helped me to write and edit this book. Dr. Alexandra Davis, who was the first to see every word; my amazing Editor, Jason Myers, who did yeoman work on the edits and kept me on the straight and narrow; the multiple good friends who agreed to read and comment on the early draft, and Dane Low, (www.ebooklaunch.com), who helped me design the distinctive cover.

Thank You All.

Davis MacDonald

This is a Work of Fiction

The Lake is a work of fiction. Names, characters, businesses, organizations, clubs, places, events and incidents depicted in this book are either products of the Author's imagination or are used fictitiously. Any resemblance or similarity to actual persons, living or dead, or events, locales, business organizations, clubs, or incidents, is unintended and entirely incidental. Names have been chosen at random and are not intended to suggest any person. The facts, plot, circumstances and characters in this book were created for dramatic effect, and bear no relationship to actual businesses, organizations, communities or their denizens.

About Davis MacDonald

Davis MacDonald grew up in Southern California and writes of places about which he has intimate knowledge. Davis uses the mystery novel genre to write stories of mystery, suspense, love, and commitment, entwined with relevant social issues and moral dilemmas facing 21st Century America. A member of the National Association of Independent Writers and Editors (NATWE), his career has spanned Law Professor, Bar Association Chair, Investment Banker, and Lawyer. Many of the colorful characters in his novels are drawn in part from his personal experiences and relationships (although they are all entirely fictional characters).

Davis began this series in 2013, with the publishing of THE HILL, in which he introduces his new character, the Judge. Here is a bit about each book in the Series, in the order they were written:

THE HILL. The Hill is a murder mystery and a love story which also explores the sexual awakening of a young girl, how sexual manipulation can change lives forever, and the moral dilemmas love sometimes creates.

THE ISLAND, set in Avalon, Catalina, continues the saga of the Judge and his love Katy, as the Judge finds himself in another murder mystery, and forced to make some key decisions about his relationship with Katy. The story explores the dysfunctional attitudes of a small town forced to drop old ways of thinking or face extinction.

SILICON BEACH, set in Venice, Santa Monica, Playa Vista and Marina del Rey, opens with a sundown attack on the Judge on the Santa Monica Beach, and carries the reader through the swank and not so swank joints on the Los Angeles West Side, as the Judge tries to bring down killers before they bring him down. The book takes a close look at the homeless, who they are, where they came from, what their lives are like, and offers a novel political solution.

THE BAY, set in Newport Beach, Balboa, and the Orange County Coastal communities, finds the Judge pressed into service by the FBI to solve a murder of one of their own, stumbling into a terrorist plot that could devastate Orange County. The story takes a close look at Islam in its many strains, as it exists in the United States.

CABO, set in Mexico, finds the Judge and Katy on a holiday in Cabo San Lucas which turns deadly as they unravel a stealthy double murder, and go head to head with human traffickers in Baha California.

THE STRAND, set in Manhattan Beach, Hermosa Beach, and Redondo Beach, tracks a murder. And also a controversial case centered on a pre-school and alleged child-abuse. A case that triggers prosecutorial misconduct and a rush to judgment by the D.A.'s Office and the Press, ruining reputations and destroying the lives and asset of the accused in reliance on 'creditable' sources that are not creditable, long before the defendants are ever brought to trial.

THE LAKE. A best friend dying in your arms. His last desperate words a cryptic message of death to thousands. What would you do? The Judge sleuths out the facts, exposing the shocking private lives of people he thought he knew. Uncovering the greedy that would risk the world for financial gain. Blind-sided along the way by Katy's sudden unhappiness, the love he expected to last forever seemingly unraveling, the relationship wobbling. What are the right words, the right steps, to touch her heart again? To put something fragile back together and fuse it so strong it lasts a lifetime ? Can the Judge hold off the dark in his personal life, while exposing killers so cold, so calculating, they give the word Evil a new meaning?

THE CRUISE, a murder mystery set on the high seas, will be published in the Fall of 2020. The first Chapters of THE CRUISE are included at the end of this book

All books are available on Amazon on Kindle and in paperback, and other fine bookstores, and available at online shopping platforms. Audio books are available for the first four books in the series. Watch for Audio Books to come out regularly on the remaining books in the series.

HOW TO CONNECT WITH
Davis MacDonald

Email: Don@securities-attys.com

Website: http://davismacdonald-author.com/

Twitter: https://twitter.com/Davis_MacDonald

Facebook: Davis MacDonald, Author

Blog: http://davis-macdonald.tumblr.com/

LinkedIn: Davis MacDonald

Amazon Author's Page: Davis Macdonald-Author

The Lake

New in 2020, THE CRUISE

Look for **THE CRUISE** from Davis MacDonald, book EIGHT in the Judge series, to be published in the Fall of 2020.

What follows are the Prologue and First chapter of: **THE CRUISE**

THE CRUISE

By

Davis MacDonald

Prologue

The man had just drifted off to sleep beside his wife. It had been a late night; difficult business decisions to make. He'd had to cut some partners loose, discipline others, re-set the priorities among his minions. His instructions would be drifting down, percolating through the organization, reaching the overseas branches in the Far East and being read even now. Later, London would open to the news, and then New York. Here, in the Valley, part of the great Los Angeles sprawl, his immediate staff would be the last to know.

He'd just entered REM sleep when a disturbance in the ether brought him back to consciousness with a start, his eyes fluttering open, trying to focus. Someone was sitting beside him on his bed, shaking him awake. Through the blur and the scant illumination trickling in the bedroom window from the city lights across the Valley he made out the shape of his son, Jay.

"Dad, Dad. Wake up. I've got something to show you. It's very important. You must come and look."

Jay sounded excited. But then he tended to be an excitable young man. Twenty-two, his youngest, and still living at home. Floundering around UCLA, trying to decide what to do with his life. An artistic and sensitive soul, favoring his mother.

Jay would be a taker, never a producer, in this family. Shirt sleeves to shirt sleeves in three generations. That's what they said. Someone pulls himself up, makes a lot of money, is hugely successful through pure grit, hard work and enormous focus. Then his children come along and are the spenders, living lavishly under his tent, spending their inheritance willy-nilly, accomplishing little. And their children, the grandchildren; well it's back to the street for them. Back to shirt sleeves. Back to scrabbling around in the herd, trying to make ends meet, trying to satisfy a dominant boss at work, trying to scratch together some money here and there for a modest vacation, and to put something away for savings and for retirement. It was the way of the human tribe.

He didn't understand people like that. People like Jay. Helpless people with no vision and no drive. He'd tried to educate by example, but he'd failed. If a person had no fire in their belly, you couldn't manufacture it there. He was older now and had pretty much given up on changing the nature of the family around him. Or lighting a spark in the grandchildren coming up. Spenders all.

"Come on Dad, hurry up. This is important. Just throw your robe on. It'll only take a minute."

He rolled out from under the covers with a sigh, nude as he always was when he slept, cast an envious glance at his wife still sound asleep and purring slightly, threw on his robe, and slid into his slippers. This had better be good.

"It's down here dad, downstairs, out on the driveway. Hurry!"

"Jesus Christ … on the driveway?"

Jay led the way down the stairs, across the sprawling living room, and out the front door, which for some reason was standing open. He reluctantly followed, shaking his head.

"You stand here, Dad. Right here. See. I've made a little mark on the driveway with pink chalk."

He stumbled out of the front door, across the grand porch, down the steps, and stopped at the pink X faintly visible on the driveway, muttering to himself under his breath, in many ways still half asleep. He was a big man, six-foot four, broad shoulders, and a prodigious stomach which required suspenders to keep his pants up. He loved to eat. His bulk cast a shadow in the moonlight, hiding his pink X, forcing him to guess more or less where it was. Where he was supposed to stand. Hair-brained!

Jay had crossed diagonally to the other side of the driveway, twenty feet away now, stopping beside a Folgers Coffee can sitting there, the top missing. It looked empty. He put his hands out, palms up, flat. "You stay right there, dad. This will only take a minute."

He'd already heard that before, five minutes ago, when he was awakened from his sound sleep. Humph.

Jay reached into his pocket and brought out a silver lighter. Shit, that was his lighter. It'd gone missing a week ago. Damn it. His kid was turning into a kleptomaniac.

Jay paused for a minute, looking like he was almost hyperventilating. Then spoke.

"Dad. It's all about the money for you. Money this… Money that. Fuck everybody, destroy the planet, but make the money. I can't deal with it, with our family, with our life, always built on the money. I can't deal with you anymore."

In one fluid motion Jay reached down and scooped up the coffee can, which turned out to have liquid in it. Jay dumped the contents of the can over his head, dousing his hair and face; liquid running down Jay's grey workout suit, soaking the fabric. The man could suddenly smell gasoline permeating the air.

Then Jay lit the silver lighter and set himself on fire.

Chapter 1
Six Months Later

As the cruise ship started to steam out of the first port on its itinerary, the Judge leaned on the pool deck rail and watched the harbor slide by. The Judge wondered if he'd be able to keep himself busy for the full week aboard. There wasn't much to do. He could eat himself into oblivion. He could lay beside the pool and get a sunburn. Or he could drink himself under the table to assure he got his money's worth from the expensive drink packages he'd been pressured to buy.

Katy had signed herself up for a spa treatment every day. Good for her, that was her thing. But the Judge had no interest in being pummeled and beaten by some overly steroidal Polack who was a woman but looked like a man. Certainly not on a daily basis. Life was too short to tolerate such abuse.

The trip had been Katy's idea. She'd lobbied long and hard, determined to get him away all to herself, she said. Of course, they were hardly by themselves, packed in this giant sardine can with another three thousand souls determined to have artificial fun eating, sunburning, drinking, gambling and… and yacking. That was the worst. It was like being penned up for a week in an overcrowded chicken coop.

The first night Katy and the Judge sat at dinner with eight retirees and got to hear about their medical problems and surgeries. Through the cocktails and appetizers and extending through the salad course, Katy and the Judge were pretty much brought up to speed on their dinner companions' entire medical histories in vivid detail. With the second course they got to hear the medical histories of their companions' parents, mostly deceased. "Genes are important you know, and deceased parents can portend what the future may hold." By the time the dessert menus were passed, their fellow diners had moved on the operations and medical issues of brothers, sisters, and cousins, some alive, some not. The Judge was now so enlightened he was certain he could pass the Medical Licensing Examination himself and enter the practice of medicine.

The Judge excused himself after dessert and had a discrete pow wow with the maître d'. After two large bills smoothly changed hands, Katie and the Judge were reassigned to a new dining table group for the balance of the cruise, starting the second evening.

In telling the story later, the Judge would usually mutter at this point, "Out of the frying pan, and into the fire!", accompanied by a little eye-rolling for effect.

They were completing their second day 'at sea', a polite description for a day spent traversing ocean, no stops, no sightseeing, nothing but a boring blue horizon, a rash of gin and tonics, a parade of overfed people prowling around the floating cork that was the ship, stepping on each other's toes, and sun burning. Oh. And it was accompanied by loud and raucous music piped everywhere, making it impossible to hold a conversation with anyone.

The Judge wandered around aimlessly in bright orange trunks that wouldn't stay wet. Trunks he'd cut the inside netting out of because it was fouling his plumbing. Katy was appalled. She scolded him for it; demanded he sit in chairs more carefully in public, and sprawl on a lounge chair with his knees together. She said his shortcomings were not to be exposed. Frankly, he didn't give a damn. But when Katy was around, he tried to obey her rules. Keep her happy.

His ensemble was completed by a triple-large puke-green T-shirt of doubtful pedigree, which hung over his paunch like a tent, mostly hiding his snazzy trunks. It was one of his favorite shirts, perhaps because Katy was so appalled by it. And because it had a breast pocket, into which he'd stuffed his passport, reading glasses, sunglasses, pens (black and blue), a pencil, an Indian Ink marker and a small spiral notebook in case an idea came to him he wanted to jot. The poor pocket bulged with complaint, sagging and looking very pregnant, even past due.

He wore a canvas hat, a Tilly, but so old the label was long gone, and sun was starting to show through the threadbare material in splotches here and there. The chin strap was missing too, requiring him to periodically scrunch the hat hard down hard on his head against the breeze, often making it difficult to see out under the brim. He hadn't walked into anybody yet, but it was so crowded around the pool deck, what with people carrying heaping plates of sloppy food, pizza, drinks and what not, there'd been some close calls. God could his fellow passengers eat.

He was confident he projected a certain elegant style as he wandered around the pool deck. He could tell because he could see heads turn and eyes start here and there as he walked by. But no one approached to talk.

Well, you couldn't talk anyway. Not over the trashy noise they were streaming out, pretending it was music, from some punk band one deck up. A stacked, sweaty blond and an anorexic Indian kid were setting up microphones at the pool's edge, readying themselves to begin blasting stupid games for the pool crowd. The Judge was already grinding his teeth but could see things would only get worse. He beckoned a passing waiter for another Piña colada he been assured by the staff were 'low-cal', his fifth. It was amazing they tasted so good for being so low-calorie. Almost like ice cream. He hoped to numb the onslaught of music and games to come.

Later that evening, as the Judge and Katy walked up to their new table, the Judge had immediate misgivings about their revised assignment. It was a family table, with two open seats available to be filled. As the Judge circled the table shaking hands and vainly trying to remember names, its members looked at the Judge and then Katy with curiosity.

Who were these interlopers who were braving Dad's table, and what did Dad think about it? They invariably turned after their introduction to glance at Dad for direction. Welcoming?... Or cold shoulder?

'Dad', Charles (Charlie) Waxman, the third, sat at the head of the table, which was oblong in shape, and had examined the Judge with cold grey eyes as the Judge and Katy approached. He'd not bothered to rise, but lifted a meaty paw up, across his forehead and behind his right shoulder to disinterestedly shake the Judge's hand.

He was a bulk of a man; tall, broad shoulders, with a big chest and belly to match. He obviously liked his food and wine. A little older than the Judge, late fifties, he had iron grey hair, and plenty of it, worn long and streaked back along either side of his square blocked head. His features were mostly lost in his fleshy face, except for the eyes, which were the eyes of a predator, moving constantly, seeking advantage. He wore grey slacks and a black sports jacket that fit him perfectly, custom made and expensive. It was worn over a light grey silk shirt with an over-large collar, open at the neck.

The Judge moved over a step to meet Waxman's wife sitting to his left, Alice Waxman, who stood to greet the Judge, a short blonde with cropped hair, faded blue eyes, and squint lines that burst out as she produced a perfunctory smile. She looked late forties, and hard rid, pouches under her eyes, lips that fit together in a grim smile that was almost a grimace. The layer of pancake cosmetics on her face only emphasized the lines of pain and frustration etched there. She wore an expensive silk cocktail dress, metallic cobalt blue, open at the neck with a long patch of bare skin extending down almost to her navel. Small rises tucked under the silk to either side.

The chiseled bones of her throat and chest protruding here and there across her bare expanse suggested a scrawny creature underneath.

To the left of Alice Waxman sat her daughter, Laura Waxman, late twenties, a younger, taller version of her mom, streaked blond hair turning to brown. Blue eyes again, watching the Judge suspiciously as she extended her hand to briefly touch his before yanking it away as though scalded. She was dressed in a white linen skirt and a bright yellow blouse buttoned up to her neck.

To Charlie's right sat a man of similar age, as tall, but thin, almost bird like, stooped a little after he'd risen to shake the Judge's hand. Beady brown eyes peered at the Judge through thick coke-like glasses, a perfunctory smile pasted on his face. He wore a brown tweet sport jacket over a pale brown shirt that matched his deep tanned complexion, and clashed with his grey slacks, suggesting he might be color blind.

"My CFO." Muttered Charlie, by way of offhand introduction.

The man softly said his name as they shook, hardly auditable over the racket of the dining room as one hundred people slurped their soup, crashed their silverware together, and made an effort to restart empty conversations begun the night before. "George Walker, Chief Financial Officer for ANG International.

"And my COO," muttered Charlie again, pointing with his soup spoon at the man sitting next to George Walker, "Jack Hamilton".

Hamilton mimicked his boss, extending a thin spidery hand back over his head, not bothering to stand, his handshake little more than a sliding of dry slippery skin across the Judge's palm. The Judge repressed his intense desire to wash his hands. Hamilton had a lean face, defined by his hawk like nose and prominent jaw. Cold grey eyes appraised the Judge. He cranked his head around in his chair to get a better look at his victim. The Judge had seen friendlier eyes in the snake cages at the zoo.

"And my number two worthless son" said Charlie, nodding across the table at a young man next to the daughter, Laura Waxman, Charlie's mouth twisted in a smile, suggesting he was joking. A smile that didn't reach Charlie's eyes.

The number two son looked to be mid-twenties and favored his mother. Not particularly tall, thin, faded blue eyes, an open face, flushed now at his dad's joke/criticism. He bounded to his feet to extend a hand across the table to the Judge, introducing himself as Daniel Waxman or "Just Dan". He sported a corduroy jacket in dark blue over a paler blue dress shirt, no tie, and soft charcoal slacks. There was a sadness in his face that stained his eyes and was repeated in the beginning nasolabial folds around his mouth, despite the brave smile pasted across his lips. His handshake was determined.

"And my treasurer", muttered Charlie again, spoon-pointing to the man sitting next to son Dan. The treasurer also stood, a plump man in his late forties, dressed in a white shirt, grey suit, and red bow tie. He had a jolly smile on his face that easily covered all emotion, given his round chubby features. But the dark,

dark eyes that glowed from his face reminded the Judge of a grizzly, recently disturbed from its winter slumber. He wasn't the sort of man the Judge would turn his back on. He stated his name to be Kenny, not bothering with a last name.

Katy was behind the Judge, dutifully shaking hands in turn after him, and then settling herself at the far end of the table, as far away from Charlie as she could get, next to a third young woman in her early twenties who introduced herself as Charlie's other daughter, Nancy

This left the Judge with the only remaining empty seat, next to the COO, Jack Hamilton. He plunked himself down into the chair with a sigh, hoping these people didn't have medical problems to relate, secretly wishing he'd been successful in talking Katy out of her cruise and into flying to the Far East for their offshore adventure.

The soup course arrived, a delicious-smelling Crab Bisque. The steaming bowls were immediately dug into by the entire table, the music of soft slurping joining the similar ambiance of the rest of the busy dining room.

"You always take your staff along when you cruise, Charlie?" Asked the Judge, making his voice light-hearted and conversational, trying not to get off on the wrong foot. He apparently failed, wincing as Katy's elbow sliced into his ribs beneath his arm resting on the table. Christ, he'd get to the table early tomorrow and choose a seat between the daughters, away from Katy's elbows.

Charlie's eyes raised from his soup to the Judge's. Examining the Judge as though he were some sort of newfound beadle, some slight interest beginning in the back of Charlie's eyes.

"Yes, err.. Judge, you said your nick name was Judge, right? I like my staff handy. I never stop working… Judge. To do so is to risk your entire business. The World moves at an extremely fast pace these days. And competitors are in the wings always, ready to pounce on your smallest mistake.

And what is it exactly that you do?"

"I mostly lawyer these days, Charlie. It's good fun and it pays the rent."

"A lawyer, huh. Don't have much use for lawyers. My experience is you pay them a lot of money, only so they can make a lot of trouble for you, thereby requiring more of their time to fix the trouble they've made, and so you have to pay them more money again. Kind of a closed circuit, and expensive. Lawyers are useless creatures who produce nothing of value. Like a leech; they attach themselves to your business and then just suck."

"So, you don't use lawyers?" Asked the Judge.

"Oh yes. I have to. I use a lot of them, and all the time. Trapped into it because I'm in business. I just don't like them."

"They probably don't like you either, Charlie."

Jesus, Katy's jab was even shaper this time.

"What kind of business are you in, Charlie.

Plastics. Anything plastic. My company makes it, markets it, distributes. I'm the largest plastic manufacturer in the World."

"Is that a profitable business?"

"Oh yes. Very profitable. I've got more money than God as a result."

"And what do you do with all your money, Charlie?"

"What? What do you mean?"

"How do you spend your down time, Charlie? What do you do for fun?"

"This isn't a date, Judge. Making my money is my fun time." Charlie snorted at the stupidity of the Judge's question, turning back to his soup.

As the soup was finished, the bowls empty with spoons carefully set inside, Kenny the treasurer suddenly gave a strange gurgled cry.

"Ahhh...aaa...oof...oof"

Kenny staggered from his chair, pressing his hands to his throat, his eyes bulging with pain. One shaking hand reached into his inside coat pocket and came out with an EpiPen. He desperately fumbled its cap off and plunged the pen through his slacks into his outer thigh with vengeance. He stood there, panicky, waiting for the epinephrine to work, his face turning from bright red to purple.

Alice, Charlie's wife, jumped up, screaming, "Oh no. Oh my God. Help! Someone help him. He's got a nut allergy. He told them no nuts."

Kenny suddenly threw his head back with a final strangled cry, then fell forward, sprawling head-first across the table, his face crunching and scattering china and stemware in all directions. A veritable flood of water, coffee and cocktails slid like a tsunami across the table and over its edge, soaking the Judge's crotch.

The Judge stood up and moved to help, as did Dan Waxman, Charlie's son.

They pulled Kenny back up off the table, and sat him in his chair again, leaning his head back to hopefully clear his air passage. But he didn't look good. His face was white now, his eyes rolled back in his head. He wasn't breathing.

A man from a nearby table appeared at the Judge's arm, said he was a doctor, grabbed Kenny's head, and put two fingers to his neck for a pulse. But it was too late. The doctor looked up and shook his head at the shocked faces. "He's gone."

XXXX

Look for the Mystery Novel, **"THE CRUISE"** to be available on Amazon in the Fall of 2020.

A Personal Note from the Author

I hope you enjoyed your read. Here are the other books in the Judge Series, (in order). If you've enjoyed one or more of these Mystery Novels, please leave a Review on Amazon and help us spread the word.

Davis McDonald

THE HILL
THE ISLAND
SILICON BEACH
THE BAY
CABO
THE STRAND
THE LAKE
THE CRUISE

Made in the USA
Columbia, SC
20 June 2021